The Ancient Curse

Valerio Massimo Manfredi is an archaeologist and scholar of the ancient Greek and Roman world. He is the author of sixteen novels, which have won him literary awards and have sold 12 million copies. His Alexander trilogy has been translated into 38 languages and published in 62 countries and the film rights have been acquired by Universal Pictures. His novel *The Last Legion* was made into a film starring Colin Firth and Ben Kingsley and directed by Doug Lefler. Valerio Massimo Manfredi has taught at a number of prestigious universities in Italy and abroad and has published numerous articles and essays in academic journals. He has also written screenplays for film and television, contributed to journalistic articles and conducted cultural programmes and television documentaries.

Also by Valerio Massimo Manfredi

ALEXANDER: CHILD OF A DREAM

ALEXANDER: THE SANDS OF AMMON

ALEXANDER: THE ENDS OF THE EARTH

SPARTAN

THE LAST LEGION

HEROES
(formerly The Talisman of Troy*)*

TYRANT

THE ORACLE

EMPIRE OF DRAGONS

THE TOWER

PHARAOH

THE LOST ARMY

THE IDES OF MARCH

ODYSSEUS: THE OATH

ODYSSEUS: THE RETURN

Valerio Massimo Manfredi

THE ANCIENT CURSE

Translated from the Italian by Christine Feddersen-Manfredi

PAN BOOKS

First published 2010 by Macmillan

This edition published 2016 by Pan Books
an imprint of Pan Macmillan
20 New Wharf Road, London N1 9RR
Associated companies throughout the world
www.panmacmillan.com

ISBN 978-1-5098-0119-0

1 3 5 7 9 8 6 4 2

A CIP catalogue record for this book is available from the British Library.

Typeset by SetSystems Ltd, Saffron Walden, Essex
Printed and bound by CPI Group (UK) Ltd, Croydon, CR0 4YY

To Annamaria

1

FABRIZIO CASTELLANI arrived in Volterra one October evening in his Fiat Punto, with a couple of suitcases and the hopes of securing a researcher's position at the University of Siena. A friend of his father's had found him cheap accommodation on a farm in Val d'Era, not far from the city. The farmhouse had been vacant since earlier that year, when the previous tenant had left, having given up on the owner's grand but sketchy plans to restructure the building and sell it to one of those Englishmen so enamoured of Tuscany.

The house had been added to in various stages over time around a core dating back to the thirteenth century. The oldest part was of stone, covered with ancient handmade roof tiles lichen-stained yellow and green on the north side, while the newer part was in brick. There was a pretty courtyard at the back, a tool shed and a hayloft. The land to the south hosted a dozen rows of big gnarled olive trees laden with fruit, as well as low vines still hanging with clusters of violet grapes and leaves that had started to turn bright red. The drystone wall that skirted the property was crumbling and needed fixing. Beyond the wall stretched a wood of oak trees that covered the hill all the way to its peak in a brilliant sweep of ochre, interrupted here and there by the red and gold of the mountain maples. An ancient box tree stood at the front entrance and a couple of cypresses, taller than the house's roof, swayed on the other side.

A sparkling brook gushed from a spring close by, flowing over the clean gravel until it disappeared into the ditch at the roadside, only to re-emerge further downstream before descending to the Era. A thick blanket of vegetation hid the river itself, but its voice could be heard mixing with the rustling of the oaks and poplars.

He liked the house instantly, especially the scent of hay, mint and sage that rose through the evening air to meet the flight of the last swallows of the season, still reluctant to abandon their empty nests. Fabrizio set his suitcases down at the threshold and decided to stretch his legs on the pathway that crossed the property from one end to another, dividing it into two nearly equal parts. Then he sat on the stone wall and took in that twilight moment of peace and serenity, suspended in time, a little unreal, as he idly waited for night to fall.

Fabrizio was thirty-three but he still couldn't count on a steady position, like so many of his friends and colleagues who had embraced the science of the past with a passion, not realizing how difficult it would be to make a living out of archaeology in a country with 3,000 years of history. And yet he was neither discouraged nor demoralized. All he could think of, actually, was that he might soon be encountering the object of his most recent enthusiasm and interest: the statue of a young boy housed in the Etruscan museum at Volterra.

A great poet had given the statue a haunting, evocative name: the 'shade of twilight'. Right, poets can dream, mused Fabrizio, but not scholars. Time to get down to work. He shook himself out of his reverie and walked back towards the house that he would be calling home, at least for a couple of weeks. Long enough to finish his research and to gather the information and materials necessary for a publication that might, with luck, even cause a bit of a stir in the field.

His interest in the piece had come about totally by chance. He'd been in Florence at the National Restoration Institute, studying the most recent techniques in treating and conserving ancient bronze, when he'd happened upon a set of X-rays of the

Etruscan statue, perhaps taken in view of a possible restoration. The X-rays had been stuck into a file at the bottom of a drawer and would have remained there who knows how long, waiting perhaps for financing from some ministerial project. Fabrizio had been struck by a strangely shaped shadow that showed up in the plates right where the boy's liver would have been. From a certain angle, the shadow took on the shape of a longish, pointed object.

He hadn't breathed a word about his discovery to anyone. There was no mention of the shadow in any file or description of that unnamed masterpiece of Etruscan art. He'd had copies made of the X-rays and had scanned them on to a couple of files that he could analyse on the computer. But the more he looked at them, the more Fabrizio became convinced that he needed to examine the object itself to get to the root of the mystery, and he had requested permission to analyse the statue itself. He figured that a move to Volterra would make it easier to carry out his research on an intensive basis. What he really wanted to do was an MRI; the results would certainly complete the overall picture and provide the key for explaining the irregularity in the bronze cast.

He'd examined the hypothesis of a flaw in the bronze fusion or a defective weld, but neither made much sense since the area of the statue he was interested in was made of flat, relatively regular surfaces where the liquefied metal would have been free to flow smoothly when the statue was being cast some twenty-four centuries ago.

As he was driving in earlier, he'd stopped at a grocery shop to buy bread, cheese, prosciutto and a flask of Chianti. He went into the big kitchen and sat at a table shiny with centuries of use, opening a book by Jacques Heurgon on Etruscan civilization for company as he enjoyed his makeshift dinner. He'd made up the bed with clean sheets he had brought from home and around midnight he lay down in a room that smelt of fresh plaster, stared up at the ceiling beams and listened to the song of a nightingale rising from the locust trees and laburnums that flanked the little brook.

Elisa, his fiancée, had left him three months before and he hadn't quite got over it. A classic tale of woe, really. A bit spoiled, Elisa, and lacking the guts to defend her relationship with a good guy like himself – agreeable and attractive, with a solid background and a promising future, or so he liked to think – against her wealthy, stuck-up parents' protests that he didn't have much in the way of job prospects; that he didn't dress with much class. He was bitter about the break-up, that much he would admit, mostly about how he'd deceived himself into thinking that he was up to their standards, to anyone's standards. He had felt so humiliated by her rejection, their rejection, that he hadn't made love to anyone since Elisa had left. Basically, his psychological well-being had been shot to hell. But now that he'd left the city and found himself in such a different atmosphere, so intensely pervaded by simplicity and austerity, he was beginning to feel at peace with himself. He felt rather like an athlete gearing up for a crucial meet.

He wondered whether this fortuitous state of grace would hold up in the medium and long run, or whether such isolation would shortly produce the opposite effect, driving him to flick through his address book in search of the mobile number of a tender-hearted female friend. In the end, the emotion of finding this haven and of being on the threshold of what he hoped would be an important discovery, plus the snug warmth of his bed, won out over his agonizing.

THE NEXT MORNING he introduced himself to Nicola Balestra, the regional director of NAS, the National Antiquities Service, who, it turned out, had just arrived himself a couple of weeks earlier, temporarily abandoning his main office in Florence but leaving his secretary behind to transfer important calls and forward urgent papers. Balestra had a dry, taciturn manner, and was famous for being disagreeable to the uni.ersity crowd and keeping them at arm's length, especially those – wagging tongues would have it – who prided themselves on being talk-show darlings.

'Good morning, Castellani,' Balestra greeted him, extending his hand with a certain cordiality. 'Welcome to Volterra. Have you found a place to stay?'

'Good morning, sir. Yes, thanks to my father. A nice little house on the Semprini farm in Val d'Era. It's not far from the city but very peaceful. I think I'll like it very much.'

'I've had a look at your request. I see you are interested in a very important piece. That's fine with me. It's only right that a young man like yourself should aim high; do something that will get you noticed. I just hope you've taken a careful look at the existing bibliography. There's quite a bit of high-calibre material, as I'm sure you'll have realized.'

Fabrizio had the impression that Balestra was feeling him out; trying to understand what was behind his request.

'I've been working on this for quite some time and I've thoroughly examined all the material I've found,' he answered. 'I'm eager to begin my own personal research. I don't foresee any problems and, with a little bit of luck, I should be able to complete my studies in no time. If everything goes smoothly, of course.'

Balestra offered him a cup of coffee, a very good sign indeed according to the grapevine, and after drinking it and exchanging a few more pleasantries Fabrizio made to take his leave.

'The permit I've given you is quite wide-ranging, Castellani, allowing you to remain in the museum even after closing hours. Mario, the security guard, will show you how to set the alarm and turn it off, and he'll give you an emergency number for the Carabinieri, just in case you should need it. I hope you realize what a privilege this represents. I'd ask you to respect this show of trust and to be as responsible and careful as possible.'

'This is quite an opportunity for me and I can't tell you how grateful I am, sir. You have my word that I'll take every precaution and won't cause any problems for you. When I've finished, if my research produces the results I'm hoping for, you'll be the first to know.'

Balestra gripped his hand and accompanied him to the door.

Fabrizio spent the rest of the morning organizing his files and settling into the little office they'd set aside for him, all of three by two and a half metres, a tiny space carved out of a blind archway that must have been part of an ancient structure adjacent to the museum. He then consulted the museum library to make sure that he hadn't missed anything that had been written about the young lad of Volterra.

At closing time, five o'clock, Mario painstakingly repeated everything there was to know about the alarm system. 'Just between the two of us, even if you should forget to set the alarm as you're going out, there's a backup system that sounds directly at my house, which is just around the corner. For when I'm not at home, I've rigged a receiver that I wear around my neck. If it goes off, I'll rush right over. Obviously, I'd prefer not to be rudely awakened at one or two in the morning by a false alarm, that's all.'

'Can I ask you something, Mario?' Fabrizio said after listening to the man's lengthy explanations.

'Of course, Professor.'

'I've heard that the director left Florence a while ago and that he plans on staying here another two or three weeks. If I've understood correctly, it's a little unusual, isn't it, for a man in his position, with all the responsibilities he must have back in Florence, to leave his main office for such a long time? Do you have any idea why?'

Mario gave him a knowing look, as if to say, 'Wouldn't you like to be in on this, my boy?' but he answered, 'You know, the director makes his own decisions. We on the staff aren't often privy to the whys and wherefores. What I do know is that he's always in his office and we've been told not to interrupt him unless there's some urgent paper that needs signing. He only takes phone calls from eleven thirty to noon, unless it's the Minister himself on the line.'

'There must be some pressing business that's keeping him here,' mused Fabrizio. 'Well, Mario, you take it easy, then, and have a good evening. Oh, and if you know of a nice trattoria near here that's not too pricey, I'll take a break at about seven and then come back here later to finish up.'

Mario recommended Signora Pina's place, not far from the ring road. Pina served all the local specialities, made with her own hands, mind you, and at a good price to boot. He said to be sure to tell her that Mario had sent him and he'd get a special deal, just like everyone who worked at the NAS.

Fabrizio thanked him and plunged back into his work. There was nothing better than being completely on your own, without phones ringing or people bustling in and out of offices. By seven he had finished checking the library files that contained publications on the lad of Volterra. All he'd turned up was a couple of articles by local scholars, the kind of thing that you'd expect to find in a museum collection. Nothing new in terms of information.

SIGNORA PINA found him a table in the courtyard behind the trattoria, hemmed in between the back of an old convent and an L-shaped portico that had once been part of the cloister. An archway in the portico led to a little square that was closed off at the opposite end by the striking and rather imposing bulk of a very ancient building, probably a fortified house partially restructured during the Renaissance.

'What is that place over there?' he asked as Signora Pina brought him a plate of pasta e fagioli.

'What, you don't know anything?' said the woman, speaking in a strong local accent.

No, he didn't know anything, explained Fabrizio, because he'd just arrived and moved on to the Semprini farm only last night. So Signora Pina, seeing that it was low season and her regulars wouldn't show up for at least an hour or so, sat down to keep Fabrizio company and began to tell him the story of the palace of the Caretti-Riccardi princes, empty for the last forty years except for a brief period when the current owner, Count Jacopo Ghirardini, had moved in, four or five years ago. He had taken in a woman, a cleaning lady supposedly, but everyone said she was more of a witch, and then he'd vanished. Just like that. Into thin air. No one had heard of him since. The woman, she was still around, she'd opened a tavern outside of town at a place called Le Macine. Since the count's disappearance, not a living soul had set foot inside. A pity, wasn't it, a sin, such a big, beautiful palace with no doubt a fabulous view from the top floor of the entire valley?

'Must be full of ghosts, then,' suggested Fabrizio, giving her a little rope.

'It's no joke, Doctor,' replied Pina with a touch of indignation. 'I, who have lived here since I was born, can tell you that anyone who has gone into that building has heard things and seen things. And how! Why, ages ago, there was a porter working at the mill over at La Bruciata, strong as an elephant and built like an ox. Well, he was always boasting about how he was afraid of nothing, and one day he made a bet with his friends at the local tavern that he could spend the night there—'

'And when he came out in the morning his hair had turned white overnight,' suggested Fabrizio, interrupting her story.

'How did you know that?' asked Pina with genuine surprise.

Fabrizio would have liked to tell her that stories such as hers were told in every region of Italy, tales of hidden treasure, of secret passageways stretching out for kilometres underground that linked one building to another, of golden goats that appeared at night to solitary wayfarers in the vicinity of a crossroads. An entire arsenal of stories and legends invented over the centuries before television started muddling people's minds.

'What I'd like to know is . . . how did this porter get into the palazzo anyway, since it's been closed and locked up all these years?'

'Well, you see, Doctor, there's a secret passage that leads from the Caretti-Riccardi palace to the chapel of the Holy Souls in Purgatory near the Etruscan cistern. You know the one I mean, on the other side of the state road . . .'

So there you were! He would have liked to say, 'If that passage was so secret, how come even a porter who worked at the mill knew about it?' But he'd finished the bean soup and so he decided to compliment the signora on her cooking instead and to order a piece of frittata with a bit of salad.

After dinner he took a little stroll around the city. All in all, his first contacts – his chats with the museum security guard and the trattoria owner – had been very agreeable, making him feel at home in this new context, among people that he'd heard were usually not very welcoming to strangers, despite the steady stream of tourists they must have become accustomed to.

It was completely dark and there wasn't a soul on the streets by the time Fabrizio made his way back to the museum gates. He turned off the alarm, let himself in with a key and then activated the alarm again as soon as he was inside. The time had come to meet the lad of bronze who was waiting for him in the exhibition hall. He went up the stairs, took a chair, switched on the light and sat down in front of the statue. Finally.

To Fabrizio's eyes, it was the most remarkable thing he'd ever seen. The choice of the subject was incredibly original, the crafting extraordinary. The aura that emanated from the boy was intense and emotional, capturing all the poetry of Vincenzo Gemito's street urchins, the expressive punch of a Picasso, the exasperated fragility of Giacometti's most inspired bronzes. This heartfelt vision was of such creative power that it left Fabrizio feeling awed and almost daunted.

It was the tender image of a sad, slight little boy. His frail body was exaggeratedly long, while his minute face had a melancholy look that couldn't entirely mask a hint of natural light-heartedness, cut down too soon by death. A child whose loss must have left his parents in the most unthinkable despair, if they had appealed to such a sublime artist to portray him so realistically, capturing his personality, his youth, perhaps even signs of the illness that had spirited him away . . .

When the bell tolled from the tower of the nearby Sant'Agostino church, Fabrizio realized that almost an hour had gone by. He got to his feet and began to set up his camera equipment.

The photographs available on file had been wholly inadequate. Fabrizio felt the need to explore each and every detail of the statue with his lens; perhaps he'd discover aspects of the casting that the experts hadn't picked up on. He was reminded of the words of his professor and mentor, Gaetano Orlandi, who used to say that the best place to excavate in Italy was in the museums and storehouses of the National Antiquities Service.

It took him hours to set up the lights, then study the angles and shots. He took about ten rolls of slide film and the same number of photos using a digital camera so that he could analyse the images electronically. Just as he was finishing up on the figure's face, head and neck, the phone rang out in the hall. Fabrizio checked his watch: it was after one a.m. Evidently a wrong number. Who could be calling a museum at that hour? He went back to his work, intent on finishing despite his fatigue, but the telephone distracted him again only a few minutes later.

He went to pick up the receiver and began to say, 'Listen, you've got the wrong—'

But a woman's voice with a curt, peremptory tone cut him short. 'Leave the boy alone!' This was followed by the click of her hanging up.

Fabrizio replaced the receiver mechanically and wiped a hand over his sweaty brow. Was he so tired that he was hearing things? No one knew anything about his research, except for the director himself and Mario, but the security guard wouldn't have had a very clear idea of what it was all about anyway. Fabrizio didn't know what to think, and the impossibility of instantly finding a reasonable explanation behind this apparently inexplicable event annoyed him tremendously.

Could there be a rational explanation? Might one of the library clerks have heard about his research and spoken about him to some impressionable soul, one of those fanatics who live on pseudo-scientific New Age hype? Obsessed with the pyramids or – why not? – with the Etruscans. After all, the Etruscans were second only to the Egyptians in their legendary fascination with the afterlife, and famous for being soothsayers and sorcerers.

The person on the phone must have seen the light filtering from the windows of the second floor of the museum, and that meant they must be somewhere in the immediate vicinity. Without opening the shutters, he sneaked a look outside to check the buildings opposite the museum and to the sides, but he didn't spot anything worthy of attention.

As he was scanning the vicinity, another sound – even more alarming than the phone ringing and the creepy voice of the woman warning him off – broke through the still of night, invading his ears and even more so his imagination: the long, deep howling of an animal, a fierce cry of challenge and pain. A wolf. In the centre of the city of Volterra.

'Christ!' Fabrizio burst out. 'What the hell is happening?'

For the first time in his adult life, the panic and fear he'd felt as a child came flooding back, the sheer terror that had kept him nailed to his bed when the screeching of an owl tore through the night air outside the mountain house where he'd lived then.

A wolf? Wait. Really, though, why not? Fabrizio remembered

reading somewhere that recent environmental protection poli-
cies had allowed certain predators to extend their territory along
the Apennines, all over Italy. But his logic was shattered to
pieces as he heard the ear-splitting howl echo again, closer this
time, more threatening. It trailed off finally into an agonized
rattle.

He gathered up his things, turned out all the lights, one after
another, and rushed down the stairs towards the lobby. He set
the alarm and went out into the street, triple-locking the door
behind him. As he walked away, he thought he could hear the
phone ringing again inside, shrill and persistent, but there was
no way he was going back in. There was no trusting where his
imagination would take him.

His car was parked in a little square not far from the
museum, but the distance on foot down the silent, deserted
streets that separated him from his ride home seemed never-
ending. How could no one have heard? Why weren't people
turning on their lights, looking out of their windows? He
stopped more than once, sure he'd heard a pawing sound behind
him, or even an uneven panting. Each time he spun around,
then picked up his pace. When he reached the square, his car
was not there. A surge of panic sent him running from one
street to the next, this way and that, with his heart in his mouth
and his breath coming in short gasps. He could hear that
atrocious howling echoing against every wall, from every archway, at the end of every street.

He forced himself to stop and to control the panic that was
overwhelming him. It took all his willpower to lean against a
wall, take a deep breath and make an effort to think clearly.
He realized that he must have parked his car in another spot
and he tried to remember his movements with some degree of
clarity. He started walking and, as his thoughts eventually sorted
themselves out, he found himself in the square where he had
actually parked his car. He got in, started it up and began driving
fast towards the farmhouse in Val d'Era. He was starting to feel

that living in such an isolated place, buried, practically, by the vegetation all around it, was perhaps not the ideal choice for his stay in Volterra. He let himself in quickly, shut the door behind him and bolted it.

He lay down, exhausted by the violent emotions he'd experienced on his first day in the town where he had thought he'd be dying of boredom. He couldn't help straining his ears, fearing that the howling would start up again. Slowly he began reasoning with a fresh mind. The phone call was the work of some fanatic who had a friend inside the museum, while the howl . . . well, the howling could have been just about anything: a stray dog that had been hit by a car or even some circus animal that had escaped. It wouldn't be the first time such a thing had happened. As far as his car was concerned, it was simple distraction that had led him astray. It wasn't as if he hadn't forgotten where he'd parked his car before. Or looked for it in the wrong place.

Finally he managed to fall asleep, lulled by the rustling of the oaks and the rush of the river down in the valley.

2

CARABINIERE LIEUTENANT Marcello Reggiani got out of the
squad car, a Land Rover, and walked swiftly towards the site
where the corpse of Armando Ronchetti had been found.
Ronchetti was an old acquaintance of La Finanza, the Italian
customs and excise police, having been caught red-handed
several times peddling objects that had been plundered from the
Etruscan tombs in the area: vases, statuettes, even small frescoes
detached from the walls using decidedly unorthodox methods.

Ronchetti had been at the top of his game and had honed
his technique to perfection. He would roam the area with what
those in the business called a 'prodder', an iron rod used to
locate and break through the ceilings of the underground tombs.
He would circumspectly mark the site and then return later
with a car battery and a video camera, which he would drop
down into the underground chamber. The camera would be
rotated by remote control so he could view what was buried
below on a small monitor. He'd close the hole up again,
camouflage the area all around and then show the video to the
right people and auction off the tomb's contents. The best
bidder would often take the whole lot, or he might sell off a bit
at a time, single objects or fragments of frescoes, to whoever
offered the highest sum.

It was even said that he'd got one of his nephews an associ-
ate professorship by helping him 'discover' and publish the
contents of an intact tomb of great importance. Obviously with
the promise that the old man would be given the treasure trove

compensation that the NAS provided for such fortuitous finds. Quite a pretty penny, in this case. That was the only time in his whole career that the old tomb robber had earned money legally, in a certain sense of the word, besides seasonal jobs taken now and then harvesting olives when he felt the police were breathing down his neck.

Well, there he was. Ronchetti had earned his last dishonest crust.

Hell, thought Reggiani, what an awful way to end a career. He had been covered by a sheet but there was blood everywhere and swarms of flies had settled in. When the officer signalled to his men to lift the sheet, he couldn't help but wrinkle his face in disgust. Whatever it was that had attacked the man had massacred him. His neck had been devoured, leaving mere strips of flesh, his chest was mangled and one of his shoulders had been ripped away from the collar bone and was lying by his foot.

'Has the doctor seen this?' asked Reggiani.

'Yeah, he's been by, but he said he'd wait to do the autopsy at the morgue.'

'Well, what did he say?'

'Some animal with a powerful bite.'

'I can see that for myself. What kind of animal?'

'A stray dog maybe?'

'Come on. Ronchetti wouldn't have been bothered by a stray, a guy like him used to being out in the fields at every hour of the day or night. It looks like his neck and throat were torn out with a single bite. See that.'

'Yeah, and the doctor noticed these claw marks, here at his shoulder. They're too big for a dog.'

'Would have been one hell of a dog all right. This has to have been a lion or something of the sort. Are there any circuses in town?'

'No, sir,' replied the carabiniere.

'Gypsies, then. They've been known to have bears with them.'

'We'll check it out, sir. Can't say I've seen any in the area.'

The carabiniere covered the corpse with the sheet. The coroner showed up a little later, a greenhorn from Rovereto who'd been at the job no longer than a couple of months, and he gagged at the sight of the body. He took a few notes, snapped a few Polaroid photos, said to let him know when the medical examiner's report was ready, then went to vomit the rest of his breakfast somewhere else.

'So what do the Finanza have to say about this?' Reggiani asked the carabiniere.

'Well, sir, this is what I was told. A couple of special agents were searching the area in camo gear because they'd apparently been tipped off—'

'Naturally without breathing a word of it to us.'

'I'm afraid not. Apparently they notice some strange activity, hear some suspicious noises, so they move in and manage to surprise Ronchetti, along with a couple of other guys they couldn't identify, as they're opening the pot.'

'Breaking into the tomb.'

'Exactly. As soon as they challenge them, these guys scramble and melt into the bushes. As they're about to nab one of them, the guy jumps straight down off an overhang that's steep as hell, lands on his feet and hops on a bicycle that's sitting there waiting for him. He rides off, pedalling like crazy, on that steep slope that leads down towards Rovaio. At that point, there's not much the agents can do, so they leave one of their guys to guard the tomb site and go back to headquarters to draw up a report for the National Antiquities Service. At dawn they send up another agent to replace the one who was on duty all night and that's when they discover the body. They informed us and we came right over.'

Reggiani took off his cap, sat on a stone in the shade of a tree and tried to compose his thoughts. 'Did the doctor give an approximate time of death?'

'He thought between two and three in the morning.'

'And what time was it when the agents found these guys with their hands in the honey?'

'Two a.m. precisely.'

'And they didn't hear a thing? That seems impossible.'

'I don't know what to say, sir,' replied the carabiniere. 'Maybe it's best to wait for the definitive report. The medical examiner said he'd perform the autopsy as soon as he got the corpse.'

Just then a siren was heard and a four-wheel-drive ambulance climbed up the slope towards them. Two orderlies came out with a stretcher and loaded the body on to it. They took it back to the vehicle with them and drove off.

'Where's the tomb?' asked Reggiani.

'Over here, sir,' replied the carabiniere, walking first down a path and then into a cluster of junipers and oak saplings. They got to a point where several of the young trees had been recently uprooted, their leaves already wilting. An officer sporting the Finanza insignia emerged from the wood with a pistol.

'It's OK,' said Reggiani. 'It's us.'

A slab of sandstone had been moved away, evidently using a couple of crowbars that lay to the side. They could distinctly see the dark opening that led into the tomb.

'A chamber vault,' explained the officer on guard, who must have taken a quick cultural heritage course at the local university.

'Hmm,' commented Reggiani. 'Intact?'

'It looks like it,' replied the officer. 'Would you care to take a look, sir?'

Reggiani approached the entrance and sat on his heels as the officer switched on a torch to illuminate the inside of the tomb. Reggiani could see that the chamber was quite large, about four metres by three, and so must have belonged to an aristocratic family. What surprised him was the absence of any sort of treasure inside, except for a fresco on the back wall which almost certainly represented Charun, the Etruscan demon who ferried the dead to the other world. He could see nothing inside but two sarcophagi facing each other, at least from his limited viewpoint. One was topped by the figure of a woman reclining on a couch, while the other was unadorned and coarsely sculpted, about two metres long by one metre wide and covered by a plain tufa slab. The second sarcophagus had evidently been carved out of bare stone and was quite roughly hewn, as was the slab covering it, although it appeared to be air-tight.

Reggiani noticed the floor of the chamber was made of tufa, a crumbly rock typical of the area, and seemed to be marked by deep abrasions in every direction. 'Interesting,' he commented, getting back to his feet. He turned to the guard and said, 'We'll be going now. You keep your eyes open, and if you need us you know where to find us.'

'You can be sure of that, sir,' replied the officer, lifting his hand to the visor of his cap.

Reggiani then went back to the squad car and asked to be dropped off at his office in the city. He detested asking the Finanza for information, but he had no alternative now.

Once at his desk, he picked up the phone and dialled the special operations number to see if he could speak to the men who had been on duty the night before. They were unable to give him a decent description of the two bandits who had got away or of the bicycle used to escape down the path through the Rovaio woods: a man's bike, black and old, with a triangle frame and rusty handlebars. Hundreds just like it in Volterra and the surrounding countryside.

He started to search the files to see if he could turn up someone who met the description provided by the agents, while he waited for the medical examiner's report. That's what it was like working in these small provincial cities: sheer boredom for months or even years, then suddenly someone gets their head torn off with practically no hint of a scuffle anywhere near the murder site. He knew the colonel would be calling before evening to check how the investigation was proceeding and he could already hear his own answer: it appears we're groping around in the dark, sir. What else?

He nevertheless ordered the men in his unit to ascertain whether any ferocious animals had escaped from a circus or Gypsy camp or even from the villa of some eccentric local dabbling in the illegal breeding of panthers, lions or leopards. He'd heard that it was becoming fashionable to raise wild beasts in your backyard. In the meantime, he waited for the results of the post-mortem exam on Ronchetti.

FABRIZIO ARRIVED at the museum shortly before nine and sat at the desk in his cubicle to begin his work for the day. As he was getting started, there was a knock at the door and a pretty girl walked in. Dark hair, nice figure and nicely dressed as well, not the usual vestal virgin he was used to seeing wandering the halls of museums and NAS offices.

'Hi. You're Castellani, aren't you? My name is Francesca Dionisi. I'm an inspector here. The director would like to speak to you.'

Fabrizio got up and walked out with her.

'Do you live around here?' he asked as they went down the hall.

'Yes, I do. In the Oliveto neighbourhood, left of the first bend in the road that takes you to Colle Val d'Elsa.'

'Right,' replied Fabrizio. 'I'm staying in a place not far from there. At the Semprini farm in Val d'Era.'

They had almost reached the director's office.

'Listen,' he said, before they entered, 'did you hear anything strange last night?'

'No. Why? What should I have heard?'

Fabrizio was about to answer when Mario arrived at the top of the stairs.

'Have you heard the latest? They've found Ronchetti, the tomb robber, in the fields near Rovaio with his throat slashed open! His head was practically ripped off his body.'

'Who told you that?' asked a porter.

'My cousin, the one who drives an ambulance. He saw the body himself. It was a mess. They're saying it was a wild animal, a lion or a leopard or something that escaped from a circus. Remember that panther that got out last year at Orbassano? Well, it's happened again!'

'When did it happen?' asked Fabrizio, suddenly pale.

'I don't know. Two, three o'clock, depends on who you listen to. Last night, anyway.'

Fabrizio could distinctly hear in his mind that unmistakable cry of a wild animal that had split the night as he sat working in the silence of the museum. A long shiver went down his spine.

Francesca startled him. 'What was that sound you were talking about?'

'Well, a scream, I think . . . a . . .'

She looked at him in surprise and curiosity. He was pale and upset, obviously shaken by some strong emotion.

'Go on in. The director is waiting for you,' she said to relieve his embarrassment. 'Come and see me later if you like.'

She opened the door to Balestra's office and Fabrizio went in.

'Do you mind if I smoke?' the director asked him politely. 'I usually have a cigarette with my coffee.'

'Not at all,' replied Fabrizio. 'I think I need one myself, if I may. And I'd love some coffee.'

Balestra poured a cup from the pot and passed him a cigarette. 'I didn't think you smoked.'

'I don't. But sometimes I do . . . That is, when I'm tense.'

'I understand. When you're working on something import-ant, that can happen.'

'You said you wanted to see me. Is anything wrong?'

'Yes, actually,' replied Balestra. 'We've got trouble.'

'I hope it's nothing to do with my authorization.'

'Oh no, not at all. There's no problem with that. It's something completely different. I was hoping you could give me a hand.'

'With pleasure, if I can.'

'Well,' began Balestra, 'last night a couple of Finanza agents surprised some robbers breaking into a tomb and they called me right away. It was two thirty a.m. I asked them to put someone on guard and told them we'd be by this morning.'

Fabrizio wondered whether the director had heard about Ronchetti. He imagined not, but he didn't think it was his place to tell him. Mario's account was quite confused, after all, and might have been exaggerated.

Balestra sipped his coffee and took a long drag on his cigarette before he continued: 'I'm wondering whether you would consider inspecting the tomb and possibly excavating it. I can give you a couple of workers, even three or four if you need them. It's bad timing for me. I'm up to my neck in work and I have a couple of deadlines approaching. Dr Dionisi is already working on an emergency that came up in the trench they're digging for the new power lines. One of my inspectors had an accident while on a job and is at home on sick leave, and another is on holiday – well earned, poor devil, he worked all summer on the Villanovan settlement near Gaggera. I know I can trust you to do a good job; you've already written and published studies on a number of similar digs. I've tried to help you out here, and I was wondering if you wouldn't mind doing me this favour.'

Fabrizio was shocked by the proposal. It was unheard of for a regional director of the National Antiquities Service to forgo personal excavation of a possibly intact Etruscan tomb, presumably from the early period. He must be involved in something very big and very important indeed to let such an opportunity slip by.

Careful to keep his surprise out of his voice, Fabrizio replied in a solicitous tone, 'I understand completely and I'm honoured by your trust in me. Just let me know when you'd like me to begin.'

'Believe me, I'm sorry to interrupt the work you're doing

here. I know how important it is for you, but I don't know where else to turn. I could ask another one of the regional directors to send someone in, but I'd rather not do that, because they'd certainly expect a favour in return. And, to be truthful, I can't say that my colleagues . . . Well, enough said.'

'No, really,' insisted Fabrizio. 'I'd be happy to work on this project. How soon would you like me to start?'

'Right away, Castellani. You can see for yourself that it's an emergency. Talk with Dr Dionisi and have her give you the men you need.'

Fabrizio finished his coffee and took his leave.

Francesca Dionisi was waiting for him in the hall, as if she had guessed the reason for his meeting with the director.

'Well?' she asked. 'What did the boss want? If I'm not being indiscreet . . .'

'Nothing less than for me to excavate the tomb that was broken into last night.'

'Ah. The Rovaio tomb.'

'That's the one. Listen, I hope I'm not stepping on anyone's toes here. I came to Volterra for something completely different.'

'I know. You're here for the boy in room twenty.'

Fabrizio suddenly thought of the woman's voice he'd heard the night before on the telephone: could it have been Francesca? But as much as he racked his brain, he could not connect the timbre of that voice with Francesca's natural lilt.

'Cat got your tongue?' she asked.

'No, it's nothing. I'm sorry.'

'Well, then, no, you're not stepping on my toes in the least. Actually, you're doing me a favour, and I know the director will be grateful for your assistance as well. He's a man who doesn't forget people who've helped him and I know he will appreciate your willingness to give us a hand.'

Francesca invited him into her office, where a green apple

was sitting on a plate on her desk. A snack maybe, or even her lunch.

'Listen, if I can I'll come by the Rovaio site to see what's coming out,' she went on, 'but don't count on it, because I've got my hands full as it is. I'll sign the work order for the labourers. How many? One, two, three?'

'Two will be enough.'

'All right. Two.'

'Francesca?'

'What?'

'There's something I don't understand. The director leaves headquarters in Florence for weeks to come and bury himself in this provincial office. What may be an intact tomb comes to light, probably a major discovery, and he doesn't even take a look at it. He signs over the dig to someone who doesn't even work for him, an academic to boot . . . This whole thing just doesn't make sense and I was asking myself whether you . . .'

'Whether I know something? Yes, I do, but make believe you don't know that. It's something big, much bigger than anything you can imagine.'

Fabrizio thought that if she'd wanted to silence his curiosity she would have simply answered that she knew nothing about it, so he continued to push his point. 'Bigger than an intact tomb from, let's say, the fifth or fourth century BC?'

'Yes.'

'Good grief.'

'Good grief is right. Now, go ahead, collect your workers and excavate that tomb at Rovaio. Then tell me what you've found.'

'How about tonight, over pizza?'

Francesca gave a half-smile. 'Sounds like you're asking me out.'

'Well, you know, I'm new here. And I hate eating alone.'

'I'll think about it. In the meantime, be sure you do a good job. Balestra's as fussy as they come.'

'So I've heard.'

FABRIZIO went out to the street and waited for the workers to pull the truck round to the front, then he got in next to the driver. They were at the dig in less than half an hour and the cop on duty was more than happy to go back to headquarters to write up his report.

Fabrizio decided on a frontal excavation: that is, from the tomb's main entrance. As soon as he had established the position of the facade, he began removing the earth that had accumulated over centuries as the hill behind the tomb eroded. He suspected that this might not be the only tomb in the area. Maybe Ronchetti and his buddies had chanced upon a new suburban necropolis outside the city of Velathri, the ancient Volterra. Exploring the area would take months, if not years.

They spent all morning and part of the afternoon clearing the front of the tomb. The structure was carved directly into the tufa and imitated the facade of a house, featuring a double door with big sculpted ring-shaped handles and a triangular pediment with the symbol of the new moon, or so it seemed to Fabrizio. But there was no suggestion, not a clue, as to who the bodies inside the burial cell might have been.

What also seemed quite strange was the lack of debris or objects of any sort at the ground level; there were no signs of human activity outside the chamber. The Etruscans were known to have visited their tombs frequently, holding any number of religious and memorial ceremonies there, and the first things you always found on a dig were the remains of rituals and sacrifices offered in honour of the dead.

It was already starting to get dark when he had finished clearing the area in front of the door and had taken all his measurements. Not a single object had come up anywhere at the ground level next to the tomb, not even when they were removing the sedimentary deposits. Fabrizio took a deep breath and stood there for a few minutes in silence, a trowel in his hand, facing that closed door, while a host of thoughts flitted through his mind, none of them pleasant. It was a relief to hear the voice of Francesca, who had just arrived.

'Nice. Now all you have to do is open it.'

'Right. Tomorrow, if everything goes as planned.'

A Finanza squad car drove up with a couple of men ready to stand guard.

'Are you hungry?' asked Francesca.

'Very. All I had for lunch was a sandwich and a glass of water.'

'Let's go, then. I know a nice place that's not too noisy. We'll take my car and I can drive you home after dinner.'

Fabrizio got in and was about to close the door, but then he stopped suddenly as if having second thoughts. He went over to where the policemen were standing. Both were kids of no more than twenty-five, one from the north, the other from the deep south.

'Listen, guys, don't take this lightly. This place gives me the creeps. Not because of them, poor souls,' he said, pointing towards the tomb, 'they won't bother you. I'm worried about that thing that killed Ronchetti. It's still on the loose, as far as I know.'

The two young men gestured at their machine guns and the 9-calibre Berettas resting in their holsters. 'We're locked and loaded, boss. Nothing's going to happen here.'

Each lit up a cigarette and, when Fabrizio turned back, before the first bend in the road, to take a look, the embers glowed like the eyes of an animal lurking in the dark.

3

THE RESTAURANT was inside a farmhouse that had been converted into a bed and breakfast along one of the country lanes that branched off from the regional road to Pisa. The fare was rustic and very tasty, promised Francesca: local crostini, ribollita soup, salami made with wild boar and a mean Fiorentina T-bone on request.

As they were turning off the asphalt road, Francesca and Fabrizio were surprised by an Alfa Romeo carabiniere squad car darting by at top speed, its siren screaming.

'Did you see that!' said Fabrizio. 'What is going on here? I thought I was going to end up in some sleepy little backwoods town . . .'

Francesca parked her Suzuki under an oak tree, then walked with Fabrizio into the restaurant and chose a table before answering, 'Yeah, well, this place usually is a little dead. But now we've got a corpse to show for it. And maybe it won't be the last . . .'

'Let's sit down and have them bring us some wine.'

'Poor guy. Everyone knew him. Ronchetti, I mean. Here everyone knows who the tomb robbers are. Sometimes they've been at it for generations. Some of them get so caught up in what they're doing that they even go back to school to brush up on their history!'

Fabrizio seemed amused and Francesca continued: 'In general, they think of themselves as being better at their jobs and more efficient than we are at the NAS. From a certain point of view, they're right. Since they're not bound by scientific methods, they can get straight to work and dig out everything they need in a couple of minutes. Seriously, they are far superior to us in one thing: how well they know the territory. They're familiar with every centimetre of the land. They leave no stone unturned, literally. Some of them even believe they're the reincarnation of someone from Etruscan times. But I'm sure you've heard all this before . . .'

'No, not at all. You know, I've only worked at a university. Our excavations are always organized well ahead of time and are usually uneventful. You NAS people are always on the front lines. I imagine that your work must occasionally even be risky.'

'Well, it can be, although it looks like this time our rivals were the ones who met up with something really terrifying. Let's not talk about that now, though. Tell me how you're getting on with the Rovaio tomb.'

'There's not much to say. You saw yourself that I've cleared the facade. But I found nothing in the sedimentary layer. Just earth. And nothing at the ground level either.'

'Either they were cleanliness fanatics or no one ever came by . . .'

'That's what has me wondering. You know, cemetery sites always show signs of being well visited. Flattened areas where people have beaten a track, little objects that people lose over time and that get crushed beneath their feet. I saw absolutely none of that there. I'm sure about the layer. I got to the base of the monument, so there's no doubt about that. So how could that be?'

The waiter brought the wine and a plate of salami. Francesca put a slice into her mouth, savouring the strong flavour of the boar meat.

'It's too soon to say,' she said, 'but you're right. The path leading to a tomb is always well worn, and that's noticeable. That's where you tend to find things. So these people never had a living soul come by with an offering or a prayer, as we'd say today. Did you see any marks on the stone?'

'The only marking seems to be the sphere of the new moon.'

'The dark moon, then.'

'So something's not right, you're saying.'

'Listen, it's no use guessing. Tomorrow you'll open the tomb and you'll see what you find. I'm really sorry I won't be able to be there. At least, not before noon.'

'Do you want me to wait? I can finish the site survey, clean up a little . . .'

'No, it's already clean enough as it is. No, you go on with your work. You must be eager to get back to your research at the museum.'

Fabrizio tried to shift the discussion around to more personal things, but Francesca was politely defensive and kept her distance, deftly steering him back to neutral topics. He felt discouraged and lonely, not seeing the point in continuing with such superficialities.

'I was really scared last night,' he said suddenly.

'That's right, you said you'd heard something.'

'A scream or a howl. I really can't describe it. It was atrocious. It didn't sound human, that's for sure. And it made my hair stand on end.'

'And you think it's connected to whatever killed Ronchetti.'

'What do you think?'

'I stopped at the place where it happened before coming to meet you. There's not a sign on the ground. The bushes all around are untouched. If it had been an animal, I think you'd see something. You know – broken branches, clawed-up earth . . .'

'Well, then?'

'I have my suspicions.'

'I'd like to hear about them. Maybe it would make me sleep easier tonight, in that isolated farmhouse! More wine?'

Francesca nodded. 'There've been Sardinian shepherds around, from the Barbargia region. Tough characters.'

'Yeah, I've heard about them.'

'Let's say that Ronchetti had set up shop with one of them and that the deal was that they would act as look-out for him—'

'In case of a Finanza raid?'

'Could be. You know how shepherds go everywhere. They'd be able to let him know if there was anyone coming . . .'

'Go on.'

'Well, let's say that Ronchetti tried to cheat one of them. Refused to share the booty, or simply didn't inform him about this last find. So this guy kills Ronchetti, strangles him, then carries the body somewhere else and lets one of his dogs loose on it – they're very ferocious, you know. The dog mangles the body and destroys any sign of the strangling.'

'And that sound I heard last night?'

'I'm not sure . . . Why didn't anyone else hear it?'

'How do you know that?'

'This is a small town. People here get upset over the sound of a leaf falling, let alone some horrible howling in the middle of the night. The next morning everyone would be talking about it.'

'So I dreamed it, then?'

'I'm not saying that. But sounds . . . sensations . . . are magnified at night. Even the howling of a stray dog, when everything else is perfectly silent.'

'That may be, but I have a shotgun and I'm going to keep it loaded.'

'Do you hunt?' asked Francesca.

'I like hunting hares sometimes. Why, are you against killing animals?'

'I just ate a big steak, didn't I?' she said with a touch of feline satisfaction.

Fabrizio fell silent for a little while without looking at her, then continued: 'What about this mysterious project that's keeping Balestra glued to his desk here, so far away from Florence?'

'I'm sorry, I can't tell you that. I would just risk saying something stupid, because I don't have any first-hand information myself. Just what I've heard in the hallways.'

Fabrizio nodded, as if to say, 'I won't insist.'

Francesca ordered coffee. 'How do you like it at the Semprini farm? It's nice and big, isn't it?'

'Too big,' replied Fabrizio. 'It's one of those traditional family homes, at least six bedrooms. Wasted on a single guy living alone.'

'Doesn't your girlfriend ever come down to visit?'

Fabrizio was surprised at her personal question, after she'd skirted all of his. She evidently didn't like talking about herself but didn't mind poking into the lives of others.

'No, since I don't have a girlfriend. She left me a few months ago. A question of class, you might say. As in my class not measuring up to her economic expectations. Not husband material, I guess.'

'She sounds nasty,' commented Francesca.

Fabrizio shrugged and said in a firm tone of voice, 'Happens. I'll survive.'

He insisted on paying the bill and Francesca thanked him with a smile. At least she wasn't a diehard feminist; who knows, maybe she even wore pretty underwear under those jeans of hers.

They left the restaurant around eleven and got into the car, continuing to chat until Francesca pulled up at the museum entrance, where Fabrizio had parked his Punto.

She didn't seem to expect a peck on the cheek, so Fabrizio didn't try, saying only, 'Goodnight, Francesca. I had a nice time. Thanks for the company.'

She brushed his cheek with her hand. 'You're a good guy.

You deserve to go places. I had a nice evening too. I'll see you tomorrow.'

Fabrizio nodded, then got into his car and headed towards the farmhouse. Fortunately, he'd left the front porch light on.

AT THAT same moment Lieutenant Reggiani was entering the forensics lab at Colle Val d'Elsa. Dr La Bella, a stocky man of about sixty, came to meet him, still wearing a bloody apron.

'I got here as soon as I could,' said Reggiani. 'Well, then?'

'Come,' replied the doctor, and motioned for the officer to follow him first into the locker room and then into his office. The smell of dead bodies saturated the place, overwhelming even the stink of the cigarette butts piled up in a couple of ashtrays on the desk. La Bella lit up a non-filter Nazionale Esportazione, a cigarette that was practically unfindable. A serious professional. Reggiani was impressed.

'I've never seen anything like it and I've been in this line of work for thirty-five years now,' he began. 'When I put the scalpel into the wound it went in this deep,' he continued, his fingers indicating a length of six or seven centimetres on a convenient pen. 'No dog that I know of has fangs this long. The entire solar plexus was disarticulated, the upper ribs were torn from his sternum, the collar bone was snapped in two. Almost nothing remains of his trachea. I don't even know if a lion or a tiger could do this kind of damage.'

Reggiani looked straight into his eyes and spoke slowly. 'There are no lions in the area, or panthers, or leopards. I've had half of the province inspected. I've alerted all our stations, the police, the traffic authorities, even the fire department. There are no circuses or Gypsy camps, no reports of private residences keeping exotic animals. I've gone down the list of animal food stores, butchers' shops, slaughterhouses to check if anyone's been buying suspicious quantities of meat. And I've turned up nothing.'

La Bella lit another cigarette with the stub of the first, making the air in the little room unbreathable.

'I know I'm not wrong,' he insisted. 'Find the animal that did this, Lieutenant, or I'll soon be slicing into someone else here on my table.'

'What about the time of death?'

'There's no doubt about that: between two and three o'clock last night.'

'Aren't there any other tests that could be done – I don't know, the DNA of the animal's saliva – so at least we know what we're looking for?'

La Bella put out the second cigarette and burst into a hacking cough that seemed to suffocate him while it lasted. When he could breathe again, he said, 'You must have seen that in some American movie, Lieutenant. Before the file is closed, there won't be anything but the bones left on this one. The kinds of tests you're talking about cost a lot of money. They're only done if there's been a sexual assault, rape. This is just a poor tomb robber who no one could care less about.'

'We'll see,' said Reggiani. 'Have you already written a report?'

La Bella opened a drawer and pulled out a folder. 'Here you are, Lieutenant.'

Reggiani thanked him, shook his hand and said goodbye. As he was leaving he turned, gripping the door handle. 'You must have some idea, right?'

'I do,' replied La Bella. 'If I had to picture it, I'd say an animal weighing at least a hundred, a hundred and twenty kilos, with powerful claws and fangs six or seven centimetres long, jaws strong enough to break a bull's backbone. So . . . a female lion, for example, or a panther. Oh, by the way, I had the crime lab check for hairs, but they found nothing. Isn't that incredible? Not a single hair. What about you? Did you sweep the site?'

Reggiani shook his head in commiseration. 'That's the first

thing I did. The ground was inspected over an area of four or five metres all around the spot where Ronchetti's corpse was found and what we came up with was turned over to the lab.'

'Well, then?'

'Human hairs: Ronchetti's. No trace of anything else, not even cat hair.'

La Bella got up to accompany him out. 'I don't know what else to say, my dear Lieutenant. If it's so important to you, I can see about a DNA analysis.'

'Yes, please.'

'But I'm not promising anything.'

'Naturally.'

Soon his Alfa Romeo pulled out, tyres squealing, and took off in the direction of Volterra. Once he was back in his office, Reggiani picked up the phone and dialled a mobile number.

'Sergeant Massaro,' replied the voice on the other end.

'This is Lieutenant Reggiani. How are things going there?'

'Nothing's happened, sir. In half an hour the replacements should show up, for us and the Finanza agents.'

'All right, but don't let your guard down. Don't play cards, don't read comics, don't sleep in the squad car. Keep your eyes open and each other's arses covered, because you're in danger. Get that? Your lives are in danger. Is that clear?'

There was a momentary pause on the other end, then the voice answered, 'Perfectly clear, sir. We'll be careful.'

Reggiani looked at his watch: one a.m. He loosened his tie and unbuttoned his jacket, leaned back into his chair and sighed. It felt like the night would never end.

FABRIZIO left the house at seven and drove directly to the excavation site, where the carabiniere on guard greeted him.

'How'd it go last night?' asked Fabrizio.

'Fine. We didn't see a soul.'

'Thank God. If you like, you can go.'

'No, the lieutenant says it's best for one of us to stick around. You never know. Another agent's coming to relieve me in an hour's time and I'm hoping he brings coffee.'

'I have coffee for you,' said Fabrizio, unscrewing the cap of a Thermos he took from his backpack. 'I'm never awake before I've had three cups, so I always carry extra with me. I see the workers haven't shown up yet.'

He sat on a block of smooth tufa, while the carabiniere remained on his feet with his left hand resting on the trigger of his sub-machine gun as they sipped their coffee in the cool morning air. A lovely October morning, with the leaves just turning colour and the hawthorn and dog-rose berries taking on red and orange hues.

The pickup with the workers and the gear arrived and Fabrizio walked over to the driver.

'I think the door is resting on its hinges, stone on stone. We'll have to clear away at least five centimetres under the wings, then clean the hinges by hosing them down with water and hope the door will open by pushing it back.'

The workers set about the task, using their pickaxes first to prise off the latch that crossed the two wings and then their mattocks to clear away the soil underneath the door. When they had worked their way down to a thin layer of earth, Fabrizio took over, using his trowel to scrape away the last centimetres, a little at a time, until the edge slipped inside.

The air flowing out brought no particular smell to his nostrils, apart from the odour of damp earth. The unmistakable whiff of millennia, so familiar to an archaeologist's nose, had been lost when the tomb robbers broke in. When the soil underneath the door had all been cleared away, he used the nozzle of a small compressor connected to a generator and freed the hinges of encrusted dirt with a pressure wash. The time had come to open the doors.

He got to his feet and motioned for the workers to join him. One on the right and the other on the left, with him in the centre, pushing at the meeting point of the two door panels. They began applying steady, uniform pressure under Fabrizio's direction.

'Slowly, slowly, here we go. There's no rush. Just a bit more now . . .'

The two door panels finally separated from each other with a slight grinding of fine sand, letting the first beam of light into the tomb after 2,500 years. The scowl of Charun – the demon who accompanied the dead to the other world – greeted him. A fresco of good quality, the work of an artist from Tarquinia, Fabrizio thought at first glance. He had the men push the wings open further, enough to allow him to enter with ease. He turned around before he went in, remembering Francesca's words and hoping that she'd be there to share this emotional moment with him. No one.

It was twelve o'clock exactly when he entered under the sign of the new moon and stepped across the threshold of the ancient tomb. He waited to allow his vision to adjust to the shadowy light and to the contrast between the sliver of wall illuminated by the bright sun and the gloom all around.

It was on his left that he first distinguished the body of a reclining woman sculpted softly into a block of alabaster. The statue represented a person at the height of her beauty, at an age which wasn't definable, maybe thirty or so. She was resting on her right elbow so that she faced the other sarcophagus on the opposite wall. The contrast was striking: the second coffin was a bare, roughly carved block of sandstone, without the slightest embellishment of any sort.

The female figure was wearing her jewellery: a necklace, a bracelet, rings and earrings, and her hair was gathered at the nape of her neck with a ribbon. Her facial expression, in the pale flesh tones of the alabaster, was extraordinarily sweet, but a further glance revealed an intense, pained pride.

Fabrizio couldn't get over the strangeness of the situation. He walked up to the first sarcophagus and ran his hand lightly along its edge. What he discovered in doing so was even more mystifying: it was sculpted in a single block of stone, almost certainly solid, which meant that there was no one buried inside. A cenotaph: a symbolic tomb. This was rare, for Etruscan times; in fact, it was possibly the only one of its kind. Fabrizio had never seen, or read about, anything like it. He carefully inspected the sides and the back but could find no sign of a separation between the coffin and its cover. What was also very unusual was the absence of a name or marking of any kind.

He turned towards the second sarcophagus and was struck by how the floor around it was scored by deep, irregular gouges, as if iron claws had scratched away at that smooth finish. His mind was flooded with fangs and claws, with that ferocious howl ripping through the night.

Fabrizio forced himself to start taking measurements and to draw the layout of the tomb with the various objects it contained. But his eyes kept going back to that rough sarcophagus towering there in front of him and he dreaded the moment of coming to terms with what was inside.

He came out at one o'clock to have a sandwich and get a breath of fresh air. He lingered in the hopes that Francesca would turn up. He wanted her to be there when he opened the coffin. The carabinieri had a little camp stove for making coffee and Fabrizio joined them in a cup before going back in.

The workers had already been to fetch the necessary equipment. They placed one wooden horse in front of and one behind the sarcophagus, set a beam across them and hung an electric winch connected to a power generator from the beam. The cable hanging from the winch ended with a ring, on to which four more cables were attached. Each of these ended in a specially shaped aluminium bracket, which was applied to one of the four corners of the lid.

Fabrizio made sure there were no cracks in the stone and then, at exactly three fifteen, threw the switch that powered the winch at its slowest speed. The four steel cables pulled straight at the same moment and slowly lifted off the lid without making the slightest noise.

At first the inside of the big coffin was so dark that Fabrizio couldn't make out what it contained. But this time he got a good whiff of the scent of millennia: the smell of must and mould, of damp stone and dust. An indefinable odour whose diverse components had had all the time they needed to decompose and recombine a thousand times with the passage of the seasons, of the centuries. The work of ages, of heat and cold, and above all of silence.

He switched on his torch and shone it inside. The contents emerged all at once from the dark, freezing the blood in his veins and cutting his breath short. He had expected to find an urn with the ashes of the deceased, along with all the usual objects that accompanied the funeral rites. What met his eyes instead was a scene of horror, covered only by the thin veil of dust that had fallen from the inside of the sandstone lid over the centuries.

He saw a tangle of human and animal bones, all jumbled up and practically fused together by a fury and ferocity beyond any limit. Enormous clawed paws, a disarticulated jaw with monstrous fangs still attached, and a human body that was barely recognizable. Shattered bones, mangled limbs, a crushed skull whose top dental arch yawned wide in a scream of pain that could no longer be heard but was still present, desperate, immortal. Both the coffin walls and the inner lid were scored with the deep abrasions that Fabrizio had seen on the ground outside.

There was no doubt about what had happened here. A human being had been buried together with a wild animal that had torn the body apart and then tried to writhe and claw its way out of that narrow stone prison before dying of suffocation. Fragments of coarse cloth were still sticking here and there to what was left of the man's head, and this detail left no doubt in Fabrizio's mind as to the horrifying ritual that had brought about this person's death.

He pulled back from the coffin, his face pale and beaded with cold sweat, murmuring, 'Oh, Christ! Oh, my God. A . . . a Phersu . . .'

4

FRANCESCA ARRIVED at about five and saw that the workers had already loaded a sarcophagus on to the pickup and were removing the winch cables. It was a striking alabaster cenotaph coffin with the figure of a woman reclining on a triclinium. She saw that the door to the tomb was open and had been entered. Fabrizio was leaning into the other roughly hewn sarcophagus with his head and arms practically inside.

He straightened up when he heard her footsteps and she was shocked by the expression on his face. He looked as if he had been to hell and back.

'What's happened? You look horrible.'

'I'm a little tired,' he said, motioning for her to join him. 'Look at this. Have you ever seen anything like it?'

Francesca leaned over the open coffin and her smile disappeared instantly. 'Good God. It's a . . .'

'A Phersu . . . I think it's a Phersu. Look at the skull. There are still shreds of the sack they closed his head in.'

'This is a sensational discovery! I would say that this is the first time archaeological evidence of this ritual has ever been found. Up until now, we've only seen it represented in the iconography.'

'I'm sure you're right, Francesca, but I don't feel satisfied or excited. When I opened the lid and saw this scene I thought I was having a heart attack. It felt like it had just happened.'

'Well, that's only natural,' said Francesca. 'The same thing happened to me when I excavated the harbour at Herculaneum with Contini. Those scenes of death and desperation seemed crystallized in time and were still laden with human drama . . . at least for me.'

'What do you think this poor wretch did to deserve such an end?'

'Come on, you know he was already dead when they shut him in the sarcophagus.'

'All right, let's say he was dead, but what led up to this? I mean, have you seen that animal inside? I've . . . never seen anything like it.'

Francesca leaned into the coffin again to peer inside, more apprehensively this time. 'What do you think it is?'

'It looks like a dog, but—'

'Yeah, it does, but its snout is so long and it's . . . enormous. Did they have dogs that big back then?'

'Don't ask me. I have no idea. I want to contact a friend of mine in Bologna tonight. Sonia Vitali is a palaeozoologist. I'll email her a picture. Hopefully she'll be free to come here and have a look at these bones.'

'What do you have left to do here?'

'I've photographed everything, both on film and digitally, and I've recorded the position of every find inside the coffin. I just have to remove the remains.'

'Does Balestra know?'

'I called him at the office and on his mobile phone, but he's not answering. Have you seen him?'

'I haven't been at the museum today. But it seems strange you can't reach him. I think he'd like to see the finds in their original positions.'

'I'm sure he would, but both the Finanza and the carabinieri are telling me they can't ensure continuing surveillance. That's why I've had the alabaster sarcophagus loaded on to the truck and now I have to remove everything else. I can't leave things here unguarded. Not that there's anything precious, but you never know . . .'

'Then I'll help you,' said Francesca.

She set to work with Fabrizio, picking out every little fragment, every last bit of that tragedy, and packaging it all up into plastic boxes. They put little yellow tags on each with the wording: 'Rovaio tomb. Sarcophagus A. Human and animal remains.' This formulation was as vague and confused as the situation that had presented itself once the coffin was opened.

Eventually nothing remained in the big chamber except for the bare sarcophagus, whose lid had been replaced. The boxes were numbered and loaded one by one on to a foam-rubber bed in the pickup. Each box had been wrapped in sacking and placed in a plastic bag to prevent dehydration. It was seven thirty by the time everything was ready.

'What about the door?' asked Francesca. 'I know people who could sell that for a fortune to some fence in Switzerland.'

'It's awfully heavy,' replied Fabrizio. 'They'd need a thirty-ton crane. A truck that size could never make it down this path and the carabinieri said they'd send a vehicle over during the night. I think we can relax. When Balestra gets back, we'll ask him what should be done.'

Francesca nodded. 'You know, you don't seem like a bumbling academic in the least! You'd make a fine inspector!'

'Thanks. I imagine that's a compliment.'

Francesca smiled. 'Listen, you've done a great job.'

'It wasn't difficult. There wasn't any stratigraphical work, just the two sarcophagi.'

'Did you have a chance to check the surrounding area at all?'

'I did yesterday. Mostly up at the top. I found a few bucchero pottery fragments, nothing much. They're in the clear plastic bag.'

Francesca ran a final check to make sure that the alabaster sarcophagus and the boxes with the bones were safely positioned in the pickup, then asked the workers to close up the tomb. They shut the heavy stone doors and secured them, plunging the chamber back into darkness and leaving Charun the sole, silent custodian of the empty tomb.

The foreman started up the truck and drove off cautiously in first gear, followed by the carabiniere Land Rover. Francesca and Fabrizio were alone, standing in front of the closed door of the ancient mausoleum. Evening was falling and the last light was disappearing in the Rovaio woods.

'Feel any better?' asked Francesca softly.

'Sure, I'm OK.'

'I know you are, but you looked awful when I first came up. That's absolutely normal, of course. It's not every day that you see something so horrible. I must admit I was pretty shaken up myself.'

'Now I know how the scratch marks on the ground got there.'

'How?'

'The animal, when they were trying to force it into the tomb alive.'

'How did they manage that, do you think?'

'They must have tied him up, his neck, his legs . . . I can't even imagine the scene. Those claws gouged into the sandstone . . . Can you think of what they must have done to human flesh?'

'Christ.'

'Yeah.' He shrugged. 'It's not worth dwelling on it. It did happen two and a half thousand years ago, after all. Not much we can do now. Maybe he was a bastard who deserved to die. But we'll never know.'

Francesca did not acknowledge his weak attempt at humour. Instead she changed the topic. 'What about the woman?'

'His wife, I'd say.'

'Maybe.'

'Or his sister.'

'Less probable. That empty sarcophagus seems more like a declaration of undying love.'

Fabrizio looked at the photo he'd taken earlier on his digital camera and admired the sublime features of the alabaster maiden, then said, 'Let me see if I can guess what you're thinking. The Phersu was the husband of this lovely lady, who continued to believe in his innocence even after the ordeal. She would have been forbidden to have herself buried in this cursed place but she wanted her image to soothe the spirit of her husband, unjustly accused for all of eternity.'

Francesca gave him a slight smile. 'You think that's impossible?'

'No, not at all. I wouldn't know how else to explain the presence of a female cenotaph in a place like this.'

Francesca knew that Fabrizio would have liked to prolong the conversation, but she excused herself. 'I'm sorry I can't join you for dinner tonight. I have to go and see my parents in Siena. My mother's not well.'

'That's OK. We'll see each other tomorrow or the next day. I don't feel like eating anyway. I'll just drink a glass of milk and go to bed.'

'Well, bye then.'

'Goodbye, Francesca.'

The girl got into her car, started it up and pulled away. Fabrizio waited for the dust to clear on the trail before leaving as well. He could see the spread of the Suzuki's headlights about a kilometre up ahead and could still hear the sound of the engine. He decided to put on some Mozart, hoping to calm his frayed nerves. Just as he was about to turn on to the main road he thought he could hear the howl again, but no, it was a siren. He breathed a sigh of relief.

But not for long. It was the carabinieri and they were looking for him.

'Sergeant Massaro,' said the officer, getting out of the Land Rover and extending his hand. 'Thank God we found you, Dr Castellani.'

'Why, what's wrong?'

'Another one's been found, ten minutes ago.'

'Another what?'

'Another body, ripped apart by that animal. Most of his face is missing. It won't be easy to identify him. Guy named Farneti found the corpse as he was coming home from his cheese factory. We're combing the area, lieutenant's orders.'

Fabrizio lifted his eyes to the sky and saw a helicopter's searchlights scanning the area between the Rovaio woods and the eroded Gaggera hillside.

'Listen, have you seen Inspector Dionisi?'

'Yes, driving in the direction of Colle Val d'Elsa.'

'Thank goodness.'

'You didn't see or hear anything out in the fields?'

'Nothing at all.'

'Well, that's good. But I think the lieutenant will want to talk to you tomorrow morning anyway. Where will you be?'

'At the museum. After nine o'clock, I'll surely be at the museum.'

Massaro gave a little salute, got back into the Land Rover and drove off at top speed. Fabrizio headed straight home. He was utterly exhausted, but very agitated at the same time. The idea of another mangled body had totally unnerved him. He couldn't help but connect what he'd seen in the coffin with the violence that had just occurred in some lonely corner of the Volterra countryside.

He took out his phone and dialled Francesca's mobile number.

'Where are you?'

'I'm near Colle, almost at the motorway. Why?'

'Thank God you're all right.'

'Why?'

'They found another one, quarter of an hour ago.'

'What are you talking about?'

'Another corpse, maimed like the first one. Massaro told me he's missing his face, or his head – I don't remember.'

There was no answer from Francesca.

'Can you hear me?'

'Yes, I can,' replied the girl. 'I'm appalled.'

The call was cut off; she had likely moved out of range. But Fabrizio felt a little better. Francesca was at least thirty kilometres from the scene of the killing. His first thought was to call the carabinieri and ask whether the body had been identified. He was ready to swear that it would be another of the three robbers who had opened the Rovaio tomb, but he realized how stupid that sounded. He was ashamed at how foolish the idea seemed, and how incongruous it would look for an archaeologist to be raving about Etruscan curses.

Finally he arrived home. He dissolved some instant decaf in a cup of milk and sat down to work at his computer. He put on some music, started up a graphics program and began uploading the photos he'd taken of the statue of the boy in room twenty of the museum. He integrated the X-rays with the three-dimensional images generated by the program and began to rotate the figure in space, trying to make sense of the strange shape he'd noticed inside the bronze.

It was after midnight when he became convinced that the shadow he'd seen in the X-rays represented the outline of a knife. The blade of a knife that had penetrated deep into the boy's body!

He shook his head repeatedly, as if trying to banish an idea that had started to eat away at him, then got up, walked around the room and went to the refrigerator to fetch a glass of water, trying to set his thoughts straight. He'd arrived only three days ago but it felt like he'd been sucked into another world. He was losing control over his emotions and he realized that his usual manner of rationally approaching a find or a research topic was being shot to hell with this crazy whirlwind of events. His anxiety was growing and his sense of reality felt distorted.

He went back to the computer screen to watch the image of

the boy that continued to rotate in the virtual space generated by the machine as if he were floating in a timeless limbo.

What could this mean? What was that intrusion doing inside the statue and how could no one have noticed it before now? How had it been inserted, and why? Was there a reason why? Could it be a clue, or a message? If so, who was the message from, the artist or the person who had commissioned it? Unfortunately, as far as he was aware, nothing was known about where the statue came from, or in what context it had been found. His only option was to ask Balestra for permission to perform a metallographic probe, if he wanted to get to the bottom of the question and publish an article with sound documentation. Hopefully the director would be grateful to him for his work on the Rovaio tomb and would allow him to go ahead with the analysis. Just a few milligrams of material would be sufficient to let him know if he was right. He decided he'd ask for authorization explicitly the next day.

There was still one thing left to do. He connected the digital camera he'd used to take the shots of the bone fragments from the tomb, copied two or three of the photos into a file and attached it to an email to Sonia Vitali, along with an explanation.

Hi, Sonia

I'm in Volterra, where the regional NAS director has put me in charge of excavating a third- or fourth-century Etruscan tomb. I've just finished and – get ready for this – I have reason to believe it's the grave of a Phersu! Along with the human bones I found the skeleton of an animal – a wolf, or a dog, I'm guessing – of enormous proportions. Offhand I'd say about a metre ten tall at the withers and more than two metres long from snout to tail. The fangs are six or seven centimetres long. I'm attaching some pictures so you can have a look and would ask you please not to mention this to anyone. If you're interested in a closer examination, I don't think Balestra would object to you studying the skeleton and publishing it. I'll leave you my phone numbers. Let me know what you think.

Fabrizio

He felt calmer now and was about to get up and go to bed when the phone started ringing. In the deep silence of the night, the insistent trilling sounded ominous to him and alarming. An unpleasant sensation of solitude and insecurity surged through him. Logically, it could be Francesca or Massaro or maybe someone from Finanza headquarters, but Fabrizio had a gut feeling it was somebody else. He picked up the receiver and a voice he'd already heard said, 'Don't disturb the child's peace. Get out, if you know what's good for you.'

'Listen,' started Fabrizio, talking as quickly as he could. 'You're not scaring me. I . . .'

But there was no use continuing. His caller had already hung up.

Fine, he thought to himself. He'd ask Reggiani to put a tap on both telephones, the museum number and this one, and on his mobile phone as well. He let himself relish the thought of a face-to-face meeting with this crazy lady who thought it amusing to make such ridiculous threats. She must be calling him because she could see the lights on, or maybe she could even see him sitting in front of his computer screen. If only he had a dog!

To be on the safe side he closed the shutters, turned off the computer, went to the wall, took down the shotgun – an automatic five-round Bernardelli – and loaded it with five cartridges. Then he walked towards the staircase to go up to the bedroom.

The telephone rang again.

He stopped for a moment, with his foot on the step, to collect his thoughts, then turned around and picked up the receiver.

'Listen, you bitch. If you think—'

'Fabrizio! It's Sonia! I'm so sorry, but I thought you'd still be awake!'

Fabrizio let out a long sigh. 'Oh, it's me who's sorry, Sonia. I wasn't sleeping, it's simply that . . .'

'I've just got back from a conference in Padua. I saw your email and I couldn't resist . . . So who's the bitch you thought you were talking to?'

'Someone I don't know. Someone who likes to break my balls by calling late at night and—'

'Listen, I've seen the photos – they are incredible! Are you sure about the measurements you sent?'

'Give or take a centimetre or two.'

'I just can't believe what I'm seeing. Do you really think they'll let me publish it?'

'I don't see why not.'

'Will you talk with Balestra?'

'Sure. But what do you think it is?'

Sonia fell silent for a few moments. 'To be utterly frank, I don't know what to say. I've never seen an animal that big in any of the scientific literature. It's a monster.'

Fabrizio's voice became apprehensive. 'A monster? What do you mean by that?'

'Only that I've never seen such a thing. Even now, say, a Caucasian Molosser, which is gigantic, is not that size.'

'Well, then, what the hell is it? I mean, you're the expert, so how do you explain it?'

'Hey, what's wrong with you? Why are you so edgy? Are you sure I didn't wake you up? Or did I . . . interrupt something?'

'No. Listen, I'm sorry. I didn't mean to be rude. You're saying that you don't know what it is.'

'It looks like a canid, but I've never seen one so enormous. An expert is only an expert on what he's seen and studied, Fabrizio. You know that better than I do. All I can tell you is that I've never heard of such an animal, and neither has anyone else that I know of. I'd hazard a guess that it's a breed that's gone extinct and that we have no knowledge of or . . . a genetic mutation, something of the sort.'

'Right. That's a possibility, sure. Listen, try to make it here as soon as you can, and I'll talk to the director in the meantime.'

'I can leave tomorrow,' said Sonia resolutely.

'No, maybe not tomorrow. Give me a couple of days. I'll call you as soon as anything comes up.'

There was a moment of silence and in that very instant the howl that Fabrizio had heard the first night rang out loudly. A long, desperate lament that grew in force and intensity, exploding into the blood-curdling scream of a wounded beast. An atrocious wheezing that sounded nearly human.

Fabrizio stiffened as a feeling of sheer terror surged through his body.

Sonia's voice on the phone was full of anguish. 'My God . . . what was that?'

She'd heard it.

'I don't know,' replied Fabrizio mechanically. He then replaced the receiver and picked up the shotgun. It was locked and loaded.

5

Dr La Bella put out his cigarette in the ashtray, took his glasses off with a slow, studied gesture and began to clean the lenses with an immaculate handkerchief.

'Well?' asked Lieutenant Reggiani in an almost impatient tone.

'It's just as I said, my dear Lieutenant, isn't it? Remember? "If you don't find the animal I'll have more maimed bodies on my autopsy table." And here we are.'

'I want to know whether you're sure this death can be attributed to the same cause,' said Reggiani.

'I have no doubts about that,' answered La Bella, 'although that statement cannot be made with absolute certainty. Would you care to take a look yourself?'

He got up and walked towards the cooler.

Reggiani wanted to say no, he would not care to take a look, but he obediently followed the doctor. It was his job, after all.

La Bella grasped the handle of one of the drawers and pulled it towards him until the top half of the corpse, covered by a sheet, was out. He lifted the sheet.

'Dear Christ,' murmured Reggiani, looking away in disgust. 'It's worse than the last one.'

La Bella closed the drawer and locked it.

'Have you spoken to the public prosecutor?'

'You bet I have. He's been calling me every two or three hours to get an update on our investigation.'

'And what might that be?' asked La Bella mechanically.

'We don't know shit, Dr La Bella. That is the update. I have two corpses that have been ripped to shreds and not a single clue to go on. The story's bound to break, which means that in the wink of an eye this town will be besieged by a horde of reporters and TV cameras dying for a slice of the blood and mystery. Until now, I've managed to convince the prosecutor that it's best to keep this quiet to prevent the spread of panic. As luck would have it, the guy who found the second body has agreed not to spill the beans and I know I can trust my men. But I also know this can't last for long. It's bound to leak out. At the same time, I have to put maximum security measures into effect to protect local people. It's not been easy.'

As the two men neared the exit, La Bella stared into the officer's eyes with a discouraged expression and said, 'I know it's stupid to ask, but have you sent dogs out?'

'It's the first thing we did. But we didn't get anywhere. We used our best trackers, but it was crazy. They'd run off in every direction, double back, take off like wild things through the bushes and then come back again. Absurd.'

'I understand,' said La Bella. 'But you can't not warn the residents. They have a right to know, to take precautions, to protect themselves . . .'

'You don't think that's on my mind! Listen, at the start I was hoping that the first case would remain an isolated occurrence. That animal, or whatever it is, might have run off or ended up elsewhere, or have been caught or killed off, damn it. I'm about to go to the public prosecutor and submit my plan of action.'

'If I'm not being indiscreet, can you tell me what that plan is?'

'It's not that I don't trust you, Doctor, but I have to consult with the prosecutor first. Basically, we have to strive to achieve the impossible: inform the townspeople, ask the press to keep a low profile, solve the case by giving it all we've got.'

Dr La Bella patted him on the shoulder. 'I don't envy you,

Lieutenant. Good luck. I've never met anyone in all my life who needed it more.'

REGGIANI got into his car with Sergeant Massaro and drove to the public prosecutor's office. The official was exceedingly agitated and didn't even ask Reggiani to sit down.

'Maybe you don't realize this, Lieutenant,' he began, 'but from one moment to the next this situation could slip totally out of our control. The government authorities may step in and take it out of our hands completely.'

Reggiani instantly lost his temper. 'That, God willing, is the least of my problems! They're not in harm's way and have plenty of their own headaches to worry about. As far as this situation is concerned, it has already slipped out of our control! We have two cadavers at the mortuary that have been clawed to pieces and no reason to think there may not be more coming.'

'That's impossible!' shouted the public prosecutor. 'It's only an animal, for Christ's sake. You've got dogs, vehicles, helicopters, scores of men.'

Reggiani lowered his head to hide his anger and took a deep breath before he answered. 'You see, sir, all of the means that you've just mentioned have been used without achieving the slightest result. I've put my best men out in the field and on investigations. This is not just any old case. There are other matters that concern me as well and I need your help.'

The public prosecutor nodded, with an air of condescension.

'I would like you to make a personal call to the directors of all the local papers and ask for a news blackout. I'm sure you can convince them that this is necessary due to the unique, extremely serious nature of the matter. I will arrange to inform local residents regarding the nature of the threat and the precautions to be taken. A lot of unverified stories are already going around. I'll tell them the truth. Luckily, this isn't a big city. There are a given number of families that must be informed. At the same time I will reorganize my investigation, starting from another angle.'

'What angle might that be?' asked the public prosecutor.

'I want to start from the tomb,' replied Reggiani. 'From the man who opened it and excavated it. I think that's where all this began.'

FABRIZIO took a bunch of keys from the hook and went down into the storeroom. Sonia had been so excited at seeing the pictures that she was eager to start immediately. He wanted to make sure that all the material would be ready for her to begin her work. If he got this out of the way, he'd be free to return to his own studies and forget about the rest. If that was an option.

He descended a couple of floors from street level and realized he was in the middle of the ancient city: tufa walls, old substructures in ruins, foundations made of huge blocks, surely from the Etruscan age. He switched on the light and walked down a long corridor covered by a barrel vault ceiling. On either side lay the dusty odds and ends typical of the cellars of the museums and NAS facilities all over Italy: chunks of marble and stone, column segments, fragmented sculptures waiting patiently to be restored, handles and necks of vases, floor tiles and boxes. Hundreds of boxes. Yellow and red plastic stacks, each with its own label reporting the name of the excavation, the sector and the layer where the finds contained inside had been found.

The materials from the Rovaio dig, except for the alabaster sarcophagus, which had been taken to another warehouse outside the city, were at the end of the hall, sitting on top of a shelf carved of stone which created a niche in the wall. Fabrizio laid a plastic sheet on the floor and started first of all to pick out the more scattered and splintered pieces of the human skeleton. He taped to the wall an enlargement of the digital shot he had taken inside the tomb, then switched on a portable mechanic's light and began to gather the fragments, one after another, piecing them together with difficulty, seeking the lines of recomposition of a body almost disintegrated by a ravaging fury.

He patiently reconstructed shoulder and collar bones, lined up the phalanges of the fingers which were strewn in every direction. Every now and then he would glance at the blown-up photo on the wall and that awful image, that horrible tangle of bones and fangs, created a mounting sense of anxiety in him that he tried in vain to overcome. His fingers seemed to move on their own, brushing the man's skull, part of the temporal bone still bearing a strip of the sack in which his head was enclosed during the cruel ordeal. The emotion that had been simmering inside of him exploded with uncontrollable force. Those bare bones electrified him, filled him with a clear, distinct vision of those atrocious moments: suffocated, breathless panting, the crazed beating of a heart gripped with terror. Fangs sinking into live flesh as the man screamed in pain, writhing about blindly, futilely wielding the sword tight in his fist. Blood that with every bite spurted out more copiously, soaking the ground, blood that made the animal more and more excited and aggressive, feeding its thirst for slaughter. He heard the sinister crunching of bones, yielding abruptly to those steel fangs, smelt the nauseating odour of intestines ripped from the man's belly and devoured still throbbing, while he was alive and screaming, shaking violently in the throes of agony.

Dripping with sweat, Fabrizio could not control the furious beating of his own heart, nor the tears that were pouring from his eyes and running down his cheeks, nor the convulsive fluttering of his eyelids, which were fragmenting that tragedy into thousands of bloody shards that were pricking every centimetre of his body and soul.

He cried out in a hoarse, suffocated voice, the scream of a man dreaming, and he had the impression that his cry had snuffed out the bulb, abruptly plunging him into the gloom of the underground chambers. But soon that silent darkness was pierced by a mournful dirge and became animated by shadowy, sinister presences: ghosts cloaked in black carrying a litter which bore the bloody tatters of a large dismembered body. Behind them growled the beast, its eyes phosphorescent in the dim light and its mouth foaming, held tight by ropes and tethers, yanking its keepers this way and that with immense strength. They were dragging it to its final destiny: to be buried alive with the human meal that would have to satiate it for all eternity.

Fabrizio screamed again and then, tired of fighting it off, let himself sink into a well of silence.

HE WAS unaware of how much time had passed before a light stung his eyes and a voice shook him fully awake: 'Professor! Professor! Good Lord, what has happened? Are you ill? Shall I call a doctor?'

Fabrizio got to his feet and wiped his forehead. The confused image peering out at him slowly took on the familiar features of a person he knew well: Mario, the security guard.

'No, no,' he replied. 'There's no need. I must have fainted. There's nothing wrong, I feel fine, I promise you.'

Mario looked sceptical. 'Are you sure? You look pretty awful.'

'Perfectly sure. I was working down here, but it's so damp and there's no air . . .'

'You're right. This is no place for you to be working.' The security guard lifted his eyes to the blown-up photo on the wall. 'Good heavens! What on earth is that?'

'It's nothing, Mario,' said Fabrizio, swiftly rolling up the enlargement. 'Just bones. Lord knows how many you've seen.'

Mario got the hint and changed the subject. 'Listen, they're looking for you upstairs.'

'Who's looking for me?'

'That carabiniere lieutenant. His name's Reggiani.'

'Do you know what he wants?'

'He says it's just to talk with you . . . I'll bet you anything it's about that second bloke they found murdered. He's already asked me not to breathe a word about it. I don't know how he knew that I know.'

'That's his job, Mario.'

'Anyway, I haven't spoken to a soul, but people know about it. Word gets around. People are scared.'

'That's understandable.'

'You said it. So should I show him to your office?'

'Yes, do that. Tell him I'll be right there.'

Mario walked back up the stairs and Fabrizio turned to look at what he'd accomplished. Only the upper part of the human skeleton was reassembled, and only partially. He realized he might have to ask for help from a technician with expertise in osteology or he'd never manage to finish the job. There was still a lot of work to do, especially on the small fragments that were difficult to identify, and he hadn't even started on the animal, whose entire skeleton seemed to be present and was in near-perfect condition, except for some cracking and splintering probably due to exposure to freezing temperatures through the millennia. Fabrizio bent over the bones and saw that one of the four huge canine teeth had become detached from the top jaw, most likely jolted loose during transport. He picked it up and slipped it into his pocket, with the intention of observing it carefully and measuring it. He then walked up the stairs, switched off the light and closed the door behind him.

Lieutenant Reggiani was waiting in his office. When he entered, the officer got to his feet and held out his hand. 'Dr Castellani,' he started. His expression made it clear that this was no courtesy call.

'Hello, Lieutenant. Please make yourself at home,' said Fabrizio in greeting, forcing himself to appear normal. 'Would you like a cup of coffee? From the dispenser, I mean.'

'That's fine with me,' said Reggiani. 'It's not as bad as it used to be.'

Fabrizio left the room, then returned a few moments later

with two espressos and two packets of sugar. He sat down at his desk.

Reggiani took a sip of the steaming coffee and began: 'Dr Castellani, I'm sorry to be taking up your time, but the circumstances won't allow me to do otherwise. You know what has been happening in the fields around Volterra . . .'

'I don't know all the details, but let's say I'm aware of the situation.'

'You don't want to know all the details. Unfortunately, the situation is far from being under control and I've come here in the hopes that talking with you might give me some new perspective. Let me tell you briefly what's been going on. On Wednesday at about two a.m., a Finanza police team surprised three individuals trying to break into an Etruscan tomb, the one that you have since become acquainted with.'

'That's right.'

'One of them, a person that both we and the Finanza have been watching for some while, a certain Armando Ronchetti, was found dead the next day not far from the site of the break-in. The guy's throat was basically ripped out. The coroner, who's certainly used to seeing dead people, vomited his guts out.'

'I can believe it.'

'At first we thought he'd been attacked by a stray, but that seemed unlikely from the start, since Ronchetti had no doubt roamed those fields at night for years, given his line of work, and would certainly have known how to handle any dog. In fact, he had a torch with a flasher in his pocket, along with a pistol, a little 6.35-calibre Astra Llama.

'As far as we can tell, whoever murdered him didn't even give him the time to put his hand on the gun. Then, on Thursday evening, while you were completing your work at the excavation site, we found a second corpse in even worse shape than the first, slaughtered in the same gruesome way. According to the papers we found in his pocket, he was one Aurelio

Rastelli, a resident of Volterra. Like his father, he had a market stall and sold items of clothing. Nothing in his background that could justify such a bloodthirsty murder, except pure chance.'

'What you mean,' said Fabrizio, 'is finding himself in the wrong place at the wrong time.'

'We have evidence, nonetheless, that Rastelli, like Ronchetti, had been involved – although we don't know with what frequency – in the clandestine excavation and marketing of archaeological artefacts. You see, in this area, raiding tombs is like a second job for a number of people; a way to earn a little extra cash on the side. We and the Finanza do what we can, but there aren't enough of us – the territory is quite vast and the locals aren't always willing to lend a hand. I've talked to our anti-trafficking squad down in Rome and they confirm that Rastelli was picked up a few years ago for possession of stolen archaeological objects.'

'Which doesn't necessarily make him a professional tomb robber,' observed Fabrizio. 'I'm assuming you have no proof that he was at the Rovaio site with Ronchetti that night. Or do you?'

'I've had the soil from the soles of his shoes analysed and yes, it does correspond to the soil in that area. But, unfortunately, it's the same soil you'll find anywhere around here, including the neighbourhood where Rastelli lives.'

'So you're back to the starting line?'

'Yes, we are. He might have been present at the break-in, but then again, he might not. But let us suppose for a moment that, since we can't exclude the possibility, Aurelio Rastelli was at the Rovaio tomb site on Wednesday night with Ronchetti and with a third individual we have not as yet identified. At that point, the two murdered men would have something in common – that is, they teamed up in the attempt to plunder an Etruscan tomb.'

'All you need to do, then, is uncover the identity of the third man. You put a couple of well-armed units on his tail and wait until the killer – man or beast – shows up. Then you capture him or take him out.'

'I could hire you as an investigator,' Reggiani complimented him.

'Yeah, an archaeologist is a bit like an investigator, Lieutenant, but there's a difference. You arrive at the scene of a crime a few minutes or at most a few hours after the fact. We don't get there until centuries later.'

'That's true. I never thought of that. But, as I was saying, we are unfortunately not certain that the second victim is actually connected to the first and we can't afford to wait until we find the third. I've got too many people breathing down my neck.'

'How can I help you, then?'

Reggiani lowered his head as though he were too embarrassed to express his thoughts in words. 'I don't know how to say this . . . Well, I have the impression that all this originated from the opening or, if you prefer, the violation of the Rovaio tomb. I know this will make you laugh, but I can't help but wonder if . . . somehow . . . if it's not the fault of some . . .'

'Curse?' offered Fabrizio, without a trace of sarcasm in his tone.

'Well, I don't know how to explain this . . . but I can tell you that sometimes, when we don't have a scrap of information to go on, we've resorted to consulting certain individuals – you know . . . psychics, to be blunt. I can assure you that the results have been astonishing at times. It's done abroad as well, in France, the US . . .'

'Confidentially speaking, Lieutenant, there are archaeologists who consult psychics as well, though I'm not sure with what kind of success rate. Personally, I've never believed in them,' Fabrizio went on, 'but I must admit you have quite a problem on your hands. You don't know where to turn.'

'You're right. We have no trail to follow, no evidence to examine. Nothing to go on, in short.'

Fabrizio thought of what he had imagined while he was at work below and he felt a chill go up his spine. Reggiani noticed his shudder.

'What about that chase the other night?' asked Fabrizio to distract the officer from his own reaction. 'You had your guys out in full force.'

'Right, and that attracted a little too much attention. We tried to pass it off as a man hunt after a robbery. Anyway, we turned up nothing. Like looking for ghosts. There's nothing we haven't tried. This morning I saw an anatomopathologist and spoke to our medical examiner, Dr La Bella. He's a man of few words but great experience, and the results of his autopsy were, simply put, horrifying. Both men were slaughtered by an enormously powerful wild animal with huge fangs. We're talking six or seven centimetres.'

Fabrizio scowled and remembered the canine tooth he'd picked out of the box downstairs. He stuck his hand in his pocket and felt it there, long, smooth and sharp, as if twenty-four centuries had passed without making a dent. He pulled it out and showed it to Lieutenant Reggiani, holding it by the tip.

'Like this one?' he asked.

6

Lieutenant Reggiani stared in amazement at the sharp fang between Fabrizio's index finger and thumb, then raised his eyes and held the archaeologist's gaze for a long, tense, silent minute before saying, 'Yes . . . I would say so. What is it?'

'I should have an answer for that,' said Fabrizio. 'But I don't. A colleague of mine who is an expert in palaeozoology should be arriving soon from Bologna. She has studied a vast number of ancient bone fragments and skeletons of every species, both wild and domesticated. If she can't figure this one out, I know of no one else who can. This tooth belongs to a complete skeleton of which I've sent her a photograph by email, but she seemed quite puzzled. She thought it was a canid, but wouldn't hazard anything else. It's the dimensions which are astonishing, along with its uncommon anatomical features.'

'Where did you find it?'

Fabrizio opened his desk drawer and pulled out a photograph, setting it down on the table for the officer.

'In a roughly carved sarcophagus, without an inscription of any sort, inside the tomb I excavated at the Rovaio site.'

'How extraordinary,' exclaimed Reggiani as soon as he had managed to work out what he was looking at. 'But . . . what is it?'

'It's the first and only physical proof we have ever found of the most frightful rite of the Etruscan religion. This is the tomb of a Phersu. Until now, we've only suspected its existence from iconography – most notably, a fresco in the Tomb of the Augurs

61

in Tarquinia, along with a couple of others. But we've never had tangible evidence and certainly nothing so explicit.'

'Go on,' prompted Reggiani, as if he were interrogating a witness.

'Habitually it was a sort of human sacrifice dedicated to the soul of a high-ranking person who had died. The rite has very ancient roots and was performed by diverse civilizations. Even the Greeks, in the most archaic age. Do you remember the *Iliad*?'

'A little, here and there. I haven't read it since high school,' said Reggiani, certain that the professor was about to give him a lecture on classical culture.

'You must certainly recall the funeral games honouring Patroclus, including a sword fight between two men. The referee, who is Achilles in this case, interrupts the combat at first blood. But it's thought that in more ancient cultures the duellers were forced to fight on until one of them died, so that his soul could accompany into the afterlife the dead person for whom funeral rites were being celebrated. In later ages, these duels were purged of their bloodier components and became purely athletic competitions, converging in great sporting and religious performances like the Olympics. In Italy, on the other hand, the duels maintained their violent connotations and evolved into the gladiator fights of the Roman age.'

'I had no idea,' admitted Reggiani. 'So the origins of Roman combat in the arena were Etruscan?'

'Most probably. But, as I said, it started out as a religious rite, as far-fetched as that may seem to us now. Human sacrifice was a way of appeasing the gods. Usually a prisoner of war would be forced to fight against a wild animal, or more than one, under conditions which doomed him to lose.

'But what I've found evidence of here makes me hypothesize an even more cruel variant. I think that when the crime committed was beyond the pale, a real monstrosity, a horrible act that broke the laws of man and nature, the community would be seized by a kind of collective panic, fearing that the gods would not be satisfied with the sacrifice of a single life to atone for such horror and would seek to punish the whole community.

'The natural solution would be to execute the guilty party by subjecting him to the most tremendous torture. But what would happen if, let's say, the person accused of this horrendous crime declared himself innocent and that there was no definitive evidence to prove his guilt. In that case, he would be subjected to a trial by ordeal. He would be given a sword, but one hand would be tied behind his back and his head would be enclosed in a sack. Thus disabled, he would be made to fight off a ferocious animal: a wolf, or even a lion. If he managed to survive, that meant he was innocent and he could return to his everyday life, with his prior rank and rights. If he died, the beast that had killed him would be buried along with his body so it could continue to torment him for all eternity. That's what I think I see in this photograph,' concluded Fabrizio, replacing it in the drawer.

'What a nightmare,' commented Reggiani. 'I've never heard of such a thing. I have no doubt you're right about the photo. And you know, it makes me think twice about these gruesome murders. Now that I've heard this story, it almost seems that someone may be re-enacting this ancient ritual . . .'

'Seems that way to me too,' admitted Fabrizio.

'Let's say someone who learned about this discovery and got it into his head to act it out . . .'

'I can see what you're saying, but for what reason? I don't get the motive.'

'No, you're right,' agreed Reggiani. 'And Ronchetti's body was found before you opened the tomb.'

'So we're back where we started.'

Lieutenant Reggiani bit his lower lip. 'As a matter of principle, I can only consider hypotheses that are rational, caused by a natural sequence of events.'

'Do you think I was suggesting otherwise?'

'No, of course not. But why did you show me that fang then? You know it belongs to an animal that died twenty-four centuries ago, if I'm not mistaken.'

'I don't know why I pulled it out. I did it without thinking.'

Reggiani held out his hand and Fabrizio put the fang in his palm.

'You know,' the officer continued, fingering the oversized tooth, 'when you showed me this, I was reminded of something I saw on television a few days ago. It was in one of those nature programmes. They were showing the skull of a southern African hominid with two strange indentations at the top. No one had been able to interpret the marks until they found the skull of a predator from that age, whose top canines were a perfect match for the indentations.' He held out the fang. 'Can I keep this for twenty-four hours?' he asked.

Fabrizio shrugged. 'No, not really, but what the hell? If I can't trust a carabiniere, who can I trust?' Then he added, 'What are you going to do with it?'

'Show it to a friend.'

'All right. But be sure you give it back to me tomorrow. My colleague will be coming from Bologna and she'll be examining the skeleton. I don't want her to find anything missing.'

'You bet,' the officer promised. He was about to put his cap back on, when Fabrizio remembered that threatening voice on the telephone and thought it would be best to let the police know.

'Listen, there's something I wanted to mention . . .' he began.

Just then, someone knocked at the door.

It was Francesca. 'Good morning, Lieutenant,' she said to Reggiani, before turning to Fabrizio. 'The director is in his office. He wants to talk to you.'

'I'm coming,' said Fabrizio, getting up.

'Wasn't there something you wanted to tell me?' asked Lieutenant Reggiani.

'No, it doesn't matter,' replied Fabrizio. 'Some other time.'

'As you like. Goodbye, Dr Castellani.'

'Goodbye, Lieutenant. And . . . don't forget.'

'Not to worry. You'll have it back tomorrow.' He placed his cap on his head and walked away down the hall.

'What's he talking about?' asked Francesca.

'Nothing. Just something I lent him. Do you have any idea what Balestra wants?'

'That doesn't take much guesswork. You've just excavated an intact late-fourth-century tomb, haven't you?'

'Right. Now that you mention it, it's strange it took him so long to start looking for me.'

'He's been out.'

'Where?'

'He didn't say. At the ministry maybe. Who knows?'

They had reached the director's office. Francesca waved him towards the door with her hand and walked away. Fabrizio knocked.

'Come in,' replied Balestra's voice from inside.

'It must seem impossible,' began the director before Fabrizio had even taken a seat, 'but with a dig this important in progress, I haven't been able to find a moment to touch base with you.'

I'd love to know why, thought Fabrizio. Out loud, he commiserated: 'I can imagine. So many things clamouring for your attention at once.'

Balestra took half of a Tuscan cigar from a box and put it in his mouth. 'No, don't worry,' he said instantly, seeing the look on Fabrizio's face. 'I don't smoke them. So, from what I hear, the Rovaio tomb was completely inviolate. Is that true?'

'That's right, sir.'

'Why so grim, then? What you're saying is extraordinary.'

'Well, the things that have happened since that tomb was discovered would dampen anyone's enthusiasm.'

Balestra scowled. 'I can't say I blame you. I was told you've just been speaking to that carabiniere lieutenant.'

'Yes, that's right.'

'In any case, I'm looking forward to hearing exactly what you found. You can follow up with a written report at your convenience. I also want you to know that, as far as I am concerned, you can publish this on your own, if you like.'

Fabrizio expressed his appreciation for the opportunity, but politely declined. 'I'm honoured, director, but I really don't think it's my place, and besides, I already have my own research to take forward. I've limited my work to documenting the find and ensuring that the contents of the tomb are secure.'

'I insist that you publish at least a part of the findings, or at least sign the article with me, if you prefer. Let's hear, then, exactly how things have unfolded.'

Fabrizio began to detail all the phases of locating, opening and inspecting the tomb. But when he started speaking of the bare sarcophagus at the north wall of the funeral chamber, he couldn't stop his voice from cracking as his deep misgiving and bewilderment leaked out.

'I realized that I was looking at something that had never been documented,' he said. 'That sarcophagus was the tomb of a Phersu . . .'

'Are you serious?'

'Yes, I'm sure of it. The tomb contains proof of the ritual, if my reconstruction is correct. Look for yourself . . .' Fabrizio extracted a file from the folder he held and handed the director a big black-and-white print.

'See,' he began, as Balestra examined the image, 'I'm led to believe that the man is certainly a Phersu by the fragments of fabric still attached to the skull and vertebrae of the neck. I've deduced that his head was covered by a hood, or a sack on which a mask was painted . . .'

Balestra's flinch was barely perceptible, but Fabrizio was struck by it nonetheless; the director was famous for being tough and imperturbable.

'Continue,' he said, without raising his eyes from the photograph.

'What's more, the architrave at the entrance has a black moon at its centre, and the western wall a fresco of the demon Charun. The sarcophagus is roughly carved, completely unadorned and has no inscription. The other skeleton, the animal's, is largely intact, while the man's is mangled. I believe that the animal was entombed alive with the corpse of the Phersu. Actually, I'm wondering whether the man might not have been alive as well. Perhaps the ordeal was interrupted before his death in order to ensure that the punishment would fit the horror of his crime.'

Balestra was examining the photograph with a magnifying glass and it was clear that he was trying to stifle an emotional reaction. His forehead was beaded with sweat and his face had become ashen.

'That seems to be a plausible deduction,' he said curtly in a controlled tone of voice. 'Go on, then.'

Fabrizio drew a long breath, then began speaking again. 'My hypothesis seems confirmed by the fact that the tufa in front of the sarcophagus is scored with scratch marks so deep they could only have been left by the powerful claws of a baulking animal. The leather fragments that I found both inside among the bones and outside at the foot of the sarcophagus may be from the belts and straps that held the animal as it was forced to enter. I've calculated that it took a number of men to accomplish this.'

He took more photos out of the folder and laid them on the desk in front of the director. 'I've taken the liberty of contacting a colleague of mine, Dr Vitali, a palaeozoologist at the University of Bologna, and have asked her to examine the skeleton. You'll have noticed the enormous size.'

'I have,' said the director. 'The dimensions are beyond belief. Monstrous. Chimera-like, as if the parts did not come from a single being.'

Fabrizio pulled more photos out of his briefcase and placed them on the desk. These were of the alabaster sarcophagus with the reclining woman and, as he began to explain his interpretation of how the finely carved piece had found its way inside a cursed burial chamber, he realized that, despite the beauty and uniqueness of the piece, the director was no longer listening to him. He seemed distracted and preoccupied, as if some thought were tormenting him, and Fabrizio noticed that he had completely crumbled the cigar he was holding.

'Are you feeling well, sir?' he asked, hoping that Balestra might want to confide in him and let him in on the mysterious work that had been keeping him confined to his office for weeks on end, but the director instantly regained his customary aplomb.

'Certainly, I'm fine,' he replied. 'Why do you ask?'

As if you didn't know, thought Fabrizio, ready to let the subject drop. But Balestra hadn't recovered completely; he was still massaging his temples as if his head were killing him. Fabrizio realized this was the best chance he'd ever have and decided to run the risk of irritating the director. It's now or never, he thought, and took the plunge.

'Well, because a lot of things just don't add up here. The way you reacted to these photographs and to my words doesn't seem normal to me. And, if I may say so, it also seems odd that you've been away from your office in Florence for so long, and that nine times out of ten you have your secretary say you're not in, and that you don't find the time to personally excavate an inviolate tomb like the one at Rovaio, and that you turn it over to the first guy who happens to be passing through. Wouldn't it be best if both of us showed our cards?'

Balestra took another half-cigar from the box of Tuscans and put it in his mouth. He remained silent for a while, then began: 'I think you're right, Castellani. I'm willing to be honest with you.

'It all started about three years ago, when a man came to

see me, saying that while digging on a work site somewhere near the brook at Le Macine, he stumbled upon an ancient inscription, a bronze slab broken into six pieces. The landowner had apparently arranged for a fence to smuggle these pieces out and sell them to an antiques dealer in Switzerland or Luxembourg. But this bloke was ready to tell me where the pieces were if I would guarantee him a finder's fee.

'Now, this kind of thing happens very rarely – that a tomb robber, whether he's a professional or has merely chanced upon some find, comes to offer whatever it is to us. I figured he was trying to get back at an employer who wasn't treating him fairly or had perhaps dismissed him from his job. So maybe he thought he could get his revenge and even pick up a little extra money on the side. I told him that yes, there would be a reward attached to turning in an archaeological find, although I couldn't tell him how much that might be, since I hadn't seen the piece itself and had no idea of its value.

'So this character, who seemed a bit strange from the start – a bit touched, to be honest – seemed happy with my promises and told me exactly where the inscription could be found. In a plastic bag covered with sand and stones on the bottom of the stream. We went at night, with the carabinieri from the special services—'

'Was Lieutenant Reggiani with you?' Fabrizio interrupted instinctively.

'No,' replied the director. 'Reggiani is not with the special archaeological recovery service. He comes from ROS, the organized-crime division, and was moved here so he could take it easy after three years in Sicily and two in Calabria. He got here the year after this happened and I don't think he knows anything about it.

'We found the inscription and I informed my superiors: the Minister first of all, then the general director and a couple of my close colleagues. Five people in all. Six with you, Castellani. I then began to study the inscription, or rather the six fragments.

I soon realized that there was a piece missing, a seventh fragment, but I couldn't find out for the life of me what had happened to it. I questioned the finder, who – on the condition that he would remain anonymous – told me exactly where he'd dug up the slab. I immediately had the area scoured for signs of a historical context; a clue that would help me date the inscription, figure out how it got there. The investigation turned up nothing. Not a single element that referred to any historical period or place. So either this man was lying to me or the site was only a temporary hiding place where the slab could sit while the landowner was arranging to smuggle it out of the country.'

Fabrizio noticed that the director was no longer so pale and jittery. Just being able to talk about things had obviously eased the tension and anxiety that this investigation had caused for him. Fabrizio guessed that there was still more, and worse, to come.

'As I was putting out feelers to try to get my hands on the seventh fragment, if it existed,' the director continued, 'I started examining the text of the inscription as well. I soon made an extraordinary discovery. The language it was written in was quite unique. It was definitely Etruscan, but it was infiltrated, so to speak, with archaic Latin expressions that made the text more comprehensible. I feel that, once this text is published, it will be cited by philologists and linguists all over the world.'

'Do you mean you've found the key to translating an Etruscan text?' asked Fabrizio incredulously.

'I think I'm close. In any case, I've understood what it is: an *arà*.'

'A curse,' mused Fabrizio.

'Six curses in reality, one on each fragment. In all probability, the seventh is the final curse and the most dreadful of them all.'

Balestra fell silent and Fabrizio didn't know what to say.

'It can't be a curse that has you so upset,' Fabrizio said

finally, trying to help Balestra put things into perspective. 'The ancient world is full of curses that have never come true.'

Balestra's expression was detached, almost annoyed. 'This one has,' he said.

'Excuse me?'

'This could—' Balestra broke off and began again in a different tone of voice. 'Look, Castellani, it can't be anything more than a coincidence, but this curse was carved in bronze. Why? So that it would last through eternity, and that leads me to believe that the crime at its origin must have been a particularly gruesome one. I think we can assume that it took place here, that is in the ancient city of Velathri. Now you are showing me documentation attesting to the burial of a Phersu, seemingly dating back to the same era as the inscription, with material evidence hinting at an especially blood-curdling ritual. That's where we stand, isn't it?'

'I would say so, yes,' admitted Fabrizio.

'It comes naturally to connect the two, even if we might rather not.'

'It does.'

'As if that were not enough, two individuals accused of attempting to open the tomb are found with their throats ripped out and their necks and faces devoured by some beast which has left no traces of any sort. I've never heard of such a series of coincidences.'

'Have you spoken to Lieutenant Reggiani?'

'Of course. I am a government official.'

'Right.'

'Reggiani is a top-notch officer. He's got balls.'

Fabrizio was surprised by the use of such a colloquial expression by the director, who was always so proper. He interpreted it as coming from a need to confide and be consoled, which alarmed him even more. Balestra must be letting on much less than what he actually knew about the inscription. All the signs indicated that the man was scared to death.

'He may succeed in solving this thing sooner than we expect,' concluded the director.

'Maybe. But that's not the impression he gave me.'

'We'll see,' commented Balestra, nervously chewing on his half-cigar.

'We'll see,' repeated Fabrizio mechanically.

He had the feeling that Balestra still had more to say and that, if he insisted, he could tease the information out of him.

'I don't want to seem intrusive, but I wonder if you would possibly allow me to have a look at what you've managed to translate. I'd keep it completely confidential, obviously.'

'I can't,' replied the director. 'It's too soon. I'm not at all certain of my interpretation and there are still many gaps. It's quite complicated. You'll have to be patient.'

'The fragmentation of the inscription into six or seven pieces – did that happen in antiquity or was it done by the people who wanted to smuggle it out?'

'It was done quite recently, I'm certain of it. It's obvious they used a diamond-edged saw, those vandals.'

'Why did they do it?'

'For any number of reasons. First of all, to make it easier to transport. An intact object of that size is very visible and could easily arouse suspicion. In this case, I would imagine that the inscription was about to be taken out of the country. Any decent restorer would be able to weld the pieces back together. Or, even more likely, the fence, or the dealer himself, may have realized that more money could be had by selling the pieces one at a time. The curious thing is that the author of the ancient curse broke it down into blocks himself, so that the fragmentation of the slab did not create gaps in the text.'

'How do you interpret that?'

'That the author wanted to accentuate each and every part of the curse; to make it stronger, more effective.'

'Right. I agree.'

'The cutting was done by someone who was smart enough

to saw through the slab right where the six breaks in the text were . . . Listen, Castellani, I'm sorry, but I can't say anything more about it for the time being. You'll just have to be patient. We'll keep in touch. Please feel free to call me at any time if there are new developments or if you need anything.'

Balestra got up then to show him to the door, but added, 'Please remember not to mention what I've told you to anyone. I've been working on this inscription for two years and I don't want anything to leak before I've finished studying it and before . . .'

'Before what, sir?'

'Before the seventh fragment appears. I haven't given up hope.'

'You can count on my discretion.'

Fabrizio thought of the voice of that woman on the phone and for an instant was tempted to mention it to the director, but he realized that the situation was perplexing enough without this further complication. He didn't mention the call. He took the photographs from the desk and put them back into his briefcase.

'Have copies made and send them to me, please,' said Balestra.

Fabrizio nodded, shook his hand and walked down the corridor to his own office.

Francesca poked her head in almost immediately. 'What did he think?'

'He was blown away.'

'I believe it. You don't see stuff like that every day.'

'He told me about the inscription.'

Francesca seemed surprised. 'What inscription?' she asked.

Fabrizio turned and walked to the window. He stood watching people pass in the street below. Opposite was a souvenir shop with a bad copy of the lad of Volterra in the window. He said, 'Do you really feel we need to continue this game? The inscription in six fragments that Balestra is trying to translate.'

Francesca came up behind him and put her hand on his shoulder.

'Listen, it's not that I don't trust you,' she said in a conciliatory tone. 'Balestra ordered me not to breathe a word about it to anyone and I've kept my promise. It's a hot find. There's still a piece missing and he—'

'He also made me swear not to talk about it and, what do you know, here I am talking to you. I know about the missing piece.'

'Well?'

'Francesca, I want you to get me the translation. You have access to his office and you could manage it.'

'Don't even think about it.'

'Then I'll get it myself.'

'You're crazy. I'll tell the carabinieri.'

'You're a fool who doesn't realize what trouble we're in and how dangerous this situation has become. For me, especially, but for you as well. Do whatever the hell you want, but stay away from me.'

Francesca looked at him in shock and, without managing to say a word, walked out and slammed the door behind her.

7

Fabrizio gathered his papers and walked towards the exit. He stopped for a moment, instinctively, to look at the lad in room twenty. The cloudy sky covering Volterra cast a grey light through the window that enveloped the statue, spreading a pale green reflection on his scrawny shoulders. There weren't many visitors, but each one stopped and glanced repeatedly up from their guidebook, as if trying to understand what no guide could explain: the mysterious feeling of longing that hovered around the boy, as if the inconsolable grief of his loving parents still floated in the air like a light fog after thousands of years.

He walked down the stairs and was heading out when he found Francesca leaning against the door jamb.

'She must be pretty,' she commented, turning towards him.

'Who?'

'That Sonia. They're expecting her at the museum tomorrow and everyone's already having fits.'

'She does have a nice figure, but she's not my type.'

'Good.'

'Why?'

'Because. Did I make you angry earlier?'

'I made *you* angry.'

'You were very rude.'

'You let me down. I thought I could count on you.'

'That was no reason to talk to me that way. Don't try it again.'

'What's that, a threat?'

'Take it as a warning.'

'I'm upset.'

'I can see that. Get over it. I'd invite you for coffee but you're too agitated as it is.'

Francesca walked towards a cafe a few steps away and Fabrizio followed her in. They ordered a cappuccino and a tea.

Fabrizio looked into her eyes intently. 'Were you the one on the phone?'

'What phone?'

'The one that rings at two a.m. in the museum corridor and tells me—'

Francesca shook her head and looked bewildered. 'What on earth are you talking about?'

'Forget it. Pretend I never said anything.'

Francesca reached her hand across the table to touch Fabrizio's while looking out of the window as if something else had caught her attention. 'I'm willing to help you.'

'You are?'

'Yes. But it won't be easy. Balestra's files are bound to be protected by a password. He's very careful on the computer.'

'We could do it at night while I'm working on my research. I know how to turn off the alarm. We'll go into his office and—'

Francesca shook her head. 'Forget it. His office has a separate alarm that goes directly to the carabiniere station right around the corner. In ten seconds flat you'd find Sergeant Massaro at the door in full combat gear asking embarrassing questions. And don't you feel at all bad about betraying Balestra's trust in you?'

'Of course I feel bad,' replied Fabrizio, 'but I have no choice. I asked him if I could take a look at it, right there in his office, but he refused. And yet I could tell by how he reacted that he's instinctively linked the text to these murders that have taken place in Volterra. What's more . . .'

'What?' insisted Francesca when Fabrizio didn't go on.

'He's linked it to the tomb of the Phersu as well . . . at least, that was my impression.'

'It sounds to me like someone's going nuts here.'

'That's probable. But in the meantime two people have been slaughtered and I'm not sure that it's over, seeing as Reggiani is running out of ideas. So how do you say we do it?'

'Open the files? Don't ask me. I have no idea. Let me think about it. In the meantime, don't screw things up. Let me do this my way. I'm the only one who can manage it. Anyway, if I do succeed, this has to remain an absolute secret between us or I'm done for. Understand? If Balestra suspects me in any way I'm out of a job. Do we have a deal?'

Fabrizio nodded. 'Thank you, Francesca.'

'Right. Well, I've got things to do. I'll let you know when I find something.' She brushed his cheek with a light kiss, then went out.

SONIA VITALI arrived at the museum late the next morning, after checking in at the Corona, an inexpensive hotel near the fortress. Fabrizio introduced her to the director, then took her straight downstairs, where he'd set up some tables and lights to make their work a little easier.

'I started to separate the human bones from the animal ones, but I didn't get very far, as you can see.'

'Good God!' exclaimed Sonia as soon as she had seen the skeleton. 'It's even bigger than I thought.'

'How do you want to go about this?' asked Fabrizio.

'I want to reassemble it in a standing position. We'll put it on exhibit when I'm finished, with a virtual reconstruction. Won't that be something?'

'Yeah, I'm sure it will,' he replied without enthusiasm. 'How long do you think it will take?'

'I'm not sure . . . It's not something you can just improvise. It's very delicate work. I have to find all the junctures, create supports . . . You know how it is. You figure it out as you go along. So what about your statue? Is your research proceeding?'

'No. I haven't been able to get to it. This damn tomb came up and I had to excavate it, remove all the material, the whole deal. The director had too much work on his hands and his inspectors were all busy as well.'

'Well, this is one hell of a find, as far as I can tell.'

'Yeah, that's what I'm worried about. Keep it to yourself for the time being. I don't want the press in on this.'

'No problem. I just want to be able to work in peace. I'll start by taking some photographs and then we'll see. Who knows, I might get inspired.'

Fabrizio got ready to leave.

'What's there to do here at night?' asked Sonia, her eye to the viewfinder of her digital camera.

Since the tourist season was over and Volterra was settling into a wintry sloth, the question seemed entirely rhetorical, but Fabrizio made an effort not to notice.

'There are a few good restaurants and the theatre programme for the autumn isn't half bad . . . a couple of cinemas and a club or two, I think. I haven't had much time to get out.'

Sonia mumbled something under her breath as Fabrizio went up the stairs to return to his office.

REGGIANI walked in about five.

'I brought back your tooth,' he said, placing the ivory-coloured fang on Fabrizio's desk.

'Thank you. My colleague has already begun to examine the skeleton, so I'll have to sneak it back in place. Can you tell me what you needed it for?'

'I showed it to Dr La Bella, our medical examiner, and he tested it in the wounds of the two cadavers. Said it was a perfect fit.'

'Interesting, but no use for your investigation, I suppose. I wonder why you even thought of doing such a thing, since skeletons don't normally go around sinking their fangs into people.'

'Curiosity,' replied Reggiani. 'Pure curiosity. When your colleague has finished examining the bones, we'll certainly know more about this animal, but I'm afraid we may have more trouble in the meantime. By the way, you live out in the country, don't you?'

Fabrizio felt a sudden jolt of apprehension. 'Yes, that's right. At the Semprini farm in Val d'Era.'

'Be careful when you go home tonight. Park in front of the door and lock up everything once you're inside.'

'I can take care of myself, Lieutenant,' Fabrizio assured him. 'I have an automatic five-round Bernardelli and I keep it loaded. I have a hunting licence, naturally.'

'Keep your eyes open anyway. Those two I just had another look at in the cooler knew their way around, and they were armed as well. Last time we saw each other there was something you wanted to tell me. Have you changed your mind?'

Fabrizio hesitated, thinking that perhaps the voice might never bother him again, but then he decided it was best to let Reggiani in on all the strange things that had happened to him since he'd arrived in Volterra.

'It happened the first night, just after I got here. I was in the museum, working on my research: I'm studying the statue of the boy that's in room twenty. Do you know the one I'm talking about?'

'Yeah, sure,' replied Reggiani. 'It's the one that looks like a Giacometti sculpture.'

Fabrizio was favourably impressed by Reggiani's art savvy. He said, 'That's the one. There's something odd about the casting that I'm trying to figure out. Well, as I was there with the statue, absorbed in my work – it must have been some time before two in the morning – the phone rings. A woman's voice says, "Leave the boy alone," and hangs up. I was shocked at first, because I couldn't understand who it could be and how they could possibly know what I was researching—'

Reggiani interrupted: 'Dr Castellani, what exactly . . . Wait, can't we do this on a first-name basis? I don't think I'm much older than you are.'

'Absolutely, it's Fabrizio. What's your name?'

'Marcello.'

'Well, Marcello, as I was saying, I was really unnerved by that voice in the middle of the night – what the hell could they be on about? I thought, this must be a joke, but who could be joking at my expense? I'd just got here. I hadn't met a soul.'

'Well, there's no saying that the voice was referring to that "boy". Your statue, that is. It might have been some kind of weird coincidence. Have you had any more calls?'

'No, not lately,' Fabrizio lied, realizing that Reggiani must have enough on his plate without having to worry about this too.

'Then let's take one thing at a time,' said the officer. 'I'll see if I can get a tap put on your phones, at the museum and at the Semprini place. I can't imagine they'd call on your mobile phone, or do many people have your number?'

'No, just family and a few close friends. I hate being bothered at all hours.'

'Right. If we're lucky and they try again, we should be able to trace the call, figure out who's placing it. But luck is something we've been a bit short of lately.'

Fabrizio scribbled his numbers on the back of a card and handed it over.

'If they do ring back, how should I handle it?'

'Try to keep them on as long as possible so we can trace the call. A couple of minutes would be good.'

'All right. I'll do my best.'

'Well, Fabrizio, we'll be in touch soon. If you should need me for any reason, call.' He got up to leave.

'Marcello, can I ask you a favour?'

'Sure.'

'You might want to put one of your men on my colleague, Dr Vitali. She's the one who's working at reassembling the skeleton. She likes a good time and she can be a bit imprudent on occasion. Now is not the best moment to be wandering off on your own, especially after dark.'

'I've already taken care of it,' replied the officer.

He put on his cap, slipped on his black gloves and left.

Fabrizio went into the basement to put the tooth back in its place. Sonia wasn't there but she'd already started her work, concentrating on the skull, which she was assembling on a platform lit by a couple of halogen bulbs. With its hollow eye sockets and huge toothy jaw, it might have seemed a grotesque mask, if he didn't know the context it had been found in. She had applied little dots of putty along the chalk lines that she'd drawn on the skull, both lengthwise from the nape of the neck to the tip of the snout and crosswise from temple to temple. Each piece of putty held a pin half a centimetre long. The pins had different-coloured heads, depending on the line, which he supposed identified muscles or other anatomical features. Around the earholes the pins were much longer and had yellow heads.

Fabrizio knelt and very cautiously inserted the fang into its socket, then returned to his office and got back to work. The days were becoming shorter now and the small cubicle was soon plunged into shadow. When he was forced to get up and switch on the overhead light, he realized that it was already seven thirty and that the museum was empty. He wondered where Francesca might be and felt like calling her, but then reasoned that if she hadn't called him she hadn't felt the need, so why should he?

He backed up his files and rose to leave, stopping on his way out to check on Sonia.

'Would you like to get a bite to eat with me?' he asked.

She declined his invitation. 'I'm sorry, but I'm just too tired to go out. I'll just have a glass of milk at the hotel and go to bed.'

'Don't forget to set the alarm before you go,' Fabrizio reminded her.

He left the museum and headed towards Signora Pina's place for some dinner.

There were still a few tourists out and about and when he turned into Piazza dei Priori he noticed quite a few people sitting outdoors at the two main cafes, having a drink before dinner. He deliberately walked between the tables so he could hear what people were talking about in the city besieged by a bloodthirsty monster and realized it was soccer. There was an early National League game that evening: Milan versus Fiorentina. Everyone was making predictions and placing bets. No one much liked the line-ups that had been announced and everyone had a smarter strategy to propose.

There was a little breeze coming from Via San Lino, carrying the scent of hay and mint all the way to the big grey-stoned square. A radio somewhere was playing an old classic, 'Struggle for Pleasure', and the music made Fabrizio feel melancholy, despite the quick beat. It seemed crazy that he was having dinner all alone without either one of his attractive colleagues, but Sonia was too tired and Francesca must have been busy if she hadn't thought to call. He decided to take his time, strolling through the centre so he could check out the shop windows and bookshops. By the time he entered the trattoria, it was well past eight.

Pina came to take his order and brought him some bruschette and a glass of white wine to start. A group of teenage boys were already sitting in front of the TV, waiting for the whistle that would signal the start of the game, and there was a party of Germans at a long table downing one carafe after another while they waited for their food.

Pina got everyone served and came to sit at his table, seeing he was the only guest she'd be able to talk to now the game had begun and the Germans were already tipsy as well as impossible to understand.

'Want to hear the latest, Doctor?' she asked him with a mysterious air.

'I most certainly do, Signora Pina,' replied Fabrizio, imitating her tone.

'The other night I saw a light filtering out from the cellar of the Caretti-Riccardi palace.'

'Someone had gone down to get a bottle of wine,' suggested Fabrizio.

'Nothing to joke about, Doctor. A living soul has not crossed that threshold,' she said, pointing at the front door, 'since the late Count Ghirardini left, and he only lived there two or three years in all.'

'So what was it, then, ghosts?'

'Well, I certainly don't know about that, but you tell me, you who are a man of letters and have an education. Who could have been down there at one o'clock in the morning, wandering around that cellar? Just thinking about it gives me goosebumps.'

'Someone, somewhere must still own the place. Maybe he came by to pick up something he needed . . .' His voice trailed off as he realized how lame his reply sounded.

Pina shrugged. 'They say that you're studying the statue of the thin young boy at the museum.'

'That's the truth, but I'd like to know who told you that.'

'Oh, this is a small place, people talk. You're a stranger and everyone's wondering what's so special about that statue. It's been there forever and no one has ever noticed it before now.'

'You're right, there's nothing special about it. There's a publisher coming out with a book about the Etruscans and they're paying me to study a few statues at the Volterra museum. That's all, Signora Pina. If you wouldn't mind bringing my bill, I'll be off towards home, then.'

'You go right ahead, Doctor. Goodnight. Well, will you look at that?' she added, glancing out the window.

'What?' asked Fabrizio.

'Oh, nothing. It's just the fire chief, who sleeps with attorney Anselmi's wife. Oh, that's right, it's the weekend. The lawyer will have been at his other office in Grosseto yesterday and he's probably still there.'

Fabrizio shook his head and got up. Joyful shouts exploded from the group clustered around the TV, leading Fabrizio to conclude that Fiorentina had scored. He paid his bill, tossed his jacket over his shoulders and walked out towards the Caretti-Riccardi palace instead of retracing his steps. He walked along the pavement that flanked the building down the whole block and noticed that every so often there was a heavy iron grating covering the cellar's ventilation ducts.

The doors and windows were all closed and the paint was peeling. He'd walked practically all the way around the building and was approaching the facade when he heard the squeak of a door opening.

He ran around to the front and caught a fleeting glimpse of a child letting himself in from a smaller entrance next to the main door. Fabrizio saw him quite well in the lamplight: a slight, slender boy with short hair and big dark eyes. But it all happened very quickly. The child disappeared inside and the door clicked shut behind him.

Fabrizio ran to the door and knocked repeatedly but got no answer. The main door was covered with rust; it looked like no one had opened it for ages. The side door seemed firmly locked but evidently someone still had the key.

He walked off, perplexed. Who could that child be? If he'd had time, he would have been curious to go to the land registry office to find out who the current owners were. Maybe some well-heeled family from Milan living on Via Montenapoleone who had so many properties they'd forgotten about this one. Before turning on to Via di Porta dell'Arco, he glanced back impulsively at the dark mansion and saw a reddish reflection flashing briefly from behind one of the ventilation ducts on the rusticated base. He started and began to feel as if he were seeing things. He fought the urge to go back and take a closer look and turned instead towards the music that was coming from one of the little cafes in the centre, which sounded appealingly normal and real.

A more familiar glow shone from the open windows on his way and he heard the exclamations of the people inside watching the game on television. A carabiniere cruiser passed in absolute silence, as if it were running with the engine off. An old man rode by on his bicycle with a shoulder-length mane of white hair that fluttered in the breeze like a bride's veil. A dog poked his nose into a bag of rubbish that he'd managed to get out of the bin. In the distance, Fabrizio could even hear the whirring blades of a helicopter, no doubt patrolling the countryside in search of invisible monsters. Fabrizio's mobile phone rang loudly in his pocket and he jumped. In the dead calm of that sleepy city, any noise louder than a clock's ticking sounded like a trumpet blast.

'Hi, Sonia,' he said as her name came up on the display panel.

'Hi there, sweetie. I really am sorry I couldn't keep you company for dinner. I was so tired I didn't feel like eating.'

'Don't worry about it. Where are you?'

'At the hotel.'

'Good girl. Don't go out on your own or you could get into trouble.'

'I've heard. Two murders. You might have told me yourself.'

'I didn't want to frighten you.'

'Frighten me, my arse. How long did you think it would take before I heard about them? Everyone knows what's going on and they're scared shitless. Where are you?'

'Out.'

'Do you feel like coming by?'

'As in do I feel like a fuck?'

'You jerk.'

'Sorry. I can be there in ten minutes. Is something wrong?'

'I've rebuilt the animal's head. You can look him in the face. Virtually, that is.'

'You're kidding! Didn't you say you were worn out and were going straight to bed?'

'I've just got my second wind. I'm using an awesome program that I developed myself. I don't fool around when it comes to work. And I don't fuck around either.'

'Too bad. I was starting to get ideas.'

'Come on, move your arse. I'll be waiting downstairs at the bar.'

Fabrizio reached his car and set off in the direction of Sonia's hotel. She was sitting at a table, smoking and working on the laptop she had open in front of her.

'Before I show you this I want to ask you something. When I first got here, the lower left canine was missing. I went out to buy a sandwich and when I came back it was in its place in the jaw. Was that someone's idea of a stupid joke?'

'No, sorry, no joke. I had it and I had meant to put it back.'

'OK, one less mystery to explain. Ready, then?'

'Wait, so how did you do this?'

'Look,' she said as the program was loading. 'You plug in all the points at which the muscles join and then, based on the dimensions, the program recreates the muscle using an anatomy database.'

As Sonia was explaining, the skull of the animal appeared and was filled in with muscles, then veins, then skin.

'What we cannot determine, obviously, is the colour of the eyes and the fur. But let's say the fur was black – it seems to fit the situation. And we'll say the eyes were . . . yellow, for the same reason.'

The beast's head was shockingly real. Sonia picked a pose with its lips pulled back to bare gums bristling with pointed fangs, and revolved it. It looked like an enormous wolf but from some angles it shared certain features with a big cat. A terrifying combination, like some sort of bloodthirsty Cerberus.

Fabrizio shook his head incredulously. 'It's horrifying . . .' he whispered. 'But how realistic is this reconstruction? You're not playing games with the program, are you?'

'Let's say that there's a 90 per cent probability he looked like this. Obviously I can't tell whether it was a male or a female. I'm guessing male. And maybe I have an idea of what it is.'

'Well?'

'I have to check out some sources at the library first. I want to be sure. But I do have an idea. So, then, what do you think?'

'It's fantastic, Sonia. I knew you were the best.'

They ordered a couple of beers and lingered for a while, chatting, then Fabrizio had her make him a copy and said goodnight.

He went back to his car and headed home. It was past eleven when he let himself in, switched on the light and turned on his computer. He inserted a disk and watched as the image of the young lad of Volterra appeared on the screen. The shade of twilight.

8

THE THREE-DIMENSIONAL image rotated in the virtual space in front of him and the dark spot that he had noticed in the X-rays became larger in size and took on sharper contours as the resolution increased. It seemed to Fabrizio that there could be no doubt that the shape was that of a blade seemingly embedded in the boy's side. He printed a paper copy with the intention of showing it to the NAS director the next day and asking permission to micro-drill a specimen for metallographic analysis. He was practically certain that it would confirm that a different alloy was present under the surface of the statue at the point made clear in the X-ray. If Balestra refused, he would ask to explore the statue from the tenons, the pins that anchored the feet to the base – a non-invasive method that would not damage the statue in any way. But it would be costly. And problematic. It would also involve removing the statue from public show for several days for an outcome that might be less than worth the trouble.

The telephone rang. An irritating burst of noise in that silence, at that hour of the night. Could it be Sonia? Reggiani? A thousand thoughts flitted through his head in the brief interval of time before he picked up the receiver and said hello.

'I told you to leave the boy in peace! I warned you.' It was the same female voice he had heard on the other two occasions. But harsher this time, commanding, threatening.

'Listen,' he hurriedly said, 'don't hang up. I—'

But the mysterious caller had already cut the conversation

short. He replaced the receiver as well and remained standing for a few moments, deep in thought. A sudden awareness struck him and he ran over to where the switches were, next to the door, and flipped on all the outside lights. He grabbed a big torch from a drawer and raced through the door. The sound of an engine could be heard: a pickup or van passing on the road and disappearing into the distance.

She had to be very close if she'd seen him working on his computer and had seen the image of the boy on the screen. Fabrizio tore around the house, checking every corner, and kicked open the door to the stables, exploring the room thoroughly with his torch. Nothing, except for a clutch of cockroaches frozen at the centre of the floor, surprised by that sudden, noisy intrusion.

He pulled the door shut behind him and ran towards the bushes that skirted the olive grove to see if there were traces of footsteps on the soft ground. Nothing. He strained to listen for suspicious sounds. Only the flurrying wings of some startled bird interrupted the silence of the night. He slashed through the darkness with his ray of light, unwilling to believe there was nothing there. How could she have been watching him from so close without leaving any trace of her presence? Maybe she wasn't close by at all; could she be observing him from a distance, through binoculars, and using a mobile phone to call him? What kind of woman would be wandering around these deserted fields in the middle of the night without any fear of the thing everything was terrified of?

Fabrizio suddenly realized that he was almost 200 metres from the house, at the edge of the wood, when he heard a low whining at first, then a deep, rumbling snarl coming from the trees. He switched off his torch at once while a stream of adrenalin coursed through his blood and he took off towards the house, his heart hammering in his chest and pounding at his temples. He tripped in the darkness over a dry branch and pitched forward, skinning his hands, arms and chin. He stumbled frantically to his feet, slipped again, then sprinted back in the direction of the house as the low growl became a long, blood-curdling howl that spread through the gully between the two hills, as if the voice of hell were exploding in the still night air.

He flew past the edge of the wood and started down the path that led to his house, but the howl was filling his ears and he could sense the raging pace of the beast catching up on him. The door was less than thirty metres away. He'd left it half open and he could see the lights on inside the room.

He darted in, closed all the doors and windows as quickly as he could and ran over to the gun rack, but he stopped in his tracks as he suddenly heard the growl echoing inside the house. The sound was coming from the central hall, to his right. Fabrizio felt the blood freeze in his veins. 'Oh, my God. It's inside,' he said out loud, remembering the half-open door.

He took the rifle from the rack, feverishly attached the shining torch to the barrel with some tape he'd left on the table, locked and loaded the gun and headed towards the hall. He pushed open the door and moved fast to flatten himself against it. The hall was deserted and, as the torch beam took in the two doors that led to the second floor, he could see that both were shut. He switched on the light and drew a long sigh. He could plainly see the wrought-iron grating at the end of the hall which gave on to the outdoor courtyard. What he'd heard had been an echo reverberating over the curved vault of the ceiling.

He closed the door behind him and went through the house to check that the other door was bolted shut. As he passed in front of the window he noticed the headlight of a bicycle travelling down the hillside and could even hear the tinkling of its bell. 'Oh, shit,' he swore, his teeth clenched tight. He realized that another victim was about to be added to the death toll, his throat ripped out.

He ran back out into the courtyard as he jabbed Reggiani's number into his mobile phone. As soon as he heard Reggiani pick up, he screamed, 'This is Fabrizio. Hurry, for the love of God. It's here!'

'What's there?' shouted Reggiani's voice on the other end, but Fabrizio had already thrust the phone away and was advancing with his rifle levelled. He shone the beam of torch light in the direction of the bicycle and shouted as loudly as he could, 'Watch out! Get out of here!' But the man was still too far away to hear and continued at the same steady pace.

Fabrizio shouted again, but at that same moment he heard the snarl of the beast lying in wait and then the ferocious howl that had curdled his blood just a few minutes before. A huge dark mass sprang out of the woods towards the road as Fabrizio tried unsuccessfully to take aim. He heard a terrified scream, a confused clattering and then only the muffled growl of the animal as he sank his snout into blood.

Fabrizio jumped from the embankment to the middle of the road and for an instant he saw it plainly: the bristly fur, the bared fangs covered with blood, the yellow eyes. He aimed his gun and fired, but the animal was gone. It had bounded back into the woods with a spectacular leap, as light as if it were made of air.

A hail of shots exploded behind him in the same direction and Fabrizio threw himself to the ground, terrified, as the scene of the massacre was illuminated all at once by powerful beams of light. A loud screeching of tyres and Reggiani's Alfa Romeo pulled up sharply, a few centimetres from his feet. The officer burst out, pistol in hand, rapidly emptying the entire magazine of his Beretta into the woods.

Thirty or more men wearing combat gear and carrying assault rifles arrived ten minutes later and charged into the woods with a pack of Alsatian dogs. Before long a helicopter was hovering overhead, scanning the forest with its headlight.

Lieutenant Reggiani approached the body and couldn't hold back a shudder of disgust. It was practically decapitated. The neck vertebrae were crushed and the head was attached to the torso by only a few shreds of flesh. Fabrizio got to his feet, still holding the smoking rifle in his hands, and approached as well.

'I botched it,' he said, his voice cracking with emotion. 'It was so fast. I had it in front of me, in my sights . . . I fired . . . I was sure I'd hit it.'

'You saw it, then?' asked Reggiani. 'I mean, up close?'

Fabrizio nodded. 'The torch on the rifle barrel was on and I saw it for an instant in full light. This thing is monstrous . . . It's a beast out of hell . . . It's . . .'

Reggiani looked at him. Fabrizio was shaking convulsively, his face was drained of colour, his eyes were bloodshot and his breath was coming in short gasps.

The officer put a hand on his shoulder. 'You're in shock,' he said. 'An ambulance is on the way. It's best they take you to hospital.'

Fabrizio straightened up. 'I'm fine. There's nothing wrong with me,' he replied. 'I'll be fine.'

The ambulance arrived and waited as the police finished examining the scene of the crime.

'Are you sure you don't want them to give you a quick check-over?'

'No, trust me, I'm OK. But I think I'll go home. I just need to sit down. My legs are shaking.'

'I can believe it,' said Reggiani. 'After what you've been through, face to face with that monster . . . Too bad you didn't nail him. We would have been finished with this once and for all.' He turned to the sergeant standing behind him. 'Massaro, I'm going with Dr Castellani. If you need me, I'll be in the house.'

'Don't worry, sir. We have everything under control here,' replied Massaro.

Reggiani shook his head as they walked off. 'Under control my arse,' he muttered. 'As soon as the public prosecutor gets wind of this, there'll be hell to pay.'

Massaro's suddenly agitated voice called them back. 'Sir! Over this way, quick! The helicopter has found it!'

'What the fuck . . .' shouted the lieutenant as he wheeled around and ran towards his car. He grabbed the radio. 'Reggiani here. What's happening? Over.'

'We've spotted it, sir!' shouted the co-pilot, his voice unable to contain his excitement. 'Twice, we've seen it twice. With the heli's night vision. I can't believe how fast it's running, sir!'

'Shoot the fucker! Use the machine gun. What the hell are you waiting for? Over.'

'We're trying to do that, sir. We're trying . . .' The crackle of machine-gun fire came through over the radio. Then the voice of the co-pilot, shouting, 'Watch out! Watch out! Turn! Turn!'

'What in God's name is happening?' Reggiani was shouting into the microphone. 'Answer me, damn it!'

There was the co-pilot again, still shouting. 'We're yawing! Give it gas!'

Reggiani's ear was glued to the receiver and his heart was in his throat as he waited for the sound of the explosion. Instead, a few moments later, the pilot's voice came through.

'It's Warrant Officer Rizzo here, sir. We risked crashing into the mountainside. We're OK now, but we've lost it. We'll continue the search. Over.'

'Damn! Damn! Damn!' cursed Reggiani, slamming the receiver on the driver's seat. He turned to the sergeant. 'The thing got away and they nearly ran the heli into the mountain. That's all we need. You stay here at the radio, Massaro. I'm going.'

Massaro shook his head, discouraged. 'They were close, sir. They were really close . . . You go ahead. I'll call you if anything happens.'

'What happened?' asked Fabrizio.

'They nearly bagged it.'

'No!'

93

'Nearly. They spotted it twice with the night-vision beam and fired at it with the Browning. Then they lost it.'

'What the hell . . .'

'Is this thing made of flesh and blood? Why has no one been able to nail it?'

They walked into the house and Fabrizio put the rifle back on the rack, then went to a cupboard and opened a bottle of whisky. 'I need this,' he said. 'Want a drop yourself?'

'Nice gun,' observed Reggiani, looking over at the Bernardelli. 'Yeah, thanks. I don't mind if I do,' he added, dropping into a chair.

Fabrizio took two gulps, then drew a long breath. 'Flesh and blood? I don't know. Yeah, of course. But if you'd seen what I saw . . .'

Reggiani took a sip himself, then looked straight into Fabrizio's eyes.

'Tell me what you saw. From the beginning to the end,' he said.

Fabrizio took another swallow. Some colour was coming back to his face and his hands weren't trembling nearly as much.

'First of all, what is it?'

Fabrizio took another sip.

'Hey, take it easy with that stuff. It's not Coca-Cola.'

Fabrizio set the empty glass on the table and suddenly thought of the virtual reconstruction that Sonia had done of the skull taken from the skeleton buried with the Phersu.

'What is it?' he repeated. 'I . . . I don't know. All I can say is that my colleague showed me a computer-generated image of the animal in the Rovaio tomb and . . . Listen, you won't believe this, but it looked exactly like this thing.'

'But what is it?' insisted Reggiani. 'A dog? A wolf? A panther? It has to be something recognizable, damn it.'

'Yeah, well, it does look like a dog or a wolf. Only its proportions are humongous and it's capable of making huge leaps and . . . oh, shit, I don't know. It just doesn't make sense!'

'OK, let it go,' said the officer. 'The important thing is, it's not a ghost. Those boys up in the heli were close to pumping it full of lead . . . I could hear that Browning sing over the radio.'

The transmitter he had attached to his epaulette suddenly crackled with Massaro's voice. 'Sir?'

'What is it?'

'The public prosecutor is here.'

'I'm coming.'

Reggiani put on his cap and gloves and went to the door. 'I'll be right back,' he said. 'I just need long enough to tell him to fuck off if he starts breaking my balls.'

He stopped outside the door, lit a cigarette, took a long drag and then walked to the site where a couple of agents were still taking measurements and collecting evidence.

'Listen, Reggiani,' began the public prosecutor in a shrill voice.

Reggiani tossed his cigarette stub to one side, raised his hand to his visor and said, 'Yes, sir.'

'This is the third body—'

Oh, so he can count to three, thought Reggiani.

'And we're no further along than when we started. It's just an animal, for God's sake.'

'It's not just an animal, sir,' replied Reggiani, swallowing hard. 'It's a bloody monster we're dealing with here. It's some kind of dog or wolf as big as a lion, with fangs seven centimetres long, that probably weighs over a hundred kilos and runs so fast that my helicopter nearly crashed into that mountain down there trying to keep up with it. A monster. And let me tell you, my guys were this close from taking it out. The search is still under way, with men and dogs. We're giving it all we have. No one's standing around scratching his balls.'

'Lieutenant!'

'If you'll excuse my saying so, sir.'

Massaro approached with the victim's wallet.

'Who is he?' asked Reggiani.

'No ID.'

'Have you taken his prints?'

'Of course. I've already sent in the photos to headquarters to see if anyone has a file on him. Haven't got an answer yet.' He pointed to the mobile phone sitting on the bonnet of his car, connected to a laptop. They stopped a moment to watch the steady flow of forensic data filling the screen.

The public prosecutor turned to Reggiani again. 'Just what do you intend to do now?'

'We have to find out where the thing's den is. The heli is in contact with the men on the ground. They'll succeed in tracing this animal, I'm sure of it. They've seen it, for God's sake, and they've shot at it. They'll have to fix the exact point . . .'

Massaro approached them. 'We have a match, sir.'

Reggiani walked over to the computer and saw the front and side mugshots of the victim. At the bottom of the screen was a white band with the man's name and record: Cosimo Santocchi, son of Amedeo. Unemployed, no permanent residence, born in Volterra on 15/4/1940. Previous arrests: petty larceny, dealing small quantities of drugs.

'At least this one doesn't look like another tomb robber,' commented Reggiani.

'Maybe not,' replied Massaro, 'but you never know.'

'Right . . . So the fingerprints match up as well?'

'Yes,' replied the sergeant. 'Look.' He inserted a gelatin slide into a separate unit connected to the computer and the prints were instantly read and compared to those on the record. 'Perfect match.'

'I can see that,' Reggiani nodded. 'Analyse the soil on the soles of his shoes and see if there's any trace of that yellow clay from the Rovaio area. I wouldn't be surprised if he took part in that little picnic as well.'

'Right away, sir.'

'I'll be leaving, then,' said Reggiani, addressing the public prosecutor. 'I have to finish my conversation with Dr Castellani. He was a witness to the killing. I'll catch up with you later.'

'Yes, yes, go on. We still have quite a lot to do here.'

Reggiani started walking back to the house. He raised his eyes to the sky before he went in and could see clouds gathering.

Fabrizio was still sitting at the table and was scribbling on a notepad. Alongside was the printout of Sonia's virtual reconstruction.

'Is that it?' asked Reggiani.

'Yes, and look. It's very similar to the animal I saw. Identical, really. A little unnerving, wouldn't you say? This virtual reconstruction is at least 90 per cent true to an animal that died either of suffocation or a heart attack about twenty-four centuries ago. It is so singular that we've found no match for it, at least for the time being. No match, except for the beast that struck again here, which is practically a photocopy of this ancient creature and which materialized the night that the tomb was opened.'

Reggiani shrugged. 'Coincidence. What else? Ghosts – even animal ghosts – don't go around mauling people. And in my mind, an animal that kills can be killed. We have to find the den, that's all, and fill it with lead. You'll see that that will solve our problems.'

'There's something else,' said Fabrizio. 'She called again.'

'That voice on the phone?'

'Right. Ten minutes before this whole disaster happened. I tried to keep her on the line so the call could be traced, but she hung up immediately.'

'What did she say?'

'She was yelling. "I told you to leave the boy in peace! I warned you." Her tone was very threatening, very aggressive. That's all she said. I realized that she had to be somehow looking at my computer screen, and that meant she had to be somewhere close by, or maybe was using binoculars. So I ran out to search the place. That's when I heard the growling and then the howl of that beast. Christ, I swear it made my blood run cold. I ran back to the house, but then from my window I saw those bicycle lights travelling down the state road and I knew I had to warn the guy. That's when I called you on my mobile. But it was too late . . . You know better than I do what happened then.'

'You know, they may have managed to trace the call. The equipment they're using is very sophisticated. I'll let you know tomorrow if there's a lead. Now try to get some sleep. I'll put two guardian angels outside your door. I should already have thought of that. These two are quick off the mark, you—'

'No, really, it doesn't matter. I can take care of myself, you've seen that.'

'Right, but you have to sleep sometime, and when you're sleeping, you're sleeping.'

'OK, thank you, then.'

Reggiani was getting up to leave when Massaro called him again over the radio. 'The special ops guys have come back, sir, and they're ready to make their report.'

'I'll be there right away,' said the officer. Then, turning to Fabrizio: 'I was forgetting to say, you were good out there. It's hard to find people with balls these days. Goodnight.'

'Goodnight,' repeated Fabrizio, and closed the door behind Reggiani.

Reggiani went back to the site of the massacre and saw that a couple of stretcher bearers were moving the corpse off the road after having closed him up in a bag. The public prosecutor was standing to the side, taking notes.

The head of the ROS special operations group that had been patrolling the forest came over to Reggiani. He was a young sergeant named Tornese who had distinguished himself in a number of brilliant operations.

'Well, Sergeant?' asked Reggiani, bracing himself to hear about their failure.

The warrant officer put his hand to his cap. 'Sir, something very strange happened. The heli signalled the spot where the objective had been located and I had all my men and dogs converge at that point. It's a woody ridge that extends towards the Mottola wasteland. The surface is solid enough, but not hard. When we were fairly close we held back the dogs and went forward ourselves to look for tracks.'

'Excellent choice, Sergeant,' said Reggiani approvingly. 'And?'

'We found them, measured them, but . . . I'm not sure how to say this. At a certain point they just disappeared.'

'What do you mean by disappeared?'

'The footprint trail just ended. There were no more tracks in any direction. In the area we're talking about, there's a steep wall of sandstone that was about to create problems for our helicopter. That's where the forest ends. On the left there's wasteland, and on the right there's a dense thicket of brambles which is practically impenetrable. In between is a path, more of a trail really, that herders use. They take their swine through there to graze under the oak trees. The ground is stony, so if the animal went that way he certainly wouldn't have left tracks, but right beyond there's a bed of clay, the same soil as near the furrows.'

'And you saw nothing there?'

'Nothing. Just tyre tracks. But that's a place where couples go to park, driving up from the other direction, from the Santa Severa slope. Not lately, obviously.'

'Were the tyre tracks fresh?'

'Looked like it.'

'They were left by someone who's not afraid of driving around at this time of night, in this area, with that beast running around loose. That's a person I'd like to talk to. Did you take casts of the prints?'

'No, sir. We didn't know we'd need that gear. We came kitted out for a search party.'

'I understand, but I want you to put someone on that right

away, Sergeant. I'll expect a full report from you tomorrow. I want to know every last detail. Sorry, but I'm afraid you won't be getting much sleep tonight.'

'That's all right, sir. We're used to it. Trust me, we'll do everything we can.' He saluted the officer and went back to his men.

The public prosecutor approached. 'I'd say we can leave at this point. Have you arranged for surveillance for Dr Castellani?'

'I have. I'm putting two of my best men on it. But my gut feeling is that nothing further will happen. I think we've seen all the action we're going to see for tonight. Goodnight, sir.'

'Goodnight to you, Lieutenant. You know, I noticed you lighting up earlier. I didn't know you were a smoker.'

'I smoke one a day.'

'Interesting. When?'

'Depends.'

'On what, if I may ask?'

'On how pissed off I am.'

9

SONIA ENTERED the museum library shortly before ten and wandered among the shelves until she found Fabrizio intent on consulting a catalogue of ancient bronze objects.

'Is it true that another poor bloke has been killed?'

'How did you find out?'

'I guessed. Everyone's saying that the carabinieri were out on a man hunt last night, right around where you live if I'm not mistaken. They say there was a lot of shooting – doesn't sound like a picnic.'

Fabrizio put the book down on a table. 'No, it wasn't. It was horrible. But don't tell anyone I said that.'

'Will you come down for a cappuccino at the cafe?'

'Sounds good. Did you manage to find what you were looking for?'

'Maybe. Something . . . I'm not sure.'

'How are you coming along with the skeleton?' he asked as they went down the stairs and out of the museum.

'Well, I'm assembling the spinal column. It's the most exciting work I've done in my whole life. Almost better than sex.'

Fabrizio shook his head but could not even manage a smile.

They sat in a corner of the cafe and waited for their coffee to be served.

'So it was awful?' asked Sonia.

'Worse than awful,' replied Fabrizio, mixing sugar into his cappuccino. 'It was a bloodbath. You have no idea. But I saw it.'

Sonia widened her eyes. 'I can't believe it.'

'As I'm seeing you now. No further than seven or eight metres away. I had a gun and I shot at it, but it was already gone. They spotted it again from a helicopter but lost it as soon as they found it.'

'And what did it look like?'

'You're not going to believe this, but just like your virtual reconstruction. It felt like being in a video game. Or a nightmare . . . I couldn't say which. I only know I thought my heart was going to burst. So, what have you found out?'

'I'm still searching through all the archives. I've even emailed colleagues in a number of universities abroad. I believe there is a chance, albeit a small one, that I'll be able to identify the animal.'

'So far what have you got?'

Sonia took a folder out of her bag and extracted a black-and-white print depicting a menacing dog with gaping jaws. It looked like an ancient bronze. 'What do you think?' she asked.

Fabrizio observed it carefully while munching on a sweet roll. 'It resembles your reconstruction quite a lot,' he said. 'What is it?'

'It's a bronze sculpture from Volubilis, in Morocco. It may represent a race of gigantic, ferocious dogs that the Phoenicians had imported to Mauritania from a mysterious island in the ocean. They've been extinct for thousands of years.'

'Good try, but it sounds like a lot of other stories that have come down from ancient times – devoid of any basis in fact.'

'I don't think so. A passage from Pliny reports that King Juba of Mauritania used them for hunting. They were said to be gigantic.'

'So how did one of them end up in Volterra, a good four centuries before King Juba discovered them?'

'That I don't know. But I've found evidence that the Etruscans – towards the end of the fifth century BC – asked the

Carthaginians to join them in colonizing an island in the ocean. Don't you think there might be a connection?'

'You may be right. Pretty nice work for a techie who doesn't read Greek! But how could this animal still exist and be roaming the countryside, looking for people to tear into?'

'You're asking too much. I've come up with this information and it seems plausible to me, that's all. As far as existing breeds, I've found nothing that resembles the skeleton, taking into account both size and structure. And to tell you the truth, I don't know how to explain that.'

'There's got to be an explanation.'

'The only possible thing I can think of is that . . .'

'What?' Fabrizio urged her.

'It's a chimera.'

'Come on, Sonia.'

'No, you don't understand. I'm not talking about a mytho-logical creature. In biological terms, chimera means the product of genetic mutation, a fusion of two distinct sets of genes. It happens entirely by chance and cannot be replicated. It can occur in any species, animal or vegetable.'

'Like a white tiger, for instance?'

'No, that's just a lack of pigmentation, what we commonly refer to as an albino. I'm talking about a deep mutation of the genes that results in distinctive physical characteristics, particu-larly in terms of shape and size. Veterinarians in the eighteenth and early nineteenth centuries came up with the term to describe a calf with two heads or a goat born with one horn instead of two. Today we can get similar results through genetic manipulation, but sometimes the same thing occurs by chance, spontaneously.'

Fabrizio fell silent for a few moments as he looked out of the window. The weather was overcast and humid, and the light filtered in dimly through the window. Inside the cafe-goers came and went, took a look at the paper, even stopped to play a hand of cards. Everything seemed normal and yet the people around him seemed suspended in a false, temporary dimension: like extras in a film that he didn't know the beginning or the end of. He saw their lips moving but he couldn't hear what they were saying. They seemed to be hampered in their actions, to be moving in slow motion, as if the atmosphere of the cafe and the city itself had become as dense as water.

'Are you listening to me?' asked Sonia, placing a hand on his arm.

'Yes, of course. It's the coincidence that's not explicable. The live animal is identical to your virtual reconstruction. If you had seen it, I would have thought it had conditioned your work.'

'Chance events,' said Sonia in a less than convinced tone, 'can really surprise you at times.'

You could see that she didn't believe what she was saying, but Fabrizio pretended to agree. He paid the bill and they left to walk over to the museum. They parted at the entrance, Sonia heading downstairs and Fabrizio climbing the stairs to his second-floor office. He ran into Francesca as she left the restoration lab and raised his eyebrows as if to ask, 'Anything new?'

The girl shrugged and shook her head.

Fabrizio entered his office, gathered his notes and returned to the library. He'd had an idea he wanted to check out, so he headed straight for the museum catalogue and turned to the section about excavations to search for details on how the statue of the boy had been discovered. He began to read avidly, taking hurried notes now and then. When he finished, he realized that it was lunchtime and that he was alone in the library.

He looked over his notes and consulted the description of the excavation site. The brief report referred to a property owned by the Ghirardini counts, reminding Fabrizio of Signora Pina's story about the palace in town, but did not give a specific location. Strange, this lack of precision in such a serious scholarly publication.

He went to the catalogue of topographical maps, picked one

out and photocopied it. He placed it in his briefcase and walked towards the exit, stopping on the way to pick up his messages. It was almost two o'clock and he walked over to Pina's trattoria, after stopping to buy a couple of newspapers.

'What will you have to eat, Doctor?' asked the signora solicitously.

'Some vegetables will be fine, with a little prosciutto. And mineral water.'

'I'll bring you a nice light lunch,' Pina said approvingly.

Fabrizio took the newspapers he'd bought from his briefcase: a national daily and a local paper. In the former all he found was a short piece in the middle somewhere with the headline 'Mysterious deaths in the Volterra countryside – police investigations turn up no leads'. About twenty lines followed, containing very little information; the victims were identified by their initials.

Nearly half a page was dedicated to the case in the local rag, although it spoke of two, not three, deaths. Reggiani must have managed to keep the reporters away for the time being. The article reported the two murders at length, but it was evident that whoever had written it didn't know the details and that he'd been fed a line about a settling of accounts among Sardinian shepherds who frequented the area. People without family ties to the locals whose passing would not be a strong blow to the community.

Although the authorities had succeeded in keeping the situation quiet, holding back on the truth, with all its traumatic implications, the fear hovering through the city streets was palpable. People gathered in small clusters, speaking in low tones. The news would soon be out; there was no way to keep it under wraps for much longer.

He felt guilty about Francesca. He had asked her for such a huge favour but had hardly spoken to her since. He hated to think he'd involved her in such a dangerous situation and realized it was best that the two of them not be seen together too frequently. He promised himself to call her as soon as he could.

'Here you are, Doctor. Vegetables and prosciutto,' said Signora Pina, putting two plates on the table along with a bottle of mineral water.

'Won't you join me?' asked Fabrizio.

She plonked her considerable derriere on a chair and leaned two large breasts on the table. At twenty she must have had the whole male population of Volterra turning as she passed.

'There's no life in this town once the tourists have gone!' she complained. 'At the weekend, if you're lucky, a few stragglers from Pisa or Colle Val d'Elsa, but otherwise this place is dead. Will you be staying in Volterra long, Doctor?'

'At least a few more days. Maybe a week or so. It depends on my work.'

'I understand . . . but we certainly could use more young blood like you around here. You're such a nice young man and you know so many things.'

'Listen, Signora Pina, there's something I've been meaning to ask you. Do you remember telling me about the lights?'

'Ah, you're making fun of me now, but I assure you—'

'No, no,' he said. 'I'm serious, really. I was wondering whether you've seen them again. Last night, for instance.'

'Good Lord! How did you guess?'

'Guess what?'

'That I saw them again last night. Quite late at night.'

'I see. What time was it, if I may ask?'

'It must have been . . . Look, I was about to close. And so it was well after midnight, it must have been about one, I'd say. That's right. About one.'

'And what did you see exactly?'

'I told you. I saw lights blinking through the grating that covers the air vents over the cellar. Not very bright or anything. You could barely see them, actually. But, thank the Lord, my eyes are still good.'

'Did you notice anything else? I don't know, suspicious noises or anyone coming or going?'

'No, I don't think so ... Wait, I did hear the sound of an engine, like a delivery truck or something of the sort. But there's always one of those around.'

Fabrizio remembered he'd heard the sound of a car engine the evening that he left the Rovaio site and that he'd heard the same thing last night as well, before he spotted the bicycle heading down the road towards his house. Nothing but a meaningless coincidence, naturally.

'May I ask you a favour, Signora Pina?' said Fabrizio. 'If it happens again, could you call me? I'll leave you my mobile number.'

'If it happens to be one o'clock in the morning?'

'Why not? I always work until late. You won't be disturbing me at all.'

He scribbled his number on a paper napkin and handed it to Pina, who deposited it between her breasts.

'And what about this other business of the murders?' she said in a low voice and with a hint of complicity. 'Have you heard about them?'

'Murders? What murders?' asked Fabrizio, feigning ignorance.

'Goodness, you don't know? The tomb robbers they found butchered in the fields near Contrada Rovaio and in the Gaggera bush. Everyone in town knows about these murders and you know nothing? I thought you were on top of things over at the Antiquities Service.'

'I'm not with the Antiquities Service, Signora Pina, and I haven't heard about any murders. Are you sure? It's not just gossip?'

'Gossip! Around here people know who has a cold and who doesn't. These men were found with their throats cut. Or worse. I've heard things that would make your skin crawl. Well, whoever it is, they're certainly doing you people a favour – it'll be a while before anyone dares to roam the countryside with a drill looking for tombs. No one wants to end up the way they did.'

'Don't believe everything you hear, Signora Pina. It will just ruin your day. In any case, you're in no danger, are you? You're a cook, not a tomb robber. By the way, how much is it for lunch? And remember, if you see anything . . .'

'Don't worry,' replied Pina, 'I'll let you know immediately. That's eight fifty for everything, Doctor. I always give you a good deal.'

Fabrizio paid the bill and went to where he had parked his car. He decided to drive home. No one seemed to be following him; maybe Reggiani had ordered protection for him only at night.

Fabrizio pulled up in front of the farmhouse but didn't go in; he didn't feel like going straight back to work. He couldn't shake off a strange sensation. He'd been living in an unreal atmosphere for days and he continually felt tempted to leave and forget about everything, find a new line of work completely. Why not? He kept experiencing little twinges of regret over Elisa, the girl who had left him and obviously hadn't missed him at all, seeing that she'd never called once. He felt attracted to Francesca but wasn't head over heels, wasn't on fire like he'd hoped, wanted, yearned to be. Underneath it all was this annoying sensation of melancholy and depression. Basically, he felt alone and didn't expect that this would change any time soon.

It was even stranger that he should be caught up in such superficial thoughts after what he'd seen the night before. Perhaps it was a natural reaction, he told himself, a defence mechanism to head off the stress before it became overwhelming. He raised his eyes to the dense grey sky that couldn't decide whether to let through a ray of sun or dump a bucket of rain, then walked down the lane to the point where he had heard the beast prowling, hunting him down, the night before.

It seemed like all that had happened a century ago. Everything was peace and tranquillity now, and each time he took in a little bit of the scene he felt that he was snapping a photograph. Another strange sensation he couldn't explain. He walked along the stream to the road to look at the spot where the animal had laid into that poor wretch. There were still brownish stains on the asphalt, broken branches on both sides of the road and a strange odour in the heavy air, or maybe he was imagining it. He felt relaxed now, surrounded by green foliage and silence.

He returned to his car parked in the courtyard, took the briefcase with the books he'd borrowed from the library from the passenger's seat, went into the house and immersed himself in his studies.

When he started getting a bit tired, he stood up to stretch his legs and saw that it was already late in the afternoon. He remembered the messages he'd picked up before leaving the office and went to see if there was anything from Francesca. At the bottom of the pile was a sealed envelope, which he opened. All it contained was a typed address.

He was upset, but oddly not surprised, and realized it could be only one thing. In his mind he could hear the voice on the telephone. He took the topographical map he was using for his work, a military 1:25,000 chart, and identified the locality, a place he was not familiar with. Then he got into his car and set off. After a time on the regional road, he turned off into the countryside, driving along a dusty track. Every now and then he'd turn on his wipers, but there was less rain hitting the windscreen than dust in the air and the end result was a series of long reddish, semicircular streaks on the glass that prevented him from seeing out. Unfortunately there was no cleaning fluid because he'd forgotten to replace it. He had a feeling that he was being followed, but it was impossible to be sure.

He could feel his heartbeat quicken as he neared the place he'd circled on the map. When he spotted it in the distance, a kind of renovated farmhouse with a yellow neon sign in the window, he had to stop for a moment to catch his breath and calm down. Thousands of thoughts went through his mind, including either calling Reggiani or turning back entirely. But then he reasoned that all he had to go on was an address in an envelope: it could be anything at all, or maybe even a mistake. After all, it was only a tavern or a cafe; a bed and breakfast or something of the sort.

He parked on the left, joining three or four other vehicles of various types and a couple of old bicycles. He got out of the car and walked towards the entrance, but all at once heard a rustling noise coming from a hedge of laurel bushes behind the building. He wheeled around, feeling jumpy, and caught a quick glimpse of a little seven- or eight-year-old boy with short, fine hair gathered in clumps on his forehead who seemed to be watching him from behind the corner of the house. He looked remarkably like the boy he'd seen slipping behind the door at the Caretti-Riccardi palace in town. Fabrizio tried to call out to him, but he was gone in a flash.

Music wafted out of the tavern, an instrumental melody with flutes and kettledrums that blended with the low buzz of people chatting. Fabrizio went in and found himself in a big room with an uneven terracotta floor and plastered walls decorated with improbable frescoes of pseudo-Etruscan inspiration. An even less probable dancer in an Etruscan-style outfit was weaving between the tables to the notes of the New Age music. There weren't many guests, perhaps a dozen or so, all dressed on the shabby side. They looked mostly like the English or German couples who rented the farmhouses dotting the countryside. The scene was so trite and so dreary that the overall effect was unsettling.

He turned towards the bar, a Formica faux-wood counter covered with a pane of glass that had long since lost any transparency. Behind the counter was a woman of forty or fifty who was still attractive, although her get-up was so bizarre it was difficult to say for sure. Heavy necklaces and long earrings dangled at her neck and ears. Her hair was dyed a deep black, but the intense, magnetic look of her eyes and the marked wrinkles at the sides of her mouth gave her a harsh, almost bitter expression. Fabrizio wondered how the customers could seem so much at ease with this harpy behind the counter.

In the few moments that had passed since he entered, Fabrizio had regained control of his emotions as he realized that the tavern, albeit grotesque, inspired a certain sense of calm and security, although he felt out of place among the regulars. He approached the counter, drew up a stool and asked for a glass of white wine.

The woman stared straight into his eyes as she poured. 'I didn't think you'd come,' she said. 'You look like a nice boy. I'm sorry you've got yourself into such a mess ... You risk meeting a nasty end, you know that, don't you?'

Fabrizio refused to let himself be intimidated. He hung on to that sense of calm that he'd struggled so hard to create, but he could feel anxiety worming its way in. He swallowed a gulp of wine, set the glass on the counter and said, 'So you're the one who's been calling me.'

'Forget about everything and get out now,' insisted the woman, her right hand tight around the neck of the bottle. 'Leave now and ... you won't pay. It's on the house.'

Fabrizio did not lower his gaze and continued sipping at the wine. 'Don't think you can frighten me. I'm an academic and I'm not impressed by any of this,' he said, tipping his head back towards the room. 'This masquerade only makes me laugh.'

'Foolish boy,' said the woman. 'Don't you realize that opening what's under the ground is a dangerous game? You and those like you – you don't understand that you can reawaken buried tragedies, reopen cruel wounds. You're like a child, happy playing with soil until you find an unexploded bomb from some war of the past. A bomb that can blow up in your hands and tear you to shreds ...' She stared at him intensely, with a sarcastic smile. 'Boom!'

Fabrizio couldn't help but start, though he immediately regained his composure. 'I'm only doing my job,' he shot back. 'I'm not interested in any of this foolishness.'

The woman shook her head. 'I know what you're thinking,' she said. 'That I'm a hysterical bitch with a head full of rubbish. That's too bad for you.' She put the bottle down and lit up a cigarette, breathing in deeply and blowing the smoke out through her nose. The fumes surrounded her face and thick black hair, making her look like Medusa. 'Will you leave the boy in peace?' she asked in an expressionless voice.

'It's not a boy,' said Fabrizio. 'It's a statue. Archaeologists study statues ... among other things. That's all. Please don't call me again. You're disturbing my work.' He pulled out his wallet and put a note on the counter.

'I told you, it's on the house,' repeated the woman. And the tone of those apparently banal words made them sound like some obscure threat, a final sentence, in the way that you would offer a last meal or a last cigarette to a man condemned to die.

Fabrizio felt suddenly unsure of himself. He wanted to bring up the creature that was stalking the woods of Volterra, but he didn't have the courage to say another word. He hesitated a moment, with his hands resting on the counter and his head low to avoid those eyes, but then he swallowed the last of his wine and got up, leaving the money on the counter.

Their conversation hadn't lasted long, but as he crossed the room he noticed that the dancer had gone and the few remaining customers were keeping their voices low as they sipped at their wine. Fabrizio walked towards his car, but all at once the outside lights flickered off and the neon sign advertising the tavern went out, plunging him into total darkness.

Before his eyes could adapt he heard a low growling coming from his left and he realized he was dead. He dashed in the direction of the car; its light colour made it slightly visible on the other side of the courtyard. But he never reached it. A light blinded him and he felt a strong impact, an intense pain in his head and side, then nothing more.

When he opened his eyes again he saw a ghostly image in front of him, a face illuminated from below by the beam of a torch, but the voice he heard reassured him. 'My God! I saw you at the last moment. You were running straight for me! I braked, but you were already under the wheels. How do you feel? Don't move. Wait, I'll call an ambulance.'

'Oh, man, that hurt. But . . . who are you?'

'Who am I? I'm Francesca. Don't you recognize me?' she cried, flashing the torch at her face again. She started dialling for emergency assistance on her mobile phone, but Fabrizio stopped her and got to his feet, holding on to the bumper of her Jeep.

'No, it's OK. I'm fine. Just a few bumps and bruises . . .' Then, as he suddenly remembered what had terrified him, he instinctively turned his back to the car and grabbed on to the girl's arm. 'The dog . . . the beast . . . it's here . . .'

'A dog?' said Francesca. 'A herd of sheep just passed by with a shepherd's dog. You can still hear the bells ringing. Listen.'

Fabrizio heard the distant tinkling of bells as the flock wandered off.

'Good heavens!' exclaimed Francesca, shining the torch on him. 'You look awful! Come inside. You need something to drink.'

Fabrizio noticed that the neon sign had begun glowing again and soon regained full force. The outdoor lights were still off.

He shook his head. 'I just came from there,' he said, 'and I didn't like it. But what are you doing here?'

Francesca finally switched off the torch and came close. 'I was coming to see you, heading towards your house,' she said, 'when I saw you sailing down the regional road, crossing the state road and then pulling off on to that track in the middle of the fields. I tried to keep up, and I even flashed my headlights a couple of times, but you must have had your mind on something else. I guess you didn't see me. At a certain point I lost you and I took a wrong turn and ended up in the courtyard of a farmhouse. So I turned back and went the other way until, bang, I found you. I really found you. Are you sure there's nothing broken?'

'Yeah, I'm sure,' said Fabrizio. 'Don't worry. There's just this bump on my head that hurts like hell. I could do with some ice. But why were you looking for me in the first place?'

Francesca walked him back to his car. 'I've got news for you. Big news. Listen, have you eaten? We can put some ice on your head and make spaghetti at my house and I'll tell you what I've found. If you feel like driving, you can follow me. Just make sure you don't take any wrong turns!'

She gave him a kiss and Fabrizio responded with passion. The girl's scent, her soft lips, her arms around his neck gave him a sense of security and warmth that he needed desperately just then. When he pulled her close he could feel her full, round breasts pressing against his chest. He'd never suspected as much, since Francesca usually wore oversized shirts and trousers that didn't accentuate her femininity.

He said, 'Well, God bless you, Dr Dionisi. Are you still trying to kill me?'

He got into his car, started up the engine and waited until she reached her Jeep. Then, when she had pulled out, he followed her.

Once they were on the state road, Francesca turned right and then left down the local road that led to Poggetto, where she lived. She stopped to open the gate with her remote control and Fabrizio slowed to a stop as well. Just then the mobile phone rang. It was Marcello Reggiani.

'Hi there, Lieutenant. How's it going?'

'Awful. The only good news to report is that we pinpointed the source of those phone calls.'

'The woman's voice?'

'Yes, right.'

'So where is she located?' asked Fabrizio, mentally picturing the place he'd just left.

'A spot about four kilometres from your house. It's called La Casaccia and it's owned by a guy named Montanari. Pietro Montanari.'

The gate had opened and Francesca was pulling into the garage. Fabrizio was stunned at Reggiani's information.

'Are you sure?' he asked.

'Yes. At least the guys in the lab are. Why?'

'What kind of a place is it?' insisted Fabrizio, still thinking it might match up with the tavern.

'It's a farm with an old house on it. At the Val d'Era kilometre marker number five, on the left.'

Completely the opposite direction from where he'd just been. Fabrizio didn't know what to think.

He said, 'Nice work. Where do we go from here?'

'I've put a bug on the line and we're checking the area for suspicious activity. I'll keep you informed.'

Francesca had already opened the door and turned on the switch in the hall. As he drew close, the light on inside the house and the girl's smile warmed his heart.

'Come on in,' she said. 'I'll get that ice for you.'

10

FRANCESCA TOOK SOME ice cubes from the freezer and put them in a plastic bag, which she wrapped in a towel and handed to Fabrizio. He placed it on his forehead where it hurt and she started on dinner.

Francesca lived in a converted farmhouse and the big kitchen preserved all its old-fashioned charm. The stove was built into the masonry and a hearth stood at the centre of the main wall, with copper pots and pans hanging on either side of the chimney breast, as bright and shiny as if they had just been polished. The table in the middle of the room was very old and designed for a big traditional family. Francesca set it for two, placing a couple of mats, plates and cutlery at one end. The wind was picking up outside and they soon heard the tapping of rain on the porch roof and on the windowpanes.

'We needed this water,' said Francesca as she stirred the tomato sauce. 'My grapevines were dying of thirst.'

'I didn't know you had a vineyard,' said Fabrizio.

'It's my father's actually, but I'm an only child and he's quite elderly. He's been retired for years and lives with my mother in Siena. I try to take care of this place as best I can, but I don't have much time, as you know.'

Fabrizio watched her lift the pot's lid to check the boil and measure out the spaghetti.

'How hungry are you?' she asked, turning.

'Very,' said Fabrizio. 'All I had for lunch was a little prosciutto with some vegetables.'

'How's your head?'

'Better.'

'Good. Watch the pot while I go and change out of these dusty clothes. There's wine in the fridge. Help yourself, and pour a glass for me too.'

She disappeared down the hall and he could hear the sound of a door opening and closing and then the shower running. Fabrizio surprised himself by imagining her nude under the pounding water and he smiled: maybe there would be something between them after all. Or maybe there already was and he hadn't noticed. He could still taste her lips, smell the light, clean, girlish fragrance that had remained with him after their embrace in the dark. He thought of how lovely it would be to become intimate with her, in that country house that smelt of lavender, in a bed decorated with painted flowers and mother-of-pearl where her parents and grandparents had slept before her. And how lovely to wake up beside her on a sunny morning and breathe in the aroma of freshly made coffee.

He suddenly said to himself, 'Francesca, my love,' just to see what it would sound like when the day came for him to pronounce those words. It sounded good. He longed for the kind of simple feeling that would fill his soul, drive out the terror coiled just below the surface of his emotions, ready to spring and unleash such a crazy, irrational reaction in him.

The water was boiling. He set the bag of ice on the table and dropped the pasta in the pot just as Francesca reappeared at the door. Her hair was damp and combed straight back and she'd put on a light dress that fitted her nicely without clinging and showed her legs a little above the knee. He wanted to pay her a compliment, but he couldn't think of anything that sounded right and so he changed the topic rather than saying something stupid.

'What was so important that it had you driving around at night searching for me?' he asked.

Francesca drained the pasta and was enveloped in a cloud of

steam for an instant. She tossed the spaghetti with the tomato sauce, added a few basil leaves and transferred it to their plates. She put a piece of Pecorino and a grater on the table and sat down facing Fabrizio.

'I managed to get into the director's archives,' she said, grating a little cheese on Fabrizio's pasta and then on her own, 'and I found out where the inscription that Balestra is studying comes from. A place called La Casaccia, the property of a certain Pietro Montanari.'

Fabrizio, who had been about to bring the first forkful of spaghetti to his mouth, stopped in mid-air.

'Does that name mean something to you?' Francesca asked.

Fabrizio put the fork in his mouth and relished the flavour of the fresh tomato and cheese. 'Delicious,' he said. And then, right away, 'No, nothing at all. Why?'

'I don't know. You seemed surprised. Anyway, this Pietro Montanari has served time for petty theft and it was he who reported finding the inscription. The NAS has never made this public and Balestra has never announced the find, because he's convinced there's a fragment missing, the seventh piece, and that by keeping this quiet, it might turn up. Although nothing has come to light yet.'

'Right. Balestra spoke to me about it that day I saw him in his office, remember?'

'You bet. That day you told me to stay the hell away from you.'

'People say things they don't mean.'

'That's good to know. So, then, Balestra will also have told you that although they've explored the area nothing has emerged. No trace of a historical context, much less the missing piece.'

'Yes, that's what he said.'

'And that he's going mad because he can't find this final fragment.'

'I imagine he is. I'd feel the same way in his shoes.'

'Good. So . . . I think I have a present for you.'

'Don't tell me . . .'

Francesca pulled a little box out of her briefcase and handed it to him.

'This is the original text of the inscription.'

'Francesca, I . . . How can I . . . How did you do this? Did you get into the file?'

'Not in a million years. The protection is uncrackable.'

'I don't get it . . . How did you manage?'

Francesca's hands disappeared back into her briefcase and came up with an object not much bigger than a cigarette packet.

'See this? It's a digital video camera that I can operate using a remote control. Whenever Balestra goes into his office and locks himself in, saying he doesn't want to be disturbed, it means he's working on his inscription. I switch on the camera that I hid on a shelf of his library. It focuses on the computer screen exactly. And so I've filmed the whole text. What I've given you is a video tape, not a disk.'

'You're a genius,' marvelled Fabrizio. 'I would never have thought of this . . . Did you manage to . . .'

'Read it? No, I can't make head or tail of it. His transcription is still very fragmentary and very rough. There's no way I can understand it. You'll have to transcribe it yourself. Do you have a video recorder?'

'Sure. I brought a VCR with me so I'd be able to watch films, but who's had time?'

Francesca put the bowls in the sink and opened the fridge. 'All I have in here are a couple of mozzarellas and two tomatoes.'

'Sounds great,' said Fabrizio.

'What were you doing out at that place?' asked Francesca as she put the food on the table and took a packet of crackers from the cupboard.

Fabrizio didn't answer at first.

'If you don't want to tell me, you don't have to,' she said in a tone that meant exactly the opposite.

'At this point there's no sense keeping secrets. I met that woman.'

'The one who's been making the mysterious calls?'

'The same. Someone left a sealed envelope for me at the museum. There was an address inside. I had no doubt it was her and I was right.'

'What's she like?'

'Disturbing.'

'Exactly what I thought you'd say,' said Francesca with a touch of sarcasm.

'Well, I don't know how to define her. She may be crazy, or a visionary, what do I know? But she insisted. She told me I had to give up my research and leave before . . .'

Francesca seemed not to notice that he hadn't finished the sentence.

Fabrizio continued: 'Before something happens to me.'

'What do you think she was talking about?'

'I didn't ask her and I didn't even feel like asking her, but I'm sure you can guess what I thought and what I'm still thinking now.'

'The animal.'

'Exactly. What else?'

'So what's the connection between a woman who works behind the bar of a third-class establishment and that horrible murderous creature?'

'I don't know. I don't even know if there is a connection. Maybe she just wanted me to think that there was. I can't tell you why. Anyway, I was very deeply disturbed and I couldn't wait to get out of there. When I got up to leave, she said goodbye as if she were talking to a dead man. Do you know what I mean?'

'Well sure, I think so. But I wouldn't fret over it. I'm certain she's just some kind of a loser who's trying to work out her frustrations by acting like a sorceress or a clairvoyant or something. You'd be surprised how many of them there are out there.'

She got up and put the plates in the sink.

'Shall we make coffee?' asked Fabrizio, getting up to help.

'You plan on staying up late tonight?'

'Yeah, I think so. I'd like to start transcribing that inscription.'

Fabrizio drank his coffee, then got up to leave. For a moment he hoped Francesca would ask him to stay, but he immediately put the thought out of his head. She was the type of girl who only comes to bed with you if she loves you and thinks you love her. No, only if she's sure you love her. After which you start with the wedding plans. In a flash of lucidity, that all seemed incredibly premature and his enforced chastity seemed a small price to pay.

Francesca walked him to the door and threw her arms around his neck. 'If I were following my instincts I'd ask you to stay,' she whispered into his ear.

Fabrizio felt completely different from the way he had a moment before. 'But you're not going to follow your instincts, are you?' he asked.

'No, it's better we don't. We're in the middle of a very difficult situation, and you're not very clear about things, are you?'

Fabrizio didn't answer.

'Do you at least like me a little?'

Fabrizio would have preferred to be somewhere else and instead he heard the words he'd been rehearsing when she was in the shower slip out: 'Francesca, my love . . .' He held her close in the darkness as the rain beat down on the canopy over the front door and an intense odour of moss and wet wood flooded in from the nearby forest. He felt like he'd never want to leave her, that the smell of her hair and the taste of her lips were the only warmth and the only pleasure that life could give him.

He kissed her and ran off under the rain towards his car.

IT WAS POURING and every now and then a flash of lightning lit up the countryside like daylight. Further west, towards the sea, lightning bolts were streaking the sky, but the continuous rumble of thunder was muted by the distance. There was practically no one out at this time of night, in such weather, and Fabrizio fingered the tape he had in his pocket, thinking of the message it contained. Words from a long-ago era, words that formed a dreadful message, to judge from the director's self-imposed isolation and the extreme reaction he'd had that day Fabrizio had told him about the Phersu.

He turned down the Val d'Era road and had soon arrived at his house on the Semprini farm. The front courtyard and backyard were illuminated by the outdoor lights and the old bricks in the low walls gleamed in the rain. He stayed just long enough to safely deposit the tape Francesca had given him and to take his rifle from the rack, then he got back into the car and drove off in the opposite direction.

At that same moment, Lieutenant Reggiani was stretched out in an easy chair in his apartment, watching an Almodóvar film on TV and drinking a whisky on the rocks. He was relatively relaxed, given the circumstances, and jumped when the phone on the side table rang.

It was Sergeant Massaro. 'He got home ten minutes ago, went inside for a moment and then drove off again.'

'You're following him, aren't you?'

'He's just half a kilometre ahead of me.'

'Well done, Massaro. Don't lose him. If there's any reason for alarm, call me and call the squad car.' He looked at his watch. 'But where's he headed at this time of night in this storm?'

'No idea, sir. He's actually just turned right towards La Casaccia, if I'm not mistaken.'

'Right. I think I know what he's thinking, then. Anyway, you stay on him, understand?'

'Roger that, sir,' said Massaro, switching off the speaker-phone in his Fiat Uno.

Fabrizio pulled off the side of the road, got out his topo-graphical map, examined it under the dashboard lights and then picked up his binoculars. He pointed them in the direction of the open countryside to his right. La Casaccia, about 300 metres away, was an old country estate connected to the local road by a lane full of potholes that had filled with water during the storm. At the end of this path was a courtyard surrounded by the main house, which was old and dilapidated, another build-ing, where the tenant farmer must have lived, a shed with a collapsing roof and a stable with a hayloft, also in a state of disrepair. The overwhelming impression was of neglect and disuse, and the houses would have appeared uninhabited had it not been for a couple of lit bulbs dangling on the outside walls and for the light filtering out from a window on the ground floor of the tenant's house. Fabrizio was close enough to see the inside of the room and the bare light bulb hanging from the ceiling. There was a man of about fifty inside, sitting at a table with a plastic tablecloth, a flask of wine and a half-empty glass in front of him.

Fabrizio heard a dog barking and the sound of a chain running back and forth over a wire strung between the two buildings. A car was driving up and the dog was letting his master know. Who could it be so late at night in such an isolated place?

The vehicle looked like an old van. It stopped in the middle of the courtyard and a woman got out. At first, Fabrizio could not make out her features, but then the door opened and lit up her face. It was the woman from behind the bar at the Le Macine tavern!

Fabrizio realized immediately that a lot of his questions were about to be answered but unless he got closer he would miss whatever happened. He searched through his pockets and backpack for something he could pacify the dog with, but found nothing, not even a crust of bread. He aimed his binoculars and found himself witnessing – although he could not hear a word – an argument that soon degenerated into a violent quarrel. The woman stormed out, slamming the door behind her, got back into her van and drove off.

Strangely, during the whole time that the woman was inside, maybe ten minutes or so, the dog had never stopped barking. On the contrary, his yapping had become so fierce and insistent that Fabrizio could hear him distinctly, even at this distance. The dog continued to bark for a couple of minutes after the vehicle had disappeared, then stopped. Fabrizio could hear the chain sliding back and forth for a while, then nothing.

He decided to pluck up his courage and approach the man inside the house. He started up the car and drove it down the little lane with only his parking lights on. He stopped at the edge of the courtyard and got out as the dog started barking again and running up and down the muddy yard. Almost immediately the door opened and the man appeared as a dark shadow in the doorway.

'Are you back?' he shouted. 'Get out, I told you! Get the hell out of here!'

'My name is Fabrizio Castellani,' was his answer. 'You don't know me, but—'

He was not given the opportunity to finish.

'Get out!' repeated the man, and this time it was clear that the order was directed at him.

'I'm not a thief or a prankster,' started up Fabrizio again, 'and I need to talk to you, Mr . . . Montanari.'

'I know full well who you are,' responded the man. 'You're the one who doesn't understand. Get out. Leave here. Get as far away as you can, if you don't want to come to a nasty end. A horrible end.'

Fabrizio felt as if he'd been punched in the stomach. Hearing the same threat twice in the same day from two people, under such disturbing circumstances ... that phrase suddenly struck home with all its ominous implications. He felt alone and defenceless, the potential victim of a mess of his own making. He struggled to control himself and, after a moment of hesitation, took a few steps forward. The chained dog instantly charged at him, barking furiously, but when it was almost upon him, it stopped in its tracks and began to yelp as though it recognized him. Fabrizio, prey to so many conflicting emotions, managed nonetheless to stay calm and not take to his heels.

'I'm not afraid,' he said in a firm voice. So firm, in fact, that he even convinced himself.

The man approached and looked him over from head to toe. He turned to the dog, which was still whimpering softly, as if waiting to be petted, and then back to the young man. He shook his head and said, 'You're crazy, all right ... but, if you have to, come in.'

Fabrizio followed the man inside the house and found himself in a bare room with peeling, mouldy plaster. A light bulb hung from an enamelled iron plate in the middle of the room. On one of the walls was an image of the Immaculate Heart of Mary printed on a piece of cardboard that was curling at the edges with the damp. On the other walls were more sacred images, a little incongruous under the circumstances: St Rocco with a dog licking his wounds, and St Anthony the Abbot, with a horse, rooster and pig. Opposite the door stood a small cupboard topped by a glass case. Sitting on the cupboard top was an old phone, greasy and dirty. A table with two straw-bottomed chairs and nothing else. A strong odour of mildew saturated the room, a wretched place that reeked of abandonment.

Fabrizio's gaze was drawn instinctively to the glass case and on the shelf directly over the telephone he noticed several fragments of archaeological objects, in particular some bucchero pottery with traces of a painted swastika motif, the same as he had found near the tomb of the Phersu.

'You're a tomb robber,' said Fabrizio, looking straight into the man's eyes with an affirmative rather than interrogative tone, and deliberately addressing him with the familiar '*tu*'.

'In a certain sense.'

'You're the one who found the slab with the inscription.'

'I did.'

'And you turned it over to the NAS. Why? For the money?'

'It'll make a nice nest egg.'

'But you won't be getting any of it until you say where the missing piece is.'

'So they say.'

The man filled his glass and gestured at his guest to offer him some as well. Fabrizio declined politely with a shake of his head.

'Where is it?' he asked.

The man gulped down the wine in a single go and poured himself some more. Fabrizio was close enough to smell his sour breath.

'You think I'd tell you?' asked the man with a smirk. But behind his bravado, Fabrizio thought he could see a desperate need to talk to someone. To relieve himself, perhaps, of an intolerable burden.

'Probably not,' replied Fabrizio calmly. 'But I can tell you that you're the one who tipped off the police about the Phersu tomb. You were almost certainly there at the site with those poor wretches who ended up with their throats ripped out. But you slipped away before the Finanza team got there.'

The man suddenly leaned in closer. 'Then it's true that you're dangerous!' he said, gulping down more wine.

'Who told you that? The woman from the Le Macine tavern?'

'You know her? But how . . .'

'Yeah, I know her. And so do you, I see.'

The man was increasingly surprised and confounded by Fabrizio's words. He lowered his head, letting out a long breath.

'I wish I didn't,' he said. 'I'd be better off if I'd never met her.'

'Same here. But why did she come here to see you in the middle of the night?'

The man sighed again. 'Nightmares also come to visit in the middle of the night,' he replied. 'Since I found that inscription, she's changed completely. She's turned into another person.'

'She's the one who told you where the inscription was, isn't she?'

'How do you know that?'

'Was it her?'

'Yes.'

'And she has kept one of the pieces after she got you to break up the slab?'

The man nodded.

'So she instructed you to notify the National Antiquities Service.'

'That's my own fucking business!' the man responded with a flash of pride. 'They were supposed to give me a pile of money. And I was having problems making ends meet . . . I was in prison.'

'She's also the one who told you where you'd find the tomb.'

The man nodded, submissive again.

'And she'll tell you where the seventh fragment of the inscription is . . . when she decides.'

'No. She's already told me.'

'Tonight?'

The man nodded again.

'Why were you arguing?'

'Because . . . I've had enough. I can't take it any more. I won't . . .'

Fabrizio looked at him closely. His face was sallow, his brow damp with sweat. His hands were shaking uncontrollably. His eyes were wide and filled with fear. He was a sick man.

'Tell me where it is,' tried Fabrizio in a commanding tone.

But the man just shook his head convulsively, as if he were the prisoner of a force that dominated him completely.

'Tell me!' insisted Fabrizio, grabbing him by the shirt. 'You absolutely must tell me! Many human lives may still be destroyed unless you do. Can't you understand?'

The man yanked free, took a long breath and seemed to be about to say something when a long howl echoed, frighteningly close, followed by a deep snarling growl. The two men looked at each other with sudden, acute distress.

'My God,' said Fabrizio.

11

FABRIZIO SEARCHED the other man's face but found only bewilderment and a touch of madness.

'Do you have a weapon?' he asked.

The man lowered his head. 'It's no use,' he said. 'This time it's come for me. I should never have refused.'

Fabrizio grabbed him by the shoulders and shook him. 'A man like you must have a gun somewhere, damn it! Get it and defend yourself. It's only an animal. Ghosts don't rip people apart the way he does.'

But as he spoke he felt like his voice was coming from someone else's mouth, as if those weren't his own words. This feeling of alienation made him profoundly uneasy.

'You must have a weapon,' he insisted, trying hard to pull himself together. 'Get it and cover me while I try to reach my car. My rifle's inside and it's locked and loaded.'

As he spoke he could see the soft reflection of the burnished barrel in the darkness, smell the glycerine oil mixed with the persistent scent of gunpowder. All his senses were enhanced as he sought a point of focus.

The other man finally shook himself out of his trance. He got up, went towards the glass case and tried to control the trembling of his hands as he opened it. At that same moment the howl of the beast sounded even closer and was joined by the hoarse, furious barking of the dog outside. They heard the chain snapping back and forth, back and forth along the wire, followed by a fierce snarl and an immediately suffocated yelp. Then silence.

The man covered his mouth with his hand in a gesture of despair. 'He killed my dog,' he said softly. 'He's already here.' Then, with a sudden flash of conscience, he pushed Fabrizio towards a door at the back of the kitchen. 'You can get out this way. The regional road is just 100 metres away. There's always a car passing. Run.' He searched Fabrizio's face fleetingly, but then his eyes turned blank. He walked mechanically to the door that led to the courtyard and was outside before Fabrizio could stop him.

Fabrizio heard a shriek of terror, followed by the same growl he'd heard a few nights before, suffocated as the animal sank his snout into flesh and blood. He ran through the kitchen, down the hall and out the back door. He could see his car out of the corner of his eye; he knew he could make it. But as he was about to make a dash for it, he saw two headlights flare at the far end the courtyard and Francesca's little Jeep pulled up. He heard her voice calling, 'Fabrizio! Fabrizio, are you there?'

Fabrizio felt his blood turn to water and, gripped by panic, he shouted out at the top of his voice, 'Francesca! Francesca, no! Lock yourself in! Don't move!'

And he sprinted towards his own car, partially illuminated now by Francesca's headlights. But the beast instantly looked up from its victim and lunged after him. Fabrizio could feel its hot panting at his back, but he was sure he could make it. The car was there and Francesca was alive, though he could hear her terrified screaming. He opened the door, grabbed the gun, spun around and pulled the trigger. In the beam of the Jeep's headlights he saw the creature's terrifying bulk, its hackles raised, its bared bloodied fangs, and he understood he had failed in the same instant in which horror nailed him fast to the ground, slowed, almost paralysed his movements but left his mind free to race at an insane speed towards his own death.

He had no idea what was happening when the courtyard was swept by the blinding glare of another set of headlights. The dilated space of that unreal event was ripped through with agitated shouting and a burst of deafening explosions. He finally separated a voice he could recognize. It was Lieutenant Reggiani, yelling, 'Fire! Fire! Shoot to kill, damn it. Don't let it get away!'

Fabrizio heard bullets whistling in every direction, saw the dark sky streaked by vermilion tracers. White-hot stones scattered about him, filling the air with the sharp odour of burnt flint. A black mass made an impossible leap, cleared the squad-car blockade and disappeared into nowhere. Without noise, weightless, shape without substance, it seemed, until you saw the trail of blood it left behind. The man with his throat torn out was still bleeding in the glow of the headlights, his corpse jumbled up with the body of a dog, a brave little creature killed in the line of duty.

Fabrizio thought his head would explode. He called out, 'Francesca!' and the girl ran to him, threw herself into his arms and clung to him, crying the whole time.

Fabrizio touched her hair, caressed her cheek. 'Do you believe me now?'

'Looks like we got here just in time,' rang out Reggiani's voice to his right.

Fabrizio turned to face him. He was wearing combat fatigues and held two smoking pistols, one in each hand. The officer turned to the corpse on the ground.

'To save you, that is. It's over for this poor devil . . . Christ, what a horrifying death!'

Exhausted by so much emotion, Fabrizio put an arm around Francesca's shoulders and walked her back to her Jeep, trying to calm her. He turned to Reggiani. 'Could someone take my car home? Francesca can't drive,' he said, adding, 'She's in shock.' As if he were fine and in complete control of all his faculties.

Reggiani didn't miss a beat. 'Right. You go and take care of her. We'll take care of the car. Tonight or tomorrow morning.'

Fabrizio got into the Jeep and drove off at a slow pace, keeping one hand on the steering wheel and the other around

Francesca's shoulders and saying, every so often, 'There, there. It's all over now. You'll be OK.'

'Stay with me tonight, please,' said Francesca as soon as she had calmed down.

'Yes, I'll stay with you. That's why I asked Reggiani to have my car taken care of.'

He crossed the regional road and turned off on to the local road that led to Francesca's house.

Once inside, she prepared some herbal tea, poured it into two cups and sat at the table opposite him. Her cheeks were still streaked with tears, her hair was messy and her eyes were red and yet she was beautiful, with a quiet, unselfconscious beauty she seemed totally unaware of.

He drank small sips of the tea until it was gone, then got up and said, 'Come on. Let's go to bed.'

THE NEXT MORNING Fabrizio woke up early and feeling fairly normal, surprisingly so. Perhaps he had Francesca's herbal tea to thank. She was already in the kitchen, making breakfast. He could tell that last night's ordeal had affected her but not prostrated her. She was not the type to let her emotions run wild. Fabrizio was sure she was already rationalizing what had happened and searching for plausible explanations.

'Why did you follow me last night?' he asked her suddenly.

'I tried to call you, half an hour after you left, and you didn't answer.'

'That's impossible. My mobile phone never rang.'

'I'm sure you never heard it ring. You left it here!' she said, opening a drawer. 'I turned it off and put it away for safe keeping.'

Fabrizio shook his head, took the phone, turned it on and put it into his pocket.

'When I realized your mobile phone was here, I wanted to let you know and I called your home number. It rang and rang. You forgot to turn on the answering machine.'

'That's likely.'

'I tried ten minutes later, thinking you'd got held up somewhere or had a flat. Still no answer . . . so I put two and two
together. I drove by your house anyway to make sure. The
lights were on inside but your car was missing. I realized you'd
gone in and out in such a hurry that you'd forgotten to switch
off the lights. At that point I had no doubt – I figured you'd
gone looking for Montanari.'

'Right. And the carabinieri got on your tail.'

'I think they were already on yours. I'm sure Reggiani's
keeping an eye on you.'

'Hmm. They're good at it. I hadn't even noticed. But why
were you trying to call me in the first place?'

'Because I'd discovered something.'

'After I'd left your house? Are you kidding me?'

'No, not in the least. Hold on tight: Balestra's inscription is
opisthographic.'

'What do you mean? That there's writing on both sides?'

Francesca was all calm and composed. She took the coffee
pot off the stove and poured out two cups, then proceeded to
scramble three eggs while a couple of pieces of thick Tuscan
bread were toasting in the oven.

'How can you say that?' insisted Fabrizio, trying not to
appear impatient.

'I have a copy of the tape I gave you and after you left I got
curious. I couldn't resist taking a look. I was fast-forwarding it
when the cat starting miaowing from behind the door. I got
up to let him in and opened a can of cat food. As I was putting
it in his dish, I realized I'd forgotten to pause the VCR. When
I got back, the tape had gone beyond the point at which you
could see Balestra's transcription of the Etruscan text, which
was the only thing I had considered, and it picked up other
images.'

'What images?' urged Fabrizio. 'Francesca, don't make me
drag the words out of your mouth!'

'My camera kept filming for five minutes longer and captured a sequence of images that look like they were created by a scanner. Balestra has one that recognizes sixteen million tones of grey. For some reason that I couldn't fathom at first, he had photographed the back side of the inscription and then scanned the photo.'

'Are you sure?'

'Absolutely sure. The bronze surface is perfectly recognizable. It's fairly even but a little rough. You can even see where the inscription was photographed. It looks like an NAS warehouse, probably the one in Florence. There's not much depth behind the slab, but enough to let you see beyond it. I imagine that Balestra noticed something strange about the back of the inscribed slab and decided to try to get a scanned image. So what to the bare eye must have looked like shadows actually came out as lines of writing, thanks to the resolution of the scanning equipment. Look.'

Francesca turned on the VCR and played the tape. Fabrizio stared hard at the screen.

'No. Watch. I'll show you,' said Francesca, placing a mirror in front of the screen. As if by magic, a sequence of letters appeared.

'Latin!' murmured Fabrizio. 'I can't believe it . . .'

'Incredible, isn't it?' said Francesca, obviously pleased with herself. 'It's quite archaic, but it's Latin for sure. Now you know why he's kept this so secret. Balestra has the key for translating Etruscan if – as I think – this is the translation of the text on the other side.'

Fabrizio explored the paused image at length. 'Amazing!'

'How do you explain it?' asked Francesca.

'For some reason, the person inscribing the slab must have made a copy in Latin, probably using a material with a slightly different composition. The two slabs were in contact long enough for the oxidation process to create these differentiated shadows. Balestra really has some incredible equipment. I didn't realize these things were so sophisticated. He must have paid for it himself. I doubt the NAS would finance—'

'It's the same equipment,' Francesca interrupted him, 'that discovered that the shadows over the eyes of the man on the Holy Shroud are actually coins which picture the head of Pontius Pilate. Extraordinary work, done using the same machine. Now what are you going to do?'

'About what?'

'About this inscription, what else? Nothing that would detract from Balestra's eventual announcement about its discovery, I hope.'

'No. I wouldn't dream of stealing his thunder. The only thing I want to do is figure out what it says. It's the only way to understand what's happening here.'

Francesca shook her head. 'You're mad as a hatter . . . How can you possibly think there could be any connection between these murders and . . . Christ, this stuff happened two thousand four hundred years ago! It's absolutely impossible.'

'Last night you didn't seem so sure about that . . . The one thing I know is that Sonia's virtual reconstruction of the skull of the animal in the tomb is identical to the head of the animal we both saw last night.'

'So? It's a striking coincidence. That's all.'

'No, there is one more thing: an open account from the past always has to be settled. Even after two thousand four hundred years.'

Francesca had no answer for that. Even if she had known what to say, she knew Fabrizio would not listen. His mind was going in other directions.

'Well, what do you propose we do?' she asked.

'Start translating.'

Francesca widened her eyes. 'We're not philologists. We'll never succeed.'

'I was a pretty good epigraphist before I started studying statues, and we can always get help on the Internet or by asking someone who knows more than we do. Vartena, for instance, or Mario Pecci or even Aldo Prada. Why not? Aldo's a friend of mine. But we won't do that unless we're desperate. First of all, though, let me call Sonia. It's ages since I've talked to her.'

'Forty-eight hours at the most,' Francesca said sharply.

'She's a friend and she's doing an awesome job,' said Fabrizio defensively.

'About time!' chirped Sonia's voice from his mobile phone. 'Where are you? What have you been up to?'

'Looking for trouble, as usual. How's your work going?'

'Really well. I'm assembling the spinal column and the hindquarters.'

'As soon as I have a minute I'll drop in.'

'Oh, listen . . . that carabiniere lieutenant came by. He said he'd be getting your car back to you this morning. What, you were so busy smooching you didn't notice the tow truck dragging you off?'

Fabrizio ignored her comment.

'Pretty hot, your lieutenant friend.' Sonia started on a new tack. 'I wouldn't mind seeing him again outside the office.'

'To see how he handles a pistol?' Fabrizio teased back.

'You fool,' concluded Sonia. 'See you around.'

Fabrizio hung up and went straight to work, using his digital camera to photograph the images on the screen. Then he asked Francesca to drive him home.

'You could move in here for a while,' she suggested. 'We could work on it together. Cook something up when we get hungry . . .'

Fabrizio hesitated a moment, long enough for her to be offended.

'Forget it,' she said. 'Forget I even said anything.'

'It's just that I have everything I need at my house,' said Fabrizio. 'A lot of people don't have my mobile phone and they might leave me messages on the answering machine . . .'

His voice trailed off as he ran out of lies. In reality, he felt

THE ANCIENT CURSE

suddenly afraid of staying at Francesca's house, wary about continuing a relationship that had been too serious from the start. He was not at all sure he could cope. He'd felt strange for quite a while now: out of step, out of place, out of his depth. And he felt indebted to her, which made him uncomfortable. What's more, he was used to the solitary life, to working on his own. And when he thought of what had happened the night before, and might happen again, he knew it was best to keep her out of it as far as he could.

But he couldn't help but notice the disappointment in Francesca's face. 'Besides, this situation has us all acting crazy. You'd end up hating me, sooner than you think!' he continued weakly.

The girl shrugged, as if resigned, walked out front and opened the door to the Jeep. 'Go on, get in,' she said, then sat behind the wheel and, once he was in, started driving.

Neither spoke for a while, then Fabrizio said, as if thinking aloud, 'The beast seems to strike all of those who have something to do with the tomb.' Ringing in his mind were the words of the woman who had threatened him the night before. 'Or maybe even those who have something to do with the statue in the museum, like me.' He reflected in silence for a moment, then went on: 'You're not in on this threat for the moment and it's best that you don't get mixed up in it. I have a lead that I'm following and there's no reason for both of us to risk our lives. Right?'

Francesca took her eyes off the road for a moment and turned to him. 'If you love someone you take risks,' she said. 'But I understand. I'd feel the same way if I were in your shoes. I imagine you won't answer if I ask you what lead you're working on.'

'No, I can't. It's a pretty remote possibility anyway. At least for now.'

'I thought not,' she said and asked nothing further.

They got to Fabrizio's house as the carabinieri were pulling up to return his car. Sergeant Massaro handed him the keys and was joined by Reggiani, who stepped out of his regulation Alfa holding a hunting rifle. He said hello to Francesca, then turned to Fabrizio. 'Do you have half an hour to talk? Massaro has a few more photos to take at the Montanari house, then he'll be back to pick me up.'

'Of course,' replied Fabrizio, and turned to Francesca. 'If you'd both like to come in, I'll make some coffee.'

Reggiani set his gun in the rack, then sat down with Francesca at the table in the big kitchen as the intense aroma of freshly made coffee filled the room.

Reggiani put a spoonful of sugar into Francesca's cup. 'Is one good?' he asked.

'Yes, fine,' replied the girl.

'How are you feeling today?' the officer asked her as Fabrizio sat down with them and started sipping the coffee.

'Better, thank you, much better, but I've never been so scared in my whole life.'

'I can believe it. Finding yourself face to face with such a monster. As luck would have it, we got there in time. We were trailing Fabrizio at a distance when we saw your car on that side road. It was dark and I didn't recognize your Jeep, but when I saw you drive straight into the Montanari courtyard I thought I would have a heart attack. We rushed in and thank God we did. It could have been much worse.'

'What are you going to do with this fourth corpse?' asked Fabrizio.

Francesca noticed a moment of hesitation on Reggiani's part. She downed the last drops of coffee from her cup and got up to leave. 'I have things to do,' she said at the door. 'I'll see you later, Fabrizio.'

Reggiani sighed. 'We haven't let the news filter out yet. Montanari lived alone in that isolated house in the middle of the countryside. People were used to him disappearing for relatively long periods of time. He would go off looking for seasonal jobs or work of a more dubious nature. He's spent plenty of time in jail. No one will notice he's gone. At least for a while. I guess that's lucky for us, but we can't go on like this. I've spoken to my superiors and we're organizing a hunt with hundreds of men, dozens of dogs, helicopters and off-road vehicles, infrared equipment . . .'

'You'll draw a hell of a lot of attention to yourselves. You'll have the press of half the world on your backs. A story like this . . . I can just imagine.'

'I know. But at this point we have no choice. Especially because you're not being of any help. For example, what were you doing at the Montanari house?'

'You were the one who told me that those mysterious phone calls were coming from there. And are you aware that Balestra is studying an exceptionally important and very rare Etruscan inscription?'

'Of course. The guys over at archaeological heritage protection told me about it. The slab from Volterra. They were the ones who recovered the piece from an old riverbed, but it had been moved there from somewhere else, if I remember correctly.'

'You're right. That was just a temporary hiding place. It was Montanari who reported it to the NAS, saying that he'd dug it up while working in the fields. Balestra immediately ordered further investigations but they turned up nothing. This tipped them off; an inscription that important cannot be devoid of any archaeological context. It was evident that Montanari was lying and that he must have known where it had really been found and where the missing portion of it was. I thought I could get him to talk and that's what I was doing there.'

'Without saying anything to me,' commented Reggiani.

'I would have told you if I'd been successful. Anyway, you were following me.'

'That doesn't justify your behaviour. Go on.'

'What's more, inside Montanari's house I saw a fragment of

the same bucchero pottery with the swastika that I found near the Phersu tomb and I realized he must be connected to that find as well. I'll bet you he's the one who told the tomb robbers where the Rovaio tomb was.'

'And what about your colleague Dr Dionisi? What was she doing last night at La Casaccia?'

Fabrizio hesitated a moment, looking into the bottom of his cup, then said, 'She had something urgent to tell me.'

'What?' Reggiani pressed.

'It concerns a discovery she made . . . a scientific discovery.'

'That was so important it couldn't wait for today? It must have been very urgent indeed.'

'It was, but I can't tell you any more. Give me a couple of days to work on it before you order a full-scale search operation.'

'So it has something to do with this.'

'I'm not really sure but maybe it does . . . Give me the chance to find out.'

'I can't promise you anything but I'll see what I can do. I'll try to put off the operation for as long as I can, but then I'll turn this whole place inside out. I'll find that thing and fill it full of lead, then stuff it myself so I can see it hang in some museum. I saw this film the other night, a DVD that I rented.'

'Yeah? What film was it?'

'*The Ghost and the Darkness*.'

'I remember that one. With Michael Douglas and Val Kilmer. The story about those two lions that devour a hundred and thirty workers on a railroad project. In Africa, at the end of the 1800s. Is that the one?'

'Yes, that's it. You know, the film is based on a true story. Everyone thought the two man-eaters were spirits, ghosts in the shape of lions who couldn't be defeated. Well, you know what? They're now sitting stuffed in a window display in a museum in Chicago. I saw them.'

'You saw them? In Chicago?'

'No. I downloaded the image from the Internet. One of the new guys can navigate the web like a real sea wolf. So, you know what else? They don't even look scary. They are small and scraggly-looking. Doesn't that console you?'

'Not in the least,' replied Fabrizio. 'I've heard the phenomenon explained by animal-behaviour specialists. A predator, for some reason, becomes disabled. He can't run as fast as the others, or isn't as strong, and he gets kicked out of the pack. At some point, by pure chance, he kills a human being and immediately realizes that man is a slow, easy prey and, let's say, has high nutritional value. From that moment on, he hunts and eats only people. Now, would you say that our creature is disabled in some way, or is killing out of hunger?'

Reggiani shook his head, discouraged. 'I have to admit you've got a point there. In any case, I still intend to hunt it down and take it out.'

They heard the sound of an engine outside. 'That must be Massaro,' observed Fabrizio.

Reggiani got up and went to the door.

'Listen . . .' Fabrizio began.

'I'm listening,' said the officer with his hand on the door handle.

'Nothing . . . I have to check out this thing first and then I'll let you know, I promise.'

'I hope so,' said Reggiani. 'For your sake.' He started out, then turned back again. 'You know, I was wondering . . . that colleague of yours . . .'

Fabrizio couldn't help but smile. 'Francesca?'

'No, the other one.'

'Sonia?' asked Fabrizio with pretended nonchalance.

'Yeah, I think that's her name. You two aren't . . . together, are you?'

'No. We're not.'

'If I wasn't in the shit up to my eyeballs, I wouldn't mind having a go. Good God, someone like her can't just spend all her time with bones, right? She must like flesh as well, I hope.'

'I imagine she does,' replied Fabrizio. 'I'd bet on it actually.'

He closed the door behind Reggiani, went back to the table and switched on the computer.

12

HE HAD JUST sat down when the telephone started to ring. He raised the receiver after a moment of hesitation and said firmly, 'Hello.'

'This is Signora Pina,' said the voice on the other end.

'Signora! What can I—'

'It was you, Doctor, who told me to call you if I saw anything that . . .'

'Oh yes, of course, of course. You're not disturbing me at all. I was just about to start working.'

'Well, I wanted to let you know that I heard noises last night.'

'What sort of noises?'

'I really couldn't say . . . And I saw that light glowing again from down in the cellar.'

'Did you see anything else?'

Signora Pina fell silent for a moment, then spoke up again. 'Nothing. I didn't see a thing. The house went pitch dark afterwards and as silent as a grave.'

'I see. Thank you, Signora Pina. Be sure to keep me informed if it happens again.'

'You can count on it, Doctor. Nothing escapes me from here.'

Fabrizio lowered his head and sighed. He was lost in thought for a few long moments, then he shook himself and went back to work.

He scanned the sequence image by image, passage by

passage, until he had the entire inscription saved on his computer. He opened a program in which he could divide the screen into three parts and inserted the Etruscan version on the right and the Latin version on the left, leaving the centre open for his translation. He plugged in his laptop alongside, turned it on and connected it to the largest, most complete Latin dictionary that existed on the planet, the *Thesaurus Academiae Internationalis Linguae Latinae*, as well as to the *Corpus Inscriptionum Latinarum* and the *Testimonia Linguae Etruscae*. He took the phone off the hook, turned off his mobile phone and focused on the task at hand.

He worked for hours and hours with no interruption and without even getting up. He sipped at a glass of water, as he was accustomed to doing when he was dealing with a particularly thorny intellectual challenge. On the wall in front of him was a blow-up of the lad of Volterra, which seemed to fill the empty kitchen with its melancholy aura. He didn't stop until he was utterly exhausted, at nearly two a.m. He got up to stretch his stiff limbs and contemplated the screen with satisfaction. The central column was slowly filling up with Italian words, nursed along by the Etruscan and Latin texts. Word after word, the past was coming alive, one scrap at a time. He sat down again and went back to work. There were still a number of gaps, some longer than others, empty spaces that interrupted the flow, and as his frustration grew, so did his excitement. But he was feeling utterly drained and fatigue was setting in.

He got up, took an amphetamine and put on a Mahler symphony to buoy up his emotions, which were taking off every which way. The hours passed as the text was pieced together, taken apart and reassembled in an uninterrupted series of interpretative hypotheses. Streams of data filled the laptop's plasma screen: word lists, tense sequences, exemplifications, hundreds of alphabetical symbols representing all the possible variants. In Latin, in Greek, in Etruscan. Fabrizio paused only to watch the sun rising over the forested hills that loomed to the east with their curving, undulating shapes. Then, forgetting how early it was, he called Aldo Prada, his linguist friend, to consult with him about all the doubts that had emerged in his long night's work.

'I'm so sorry!' said Fabrizio when he realized he'd woken his colleague up. 'I'm so tired I don't know what I'm doing.'

'What are you doing?' asked Prada, immediately intrigued and not at all sleepy.

'I'm . . . trying to read an inscription.'

'Unpublished, right? Where did you find it?'

The telephone call was turning into an uncomfortable interrogation.

'It's not the inscription from Volterra, is it? Isn't that where you said you were going? I've heard about it, although no one has any details. I was talking to Sonia the other day and—'

'Aldo, what I need is your help, not your questions. This thing I'm working on is important and urgent but I'm afraid I can't explain.'

'You'll name me in the publication, though, right? Or we can publish it together. What do you say? You are going to publish it, right?'

'No. I'm not going to publish it. It isn't mine to publish.'

'Ah,' sighed his colleague in a tone both disappointed and suspicious.

'Listen,' said Fabrizio impatiently. 'We've always been friends, haven't we? That's why I thought of you. If you think you can help me, say so, otherwise forget it. I'll stumble through it on my own, as I have been doing.'

'Don't get angry. I was just curious . . . It's not every day you hear about an unpublished inscription. Let's start from scratch. If you're calling me, it must mean you're stuck – that is, the expressions you're trying to translate are not in established sources.'

'That's it. You're the only person who can help me right now. I'll be eternally grateful and, as soon as this thing is over,

I'll tell you the whole story. I promise you that I'm not doing anything illegal. I'm just dead tired right now and I'm not connecting. If you don't help me, I'm afraid I won't work my way out of this. But if you can't, that's all right. I'll survive, you know.'

'All right, I get it. You don't want to tell me anything, even though I'm an old friend. OK, don't worry about it. Tell me what the problem is. Although without seeing what we're talking about, I don't know—'

'Is your computer on? I'll send the parts I'm having trouble with and give you a few minutes to look at them. Then I'll call you back and we can go through them together. All right?'

'Sure. Send it right away, then.'

Fabrizio sent the file, waited nearly an hour and then called back.

'Got it!' said Prada.

'Well? What do you think?'

'Good God! This stuff is incredible.'

'It is.'

A few moments of silence, then his friend's voice rang out: 'Know something? You're pretty close. It's only that you haven't considered . . .'

'What?'

'Several variations in the formulation of diphthongs in the archaic form of the genitive, and a morpheme which I would classify as an *apax* because—'

'Aldo, please. I have no time for theory. Just correct what-ever is wrong with my fucking translation before I faint or have a heart attack because I'm so exhausted I can't think straight any more. Is that clear?'

'Clear as can be. Hold on, though, yeah, I think I'm right about that, there's a diphthong formulation here that . . .'

Fabrizio let him run on because he knew that Aldo Prada's mind was the most powerful machine in the world as far as phonetic and morphologic processing was concerned. If he couldn't manage it, no one could. Even Balestra must have had a lot of problems, if he'd been holed up in his office so long without ever appealing to anyone for assistance or collaboration.

'Give me a couple of hours,' Prada said suddenly. 'You've taken me by surprise here. I don't want to make a mistake. No one's ever seen a bilingual text before. What's strange is that the Etruscan is so clear and the Latin is so fuzzy. It looks more like spots than letters. But better than nothing, that's for sure. Good heavens, I can only imagine the clamour this will create when it's announced. If only I knew a little more about the context . . .'

'Don't even think about it. I can't tell you where it was found. You'll have to manage with what you have. Do it as a favour to me. You won't be sorry, I promise you.'

'OK. I'll call you as soon as I've finished.'

Fabrizio closed the shutters and lay down on the couch to try to recover some lucidity. He was light-headed with hunger. The strain of working through the night, along with the pill he'd swallowed, made him feel wide awake but sluggish. He felt like he was moving in slow motion, and his muscles were cramping up, along with his stomach. The sounds of early morning wafted in from outside: the rumble of cars on the regional road and the chirping of sparrows. The roosters saluted the dim light of another dreary day from farmhouses scattered around the countryside.

Fabrizio couldn't have said how much time had passed since he'd concluded his conversation when the phone rang. He started and grabbed the receiver.

'It's an *arà*,' said Aldo Prada on the other end of the line. His tone was a mix of irony and uneasy awe. 'An imprecation . . . a curse that is . . . But that's not all . . .'

'Yes, that's what I thought, but I wanted your verdict.'

'I have no doubts. It involves the ritual of a Phersu if I'm interpreting correctly. Crazy stuff.'

Deeply unnerved, Fabrizio fell silent.

'You're already on to this, aren't you?' insisted Prada.

'Yeah, I am,' admitted Fabrizio. 'I excavated the tomb.'

'Of a Phersu? Holy Christ. I can't believe you're telling me this.'

'It's complicated. Very complicated.'

'If I weren't so far away I would rush over there and force you to explain the whole story. If you let me read the entire inscription I could be of much more help to you. I give you my word of honour that I won't tell a soul.'

'I am sorry, Aldo, I can't take any risks. Consider that Balestra has been locked up in his office for weeks. If it comes out that I'm working on the same stuff . . .'

'Right. Got you. That's what I thought.'

'You'd end up confiding in someone you trust blindly, I know you – and then he would turn round and talk to someone he trusts blindly. In two days' time, everyone and their mother would know about it and that would mean big trouble. Bigger trouble than you can even imagine. Please, just send me your conclusions and don't ask me any more questions. You'll under-stand why soon enough.'

Prada stopped insisting and sent Fabrizio the passages that he had interpreted with the acumen and brilliance that made him one of the top scholars in his field.

As Fabrizio began to insert the phrases interpreted by his colleague in the gaps still scattered throughout his translation, he realized that his energy levels were totally depleted. He knew he couldn't stop yet and he swallowed another amphetamine to force his exhausted brain to bear up under the strain and get the job done. Thus, little by little, an hour at a time, a story began to emerge from the shadows of millennia. A cruel, delirious story that projected a desire for revenge so burning and intense that it could span the centuries. A story that cut him to the quick and filled him with fear and despair. He looked up from his work to contemplate the image of the lad of Volterra and it was like seeing him for the first time, as if, finally, he had met up with him on a deserted road after a long, strenuous journey, or as if he had recognized a son or a younger brother he never knew he had, and Fabrizio's bloodshot eyes were dimmed with tears.

He was certain of having concluded his work and he got to his feet with the intention of having a shower and then calling Lieutenant Reggiani or trying to locate him wherever he was. He took a few steps but his legs gave way and he slowly collapsed on to the mat that covered the floor. He couldn't have known that evening was falling again, an early, chalky dusk shot through with shudders of wind.

His body was completely motionless and the flickering reflection of the computer screen cast a spectral light on to his face. He would have looked like a dead man, were it not for the continuous rapid movements behind his closed eyelids, as in the most intense, most visionary phase of a dream . . .

The room was vast, rectangular in shape and adorned with frescoes that depicted scenes from a symposium, with guests laughing, drinking, leaning forward in conversation. A double row of candelabra with hanging lamps of bronze and translucent onyx lit up the room, so numerous that they filled the hall with an intense, golden light, like that of the sunset just passed. The dinner guests – men and women, young and old – were reclining on couches alongside tables filled with trays of food and cups brimming with wine, chatting amiably in low voices.

In the middle of the room lithe maidens danced gracefully to the sound of flutes and string instruments played by a little group of musicians. The atmosphere spoke of pleasure and celebration, of the refined amusements of an aristocratic gathering, similar, perhaps, to an assembly of immortal divinities.

Next to each one of the noble ladies participating in the banquet was an alabaster perfume jar hanging on a thin cord from the ceiling, filled with rare scents imported from the Orient. Every so often one of them dipped in her hand to spread the fragrance on her soft, white skin, her round shoulders, her breasts. The perfume saturated the air, along with the light, musky scent of the men's sweat.

At the head of the triclinium hall, at the centre of the short wall, against a curtain the colour of the night sky, reclined lauchme Lars Thyrrens, lord of Velathri, the red city of the huge gates and resplendent multi-hued temples. His full head of black hair, shining with bluish reflections, brushed the collar of golden plates adorning his neck and shoulders. He wore an embroidered chlamys open at the sides of his sculpted torso, covering only his groin. His massive build, wide shoulders and brawny arms were those of a mighty warrior, of a man accustomed to conquering by force anything that aroused his desire. Any woman would have yearned to lie in his arms and often, during a banquet, when the lights had burned low, one of the ladies present would go to stretch out beside him, covered by the same mantle, ignoring her fat and tolerant husband to become acquainted with his fierce, powerful virility. Many had done so, or perhaps all of them. Except one.

It was for this reason that the eyes of the powerful lord rested avidly, insistently on Anait, the most stunning, desirable woman in the city. So intriguing that she would make even the wisest, most upright of men lose his mind, so beautiful that she had Lars Thyrrens, the most powerful of men, in her thrall. A man who had risen to power merely, or mainly, to satisfy his own desires, to satiate any craving for food or wine or rare, precious objects, any longing for a young man or maiden in the prime of youth and beauty.

But she never returned his looks. She never tired of contemplating her own husband, Lars Turm Kaiknas, a man as handsome as a god, strong, yet as gentle and sweet as a young lad. She couldn't stop caressing his hands, his arms, his face, because he had finally returned to her after a long absence, a war campaign beyond the northern mountains, in the vast valley crossed by a great river. There, at the head of the Rasna ranks, he had fought off the hordes of blond Celtic invaders. He led the army of the league of twelve cities to the walls of Felsina, driving them onward as far as the mudbanks of Spina, a city *made of wood and straw but rich with gold and bronze, defended only by the wide swamps surrounding it.*

The party was in his honour and in his palace. Anait was impatiently awaiting the moment at which the guests would wander off, in which the lauchme would give the signal to end the festivities, so she could finally withdraw to the warm intimacy of their bedchamber and undress in front of her husband in the soft glow of the midnight lamp. She'd savoured the moment already in the ardour of his eyes. For Anait there was nothing else; no one else existed in the great festooned hall. The soft chatting of her dinner companions barely reached her ears, intent on listening only to the words of the man she loved, the man that she herself had chosen when, as a young girl, she had sent a servant with a message to his house, offering herself as his bride.

But the ardent glances of the lauchme did not escape the guests. Many of them were aware of the rumours that Anait's son, young Velies, had been conceived during one of the numerous absences of her husband; that he was the son of Lars Thyrrens. A lie that had surely originated in the palace of the king himself, to induce people to believe what he could only let himself dream of. In truth, Turm Kaiknas was the city's greatest warrior and the head of its army, so that not even the lauchme could challenge him, much less try to seduce his wife. If he wanted to take her by force, he would have to kill her husband first, a difficult, if not impossible, endeavour. Everyone loved Turm Kaiknas, for his valour, his deeds, his heroism. He would be the king of Velathri if it were up to the people.

Anait leaned close to her husband and whispered something in his ear, and this aroused Lars Thyrrens even more; he could only imagine how he would have felt with her lips so close to his face. He decided that the moment had come to carry out his plan, and he was in such a state that he never considered in the least the consequences of the evil deed he was about to enact. He nodded to one of the servant girls who stood at his side and she went off as if obeying a command. She waited until Anait was reposing again on her own kline, then she approached her and whispered something in the lady's ear. Anait exchanged a few words with her husband, who nodded as she stood and followed the maidservant out of the room.

Turm Kaiknas had more wine poured for himself and settled back to watch the jugglers and dancers who had disrobed and were now dancing naked in front of the dinner guests, especially those who had come unaccompanied. Meanwhile the lamps began to go out as the oil was consumed, a ruse that allowed even the most timid of them to pull one of the dancers over to his own couch, his sweetly scented kline.

The guests arranged at the far side of the room noticed Lars Thyrrens getting up and disappearing behind the curtain, but he was only gone for a few moments; he had soon returned to recline at his place. Only those who were very close could see that it was not him but another, an actor who greatly resembled him, garbed and made up in the same way, but they had been forewarned and none of them showed the slightest reaction. The guest stretched out at the very corner of the triclinium who could thus spy the corridor that led away from the hall itself, could see both the true Lars Thyrrens, who was walking circumspectly through the shadows, and the false Lars Thyrrens, reclining comfortably, intent on drinking wine from a cup. But he said not a word, as he too had been instructed by the master of ceremony, who had been bribed by the lauchme.

Anait soon reached the corridor which led out of the hall, preceded by the maidservant, who was still whispering, 'The child was crying, my lady, we could not calm him . . .' She could not see Lars Thyrrens waiting in the shadows, behind the door of the vestibule outside the bedroom. As soon as Anait entered he leapt upon her and threw her to the ground, covering her mouth with his hand. At that same instant, the musicians in the hall increased the volume of their instruments, adding tambourines and kettledrums, which covered the sounds of the struggle going on in the semi-darkness of the vestibule. Anait was a strong woman and she fought him off with great vehemence, but Lars Thyrrens was a monster of a man, tremendously powerful. He ripped off her clothing and tried violently to possess her.

The maidservant had hurried off, even though her malicious nature would have urged her to stay and watch, and she had not noticed that little Velies had truly woken up and wandered from his room. He stood in the vestibule, rubbing his eyes as if he could not believe what he was seeing. Anait caught a glimpse of her son, his shadow against the wall, inordinately lengthened by the light of the single lamp. She feigned submission for a moment and, as her assailant softened his grip, she bit his hand as hard as she could. The boy realized what was happening and the cruel scene distorted his delicate features into a mask of horror. He opened his mouth to scream. Enraged by the pain in his hand, aware that the child's cry would alert his father, Lars Thyrrens pulled his dagger from his belt and hurled it at the boy.

The child's cry was cut short. His face turned white in the pallor of death as a copious stream of blood ran down his side from where the dagger had stuck hilt-deep. Then the lauchme squeezed his hands around the neck of Anait, who had seen it all, trying to stop her from crying out. He tightened his grip until he felt her body collapse beneath him. Then he got up, composed himself, slipped back down the corridor and occupied the shadowy place left free by the actor, just in time.

Turm Kaiknas was no longer resting on his kline. His hearing had been honed by long hours of wakefulness at the head of his troops in the most remote, danger-filled places, where he had learned to pick up the slightest of noises. He had heard a suffocated cry coming from his apartments. His son, visited by a nightmare? And where was Anait? Why hadn't she returned?

An agonized howl burst out of the vestibule and Lars Thyrrens cried out himself in alarm. His guards rushed forward with lit torches in hand and many of the guests poured into the corridor after them. The scene they met with was horrifying. Turm Kaiknas was on his knees between the corpse of his wife and that of his son and he held a bloody dagger in his fist.

'Take him!' shouted Lars Thyrrens, and, before Turm Kaiknas could react or even speak, the guards were upon him. Although he fought off some of them with the very dagger he held in his hand and managed to twist free, others assailed him from every direction. Like a *lion caught in a net, he finally succumbed, stunned by a blow to the nape of his neck from behind.*

Lars Thyrrens shouted, 'You've seen it with your own eyes! Everyone knows that Turm Kaiknas has always despised his wife because she was unfaithful to him, because she bore him a bastard, the fruit of an illicit relationship!'

'It's true!' shouted all the onlookers. Because they were all slaves of Lars Thyrrens, the powerful lauchme of Velathri, all ready to swear to whatever he declared. No one dared to contradict him.

A single voice thundered out behind him, 'You lie! My sister never betrayed her husband! She loved him more than life itself. And Turm Kaiknas adored his son. He would never have raised a hand except to caress him.'

It was the voice of Aule Tarchna, Anait's brother, an augur who interpreted the signs that the gods sent to men, priest of the temple of Sethlans on the hill that overlooked the city. His features were harsh with indignation, but hot tears flowed from his eyes, because in a single moment he had lost everything that was most dear to him.

'No?' replied Lars Thyrrens. 'Then it will not be difficult for him to prove his innocence by winning the trial of the Phersu. You are a priest, Aule Tarchna, and know well that only the gods can judge a crime so horrendous it goes beyond all imagining.'

'Damn you! Damn you! You cannot do this. You are a shameless, sacrilegious, bloodthirsty beast. You cannot do this.'

'Not I,' replied Lars Thyrrens. 'The oldest law of our people. The most sacred. You should know that.'

'May I at least have their bodies?' cried Aule Tarchna, pointing to Anait and the child.

Lars Thyrrens regarded him impassively. 'They will burn along with this house. I will not allow you to expose them in public, nor to slander my name or accuse me of lying.'

'May you be damned,' said Aule Tarchna, from the bottom of his heart.

His eyes were dry; his burning hatred had dried his tears. He remained alone in the deserted house, which had been filled with song and joyous celebrating just moments before. He remained to weep over the bodies of Anait and Velies, until the crackling of the flames startled him, until the oaken ceiling beams began to collapse all around him. Then he stood and fled, never looking back.

He returned secretly the next day, to gather up what he could of the ashes and remains of his sister and nephew. He was not seen for days on end, but he returned for the terrible ritual, when Turm Kaiknas was pushed into the arena. With an arm tied behind his back and his head closed in a sack, Turm was made to fight against a vicious animal that the lauchme had procured from distant lands. Aule Tarchna did not cover his eyes, not even when he saw the hero bleeding from every part of his body, because he wanted his loathing to grow within him until it became an invincible force. A force that would survive for millennia.

Turm Kaiknas fought with superhuman strength. He had no other reason for being, in the short time that remained for him to live, than to cover his enemy with contempt and make sure that his blood fell on all those who witnessed his martyrdom. He struck the beast, wounding it again and again, but when he fell, lifeless, the monster was still alive and still tearing at his inanimate body.

Lars Thyrrens proclaimed that this was proof of Turm Kaiknas's guilt and he ordered the Phersu buried with the live animal, in the same tomb, so that the beast could continue to torture him for all eternity. An isolated tomb was designated for his burial, built in a solitary place, with no markings other than that of the black moon.

Aule Tarchna exercised his right to introduce an image of the family inside the tomb so that there might be a benevolent presence in that lair of cries and darkness, and he had a cenotaph fashioned in solid alabaster, portraying the likeness of Anait. Then he commissioned a sculpture of Velies that would be placed in the family tomb. A great artist cast the boy's likeness in bronze and included the blade that had murdered him. The portrait was the picture of melancholy and pain in a shape more similar to a shadow than to a living child, of a soul that had inhabited his body for too short a time and would never know the joy of love or of a family.

Inside the tomb he placed, last of all, two slabs of bronze, on which his eternal curse was inscribed:

> *May you be damned seven times, Lars Thyrrens, may your seed be damned and may all those who in this city sated your thirst for power be damned with you, may they be cursed until the end of the nine ages of Rasna. Damn the beast and damn all those who witnessed the cruel murder of an innocent man. May they experience the same end suffered by a blameless hero and may they weep tears of blood . . .*

Fabrizio awakened soaked in a cold sweat, filled with a sense of anguish. He stumbled to his feet with difficulty and went to the window. It was pitch dark outside.

13

Lieutenant Reggiani's Alfa Romeo pulled up in front of the Semprini farmhouse just before eight. Fabrizio came to open the door and invited his visitor to sit down in the kitchen. The coffee was already perking and bread was toasting in the oven. Reggiani wore jeans and a dark blue suede jacket which did not quite disguise the bulk of the regulation Beretta nestled under his armpit. He sat and watched Fabrizio from the corner of his eye as he took the bread out of the oven and set out butter, jam and honey.

'You are scary-looking,' he said. 'Looks like you spent the night in hell, actually.'

'Yeah, well, I guess you could say that,' replied Fabrizio without much emotion. He poured the coffee and sat down. 'Take more if you like,' he said. 'There's a full pot.'

'Aren't you going to tell me what happened?'

'I worked for hours and hours – all night, actually – without ever taking a break. That's why I must seem a little out of it.'

'That much I know. My guys are posted outside twenty-four seven. Nothing else to report?'

'Nothing else.'

'So what have you concluded after all this work?'

'I've translated Balestra's inscription, but no one is to know that. I just needed to understand what it said.'

'Can you let me in on it?'

'Not yet.'

'So why did you call me?'

'Because I need you to come with me. To the tavern at Le Macine.'

'To see that woman.'

'Yes. I want to ask her what Montanari couldn't tell me in time, before . . . that thing ripped out his throat.'

'Which is?'

'Where the seventh fragment of the inscription is.'

'And that's something that should interest us? Aside from its purely archaeological value, that is.'

'No. I wouldn't have knocked myself out this way for that reason. Archaeology takes time, usually. Do you know who that woman is?'

'Yes. I've looked into it. She's a widow who runs the place and usually serves at the bar. A normal person.'

'Does this normal person have a name?'

'First and last. It's Ambra Reiter.' Reggiani finished the last sip of coffee and lit up a cigarette.

'It's an early one today,' observed Fabrizio as he put the cups in the sink.

'I'm tense, all right? I'm preparing for the operation. You do remember I promised you no more than two days?'

Fabrizio didn't reply. He dried his hands on a dishcloth and said, 'Shall we go, then?'

Reggiani got up and went out to the car. Fabrizio locked the door behind him and slid into the passenger seat. 'She has a strange name,' he said. 'What else do we know about her?'

Reggiani turned on to the regional road. 'Not much for the time being. She's been here for about five years and for a while she worked as a housekeeper in a house here in Volterra. I'm trying to find out where she's from but I haven't got very far yet. I've heard she dabbles in magic – innocent stuff, reading palms, tarot cards, that kind of thing.'

It took them longer than Fabrizio expected because Reggiani's car was very low to the ground and he had to slow down at every bump and pothole. He seemed to be taking his time, driving slower than necessary. Maybe he wanted to allow time for conversation, but Fabrizio was quiet most of the way, absorbed in his thoughts, and his companion did not disturb him.

When they arrived in the courtyard at Le Macine the place was deserted. A northerly wind had cleared the morning mist and was scattering the dry oak and maple leaves, along with scraps of newspaper and bits of cement bags. A heap of freshly moved earth sat at the end of the courtyard near a digger, along with piles of bricks on one side and bags of cement and lime on the other, piled behind a fence of corrugated sheet metal.

'Work in progress, I see,' commented Reggiani. 'Business must be going well.'

He got out of the car and walked towards the building, followed by Fabrizio. He knocked on the door, which swung open at the touch of his hand. They entered and looked around in the semi-darkness. The room was empty, the chairs upside down on the tables, the stagnant air saturated with an indefinable smell in which one could make out a whiff of incense mixed with the aroma of some exotic cigarette.

'Anyone here?' asked Reggiani. No answer. 'Anyone around?' he repeated, raising his voice.

'Wait,' said Fabrizio. 'I'll take a look in the kitchen.'

He went behind the counter and inspected the room at the back. The stovetops were clean, the floor had been washed, the back door was locked and bolted.

He called out again, 'Is there anyone here?'

A spooked cat raced between his legs, miaowing loudly, crossed the room in a flash and escaped outside.

'Strange, isn't it?' said Reggiani. 'Looks like no one's here, but the door was open . . . Listen, I say we come back later. I don't like being in other people's houses when they're not around. Even though I'm in plain clothes, I'm still a carabiniere officer and—'

'Did you call?' a voice suddenly rang out behind them.

They spun around and found Ambra Reiter, who had seemingly materialized out of nowhere. She was standing still in the middle of the room and her face was wan but showed no emotion.

'I'm Lieutenant Marcello Reggiani,' said the officer with a bit of embarrassment, 'and I think you've met this fellow here, Dr Fabrizio Castellani of the University of Siena.'

The woman shook her head slowly as if awakening from a dream. 'I've never had the pleasure. Nice to meet you. Ambra Reiter,' she added, extending a hand.

Fabrizio couldn't help but blurt out, 'Excuse me, I don't know how you can say that. I came in here the other day and you served me a drink. Remember? When I tried to pay you said, "It's on the house." And you were at La Casaccia just a few minutes before that animal massacred Pietro Montanari.'

The woman regarded him as if he were raving. 'Animal? Pietro Montanari? Young man, are you sure you're talking to the right person? Lieutenant, would you mind explaining what this is all about? Are you here on official business, and if so what am I being accused of?'

Reggiani tried to explain. 'Absolutely nothing, ma'am, but my friend here says—'

Fabrizio interrupted him. 'She's the one who calls me at night and has made explicit threats about what will happen to me if I don't cut short my research.'

The woman looked at him in seeming amazement. 'I don't know what you're talking about. I don't know anything about any research and I don't even know you. You're either crazy or you've mixed me up with someone else.'

Reggiani realized that they wouldn't get anywhere under these circumstances and he gave Fabrizio a look, as if to say, 'Let's get out of here.'

Fabrizio nodded and followed him out, but before he left he turned to look the woman in the eye, to catch her off guard, to see if her expression would give her away. He saw nothing but the face of a sphinx, but before he looked away he noticed she had yellow mud on her shoes.

'Damned witch,' he said as soon as they were outside. 'I swear to you I saw her here the other night. We had a conversation, she threatened me . . . You don't believe me, do you?'

Reggiani lifted a hand to calm him down. 'I believe you, I believe you, but relax for a minute, will you? The only thing I can do is put someone on her. If she's who you say she is, she'll betray herself sooner or later. The only problem is time. That's what we're short of.'

They were about to get into the car when Fabrizio thought he heard a rustling. He turned just in time to glimpse a child rushing to hide behind the corner of the farmhouse. It looked like the same boy he'd spotted the last time he'd been to Le Macine. 'Wait!' he tried to call out, without much conviction, but the child had gone.

He got into the car. 'Did you notice her shoes?' he asked as soon as Reggiani had started it up.

'They looked like normal shoes to me.'

'They had yellow mud stuck to them.'

'So?'

'I'm an archaeologist. I'm quite familiar with the stratigraphy of the soil in this area. It's the same as the mud we saw piled up by the digger.'

'Right.'

'Do you know what that means?'

'That the woman's been walking around in this area.'

'No. She appeared out of nowhere, behind us. If she'd come from outside we would have seen her or heard her. I think she came from underground. More precisely, from a depth of two metres, give or take a centimetre. Now, if I—'

Reggiani slowed down, came to a stop and pulled on the handbrake. 'Wait. Let me guess. You want to get yourself into more trouble. Listen to me. Don't get any strange ideas about sneaking around at night to do underground reconnaissance, or anything of the sort. While this creature's on the loose you're not moving unless you've got company and unless I say so. If you want to stay alive.'

'Who's moving?' grumbled Fabrizio. 'Sergeant Massaro is always just around the bend in his grey Uno. Almost always . . .'

Reggiani drove off again, intending to drop Fabrizio off at his house on the Semprini property. Neither did much talking, as each was oppressed by his own nightmares.

'Know how long we've got to go?' asked Reggiani, turning off the engine. 'To the start of operations, that is?'

'A few hours?' asked Fabrizio.

Reggiani checked his watch. 'You're in luck,' he said. 'We've had a load of problems pulling together the necessary men and vehicles. But in thirty-six hours' time, not one minute later, the operation will get the go-ahead. If I can do it any sooner than that, I will.'

Fabrizio smiled. 'See where arrogance gets you? The other police forces not good enough to ask for help? Come on, Marcello, don't play the tough guy with me. There's got to be some flexibility built into that deadline. If I should need another two or three hours, say, half a day . . .'

Reggiani wiped his brow. He looked like he hadn't slept much the night before either. 'I trust that won't be necessary,' he said. 'I hope you realize I'm not fooling around here. When you mobilize for an operation like this one it's down to the minute. Let's get this straight. Although I hope it won't be necessary, I'm not going to bicker over minutes.'

Fabrizio lowered his head. 'Driving out there just complicated matters, didn't it?' he said. 'I never would have thought she could lie so brazenly, without letting out the tiniest bit of emotion. But that yellow mud is an important clue, you'll see. Goodbye, then. I'll be in touch soon.'

Fabrizio walked into the empty house and thought he should call Francesca, but the realization that he hadn't spoken to her for so many hours discouraged him. He didn't want to have to justify himself or get into an argument. He wasn't sure what to do next. Ambra Reiter was the only person who knew where the missing fragment of the inscription was, if Montanari had been telling the truth. And there was no way that she was going to tell him. Maybe there was no other option than to go in with the big guns, to let Lieutenant Reggiani run his operation, in the hope that that would solve matters. But Fabrizio couldn't resign himself to that.

He immersed himself in reading his translation and felt the dark vision of the night before encroaching again. Had it been extreme fatigue, the pills he'd taken to stay awake, or the influence of what he'd read or thought he understood in the inscription that had projected such images into his mind?

He felt oppressed by a sense of deep discouragement. The surveillance that Reggiani had provided to protect him made him feel like he was in prison. He couldn't move independently in any direction. He felt tormented by the confusion flooding his head, by that strange mix of reality and hallucination that hadn't left him, not even after awakening. It felt like he couldn't shake off the effects of a powerful drug. He'd experienced the feeling once before, in Pakistan, the only time he'd tried opium, out of curiosity. It had put him in a strange, black mood that hadn't left him for days.

Every now and then he looked over at the phone, thinking that he really should call Francesca, hoping that she might be the one to call him. Time stretched out in an unreal way. It seemed like months, or years, that he'd been living in this nightmare, this claustrophobic, agonizing situation.

He suddenly felt like simply walking out. He wished he could start up his car and just leave, forget about everyone, abandon the research that had brought him to Volterra, erase the inscription carved into the bronze slab by Aule Tarchna. He could find another way to make a living; become a high school teacher or a journalist.

But then he realized immediately that he didn't want to leave Francesca, didn't want to leave Marcello Reggiani or even Sonia, who was down in the basement of the museum assembling his monster. She must be well along by now. And above all he didn't want to leave that sad little boy who now had not only a face but a name, Velies Kaiknas, and a story, a story that felt to Fabrizio like it had happened the day before.

A light knock on the door made him jump. Was he hearing things? Who could be at his door, with the police outside? A soft knock, again.

'Who's there?' he said nervously, as his eye moved to the rifle glittering on the rack.

There was no answer. He got up and moved to the door. There was no one there.

'Who is it?' he repeated tensely.

And then he looked down. There was a little boy who looked like the kid he'd seen at Le Macine. Skinny, slight, with huge, expressive eyes.

'So who are you?' he asked in an amused tone.

'My name's Angelo,' he answered. 'May I come in?'

Fabrizio stepped aside and let him in. The child went straight to the table, sat down and put his elbows up as if he were waiting for something.

'Are you hungry?' asked Fabrizio. 'There's milk and biscuits.'

The boy nodded yes.

'How did you get here?'

'Emilio brought me. He delivers mineral water to the tavern. I like driving around with him.'

'How did you know I lived here?'

'Once I saw you going in the gate while I was riding around in Emilio's truck.'

'Do your parents know you're here? They'll be worried. How about if we give them a call?'

Fabrizio put his hand on the phone. The boy shook his head hard.

'You must have parents . . .'

'I live with my stepmother and she beats me for no reason. I hate her.'

'Maybe you don't do as she asks and she has to punish you.'

The little boy shook his head again but said no more.

'Why did you come all this way? You know I saw you at Le Macine.'

'Because I want to dig like you do. I want to be an archaeologist.'

'How do you know what I do?'

No answer from the child.

'Was she the one who told you? Your . . . stepmother? Or did you hear her talking to someone about me?'

The boy said nothing. He seemed intent on dipping biscuits into his milk. Then Fabrizio noticed that he was looking out of the corner of his eye at the blown-up photograph of the lad of Volterra.

'Do you like him?' asked Fabrizio.

The boy shook his head once again and then, a few moments later, said, 'So, can I stay?'

Fabrizio took a seat opposite him.

'I'm afraid not. A child has to be with his family. I'd like you to stay here, but then your mother would come looking for you. She'd talk to the carabinieri, you know? They'd call it "abduction of a minor" and you go to prison for that.'

'Better to be in jail than with her,' said the boy.

'Not you. Me. I'm the one they'd put in jail for kidnapping a minor, and that's you. You see?'

The boy shook his head again and Fabrizio sighed. How could he refuse to help this sweet child who seemed to have no one caring for him?

'Angelo, listen . . . you have to try and understand,' he began again.

The boy got up. 'I'm not going back to her,' he said. 'I'll run away.'

He started towards the door. He acted like a little man; no crying or betraying any sign of weakness. Fabrizio's heart swelled.

'Wait!' said Fabrizio. 'Where do you think you're going? Hold on a minute. Listen, for reasons I can't explain right now, the carabinieri come by here really often. If they see you here with me, they'll start to say, "Who is this kid and where is he from and who are his parents?" and so on and so on.'

He suddenly thought of Francesca and was pleased to have an excuse for phoning her.

'OK, wait. I have an idea. I have a lady friend who could maybe take care of you for a little while and then we'll decide what we should do, all right? You stay here. Don't move. I'll be right back.'

He went out into the corridor, where there was another phone, so Angelo wouldn't hear him. Francesca answered on the first ring, at her office in the museum. 'I figured if you weren't dead, you'd turn up sooner or later. I thought you were dead.'

'I'll tell you everything as soon as I see you. In the meantime, I have an emergency to deal with that might even help us out in the long run. A little boy has just shown up here. He lives with that woman at Le Macine, who he says is his stepmother. He's run away because she mistreats him. I think he may know something . . .' No answer. 'Francesca, I've succeeded in translating that thing, but I don't want to talk about it over the phone. I have to see you, as soon as possible.' Dead silence on the other end of the line. 'Francesca, please,' he added.

'All right. But you could have called me. Even just to say hello.'

'You'll understand when we see each other. Please, Francesca, come right away.'

'I'll be there in fifteen minutes.'

Fabrizio hung up and went back into the kitchen, but the

child had gone. Nothing more than an empty glass on the table and a few crumbs.

Fabrizio dashed outside and searched all around the house, calling loudly, but Angelo was nowhere to be found. Fabrizio couldn't believe he'd got so far away in such a short time. Feeling defeated, he sat on the stone bench by the front door and waited for Francesca.

'Sergeant Massaro is right out there in his grey Uno,' said the girl as soon as she arrived.

'I thought so. Come on in, please.'

Francesca continued to act a little peeved at first, but after she'd taken a good look at Fabrizio's face, she realized there was no point in staying offended. He was pale and his eyes were shiny as if he had a fever. She watched his hands shake as he passed her a cup of tea.

'I translated the inscription,' he said. 'I've been working on it since the moment I left you. That's why I guess I don't look so good. Actually, I'm exhausted . . . but unfortunately, without that missing segment, I don't know what's likely to happen next.'

Francesca shook her head, regarding him with an air of affectionate condescension. He was still seeing ancient curses everywhere.

Fabrizio told her about his fruitless trip with Reggiani to the tavern at Le Macine and then about the sudden appearance and disappearance of the little boy.

'If I try to leave in my car, Massaro will set off on my heels. You could hide me in the back of yours and we could drive down the regional road and see if we can find him somewhere. You didn't see a little boy walking all alone as you were driving here?'

'No. I would have noticed.'

'Then he didn't head back home. He must have gone in the opposite direction. I'm afraid he'll get lost. That he might meet up—'

'Yeah, I get it,' Francesca said, cutting him short to banish an ugly premonition. 'OK, let's get moving.'

Fabrizio left the light on in the kitchen, then slipped out and crouched down on the floor of the Jeep, hiding until he was out of sight of his guardian angel. They drove several kilometres before he had to admit that if the child had set off in that direction, it would have been impossible for him to have wandered so far.

'Let's try down the country roads,' proposed Francesca, resolutely pulling off on to a track heading east towards the hills.

'I have the translation with me,' said Fabrizio, who in the meantime had come out of hiding and was sitting comfortably on the back seat. 'Want to hear?'

'Of course I want to hear. I can't wait.'

Fabrizio began to read, and as the words came out of his mouth, his voice changed, distorted by the violent, unexpected emotion unleashed in his head by saying those words aloud. He had to stop more than once and take a deep breath, trying to recover lucidity and the strength to continue. When he had finished, his head dropped to his chest and he fell silent.

'My God,' said Francesca, without taking her eyes off the road, which was now running along the edge of an escarpment.

'I think that there are too many coincidences for this to be a product of chance. But even if there is no connection at all, even if we are dealing with a series of coincidences with no rhyme or reason behind them, I still think – actually I'm firmly convinced – that we have to find the seventh fragment and analyse what it says.'

'How can you say you're so sure?' asked Francesca, turning towards him. 'Nothing is certain when you're dealing with such a distant past.'

Fabrizio continued as if he hadn't heard her: 'The meaning I've been able to glean from the first part of the text will certainly help in reading the last fragment, if and when we find it. In any case, we'll have interpreted an exceptional find and turned it over to science. But if I'm right, we'll also have found a way to stop this massacre, or maybe avoid something even worse.'

They continued to search the countryside for hours and hours, stopping just once at a little shop to buy a couple of salami sandwiches. When it began to get dark, Fabrizio decided to call the tavern at Le Macine. He got the number from directory enquiries, but the phone rang twelve times without anyone answering.

'Where could he have gone?' he wondered, pressing hard on his forehead as if to crush a nightmare.

'It's useless racking your brains over it,' replied Francesca. 'He could be anywhere . . . somewhere you'd never think of. A friend's house, for instance. He's just a kid. He couldn't still be wandering out here alone in the middle of the fields at this hour. Stop worrying.'

'He didn't look like a kid who had friends to me. He looked like a kid who was always alone and never saw anyone.'

'Fabrizio, all we can do now is go back. If Massaro realizes you're gone he'll send out the troops.'

'Why couldn't I have taken a drive in the country with my girlfriend?'

Francesca tried not to smile. 'And who would this girlfriend be?'

'In the city!' said Fabrizio a moment later, in an entirely different tone of voice.

'Who, your girlfriend?' prompted Francesca.

'No, him. Angelo. My girlfriend is here, at the wheel of this car.' He squeezed her hand tightly.

'Why do you think he may be in town?' asked Francesca.

'It's only a hope, really. I remember seeing him slip behind the door of the Caretti-Riccardi palace a few days ago. Now that I think about it, I'm sure it was him.'

'You can't possibly be sure of such a thing! That old mansion has been closed for years. It's falling apart and no one lives inside. I'm very sure about that.'

Fabrizio recalled the last call from Signora Pina, telling him about the strange lights coming from the cellar, and turned to Francesca. 'Are you very, very sure?'

14

Francesca turned the Jeep around and headed towards the city.

'This way you'll be convinced that there's absolutely nothing in there and that the palace has been locked and bolted for years,' she said.

'I couldn't have dreamed of seeing the boy there,' said Fabrizio.

'I'm not saying that, but it's a fact that sometimes we see what we want to see or what we expect to see. The brain is a very powerful machine, much more so than you or I can imagine . . .'

Fabrizio looked at her with a strange expression. Could she read his mind? Was there some secret memory there, buried deep in his unconscious, that was responsible for what he'd been experiencing?

Ten minutes later they were back on the regional road and could see that the grey Uno was still parked in its place, although probably someone had come to relieve Massaro. In the distance they could see the Semprini farmhouse with the downstairs lights on.

'Do you suppose that'll be enough to keep them thinking I'm at home?' asked Fabrizio.

'Maybe yes and maybe no. But if Reggiani calls there and you don't answer he'll smell a rat. They'll be turning over the rubbish bins looking for you.'

'Reggiani's a smart guy and that agent sitting in the car is a

171

sort of alibi for his conscience. I'm sure he knows I'm out somewhere and he also knows that trying to keep me in a cage is counterproductive.'

'And the beast? Where do you suppose it is now? You know, since I saw it myself the other night, it hasn't been easy to keep it out of my mind. I find myself thinking: where's its den? What does it eat? Who's in there with it?'

Fabrizio didn't answer.

'Don't you wonder about that?'

'I do. And maybe I'm starting to form an idea, but don't ask me yet what it is. I need to get a few things straight first. What about you? Are you still so sure that these killings have nothing to do with the inscription and the finds inside the Phersu tomb?'

'You believe that the human bones you found inside the Rovaio tomb belong to that Turm Kaiknas in the inscription, don't you?'

'I'm sure of it.'

'I imagined as much. And you also believe that this stray dog that wanders around seeking prey at night is that creature reborn, the creature whose bones your friend Sonia is putting together.'

'Yeah, something like that,' said Fabrizio without batting an eye.

Francesca brought her hands to her face. 'Christ, I feel like I'm living in some kind of graphic horror novel . . . Come on, Fabrizio, I understand that all these weird coincidences are pretty spooky. But that's all they are. Coincidences. And when this whole thing is over, you'll agree with me.'

Fabrizio didn't speak. He seemed lost in thought, very far away from the present time and place. Francesca drove past the fortress and soon entered the city through the great stone arch.

VOLTERRA was deserted. Not a soul was on the streets. Even the bars were half empty; the rare customers inside sat playing cards and drinking wine in a smoky atmosphere. A carabiniere squad car passed them, its blue roof light slowly revolving to cast a spectral reflection on the ancient facades. Marcello Reggiani was keeping watch over that urban desert.

Francesca parked her Jeep at a corner, then they got out and went on foot towards the Caretti-Riccardi palace. They walked close to one another and close to the walls, as if they wanted to blend into the old city stones. Francesca held Fabrizio's arm and his hands were plunged deep into his pockets. The cold wind blowing down the narrow streets of the medieval city made the telephone lines stretching from one building to another vibrate like a harp's strings. In less than ten minutes, they'd arrived at the palazzo and Fabrizio gave the door a hard shove. It didn't budge.

'What did I tell you?' asked Francesca. 'That door has been bolted for years.'

She hadn't finished speaking when a howl sounded in the distance. It was very faint, but Fabrizio's ear was trained to sense that sound and he jumped, becoming visibly pale.

'Did you hear that?' he asked.

Francesca shook her head, but then the howl rang out louder and more clearly, carried by the wind, and she could no longer pretend not to have heard it.

'Do you hear it now?'

'I heard something,' admitted the girl. 'But I'm not sure what it was. We can't lose our heads, Fabrizio. We have to find an explanation for all this or we'll go crazy.'

'And that kid could be out there. Oh, holy Christ!' said Fabrizio, as if she hadn't spoken. His voice was shaking. 'I have to find a way to get in here.'

He looked around, examining the wall of the facade. There was no name plate, no number, no bell or even any trace of there ever having been any, as if no one had ever lived between those walls. Heavy iron grilles covered the only two windows on the ground floor, but the openings had been walled up with bricks. The windows on the upper floors were covered by heavy wooden shutters with massive wrought-iron hinges. Huge time-blackened oak beams supported the fourth-floor roofing. There was a single distinctive feature at the centre of the facade: a stone shield with a badly worn and barely recognizable coat of arms.

'It's impossible that a building of this size has no owner and that that owner never comes by,' commented Fabrizio.

'Wait,' said Francesca. 'I have an idea. My laptop's in the car and I'm practically sure I've downloaded the local land registry map. I just hope there's enough power left. You stay here. I'll be right back. Don't move!'

Before Fabrizio could stop her, the girl had already dashed across the little square in front of the palazzo and had disappeared behind the corner and down the street. He found himself alone. All he could do was strain his ears to try to make out any growling in the silence of the night. Instead he heard the whir of helicopter blades and saw a spotlight scanning the terrain to the south-west. Reggiani must have heard the howl himself and sent out his scouts. Fabrizio wondered whether he might not give the go-ahead for the operation sooner than he'd promised. On the one hand, that wasn't such a bad idea. If Angelo was still wandering through the countryside or if he'd found himself an unsafe shelter, say in a stable or sheep's pen somewhere, maybe the carabinieri would get to him before the thing did.

Francesca was back in no time with her big leather bag. She sat on the kerb, pulled out her laptop, set it on her knees and switched it on. She opened the land registry file and soon zoomed in on the Caretti-Riccardi palace.

'Here it is,' she said, beginning to enlarge the grid. 'Let's see—'

'Listen,' Fabrizio interrupted her, 'Signora Pina, the lady who owns the trattoria, told me that more than once, after dark, she's seen light from down below, from the basement of the palazzo. If she's right, that means that there are cellars down there and maybe an air shaft that connects them with the outside. That's a pretty common feature in these ancient buildings.'

'You're right about that. And it might even be that illegal immigrants have found a way to get down there and are using it as a shelter. A lot of old, abandoned buildings are occupied. OK, here you go. The property belongs, or rather belonged, to Jacopo Ghirardini, a Volterra nobleman who hasn't been seen or heard of in the last five years. Current whereabouts unknown. Apparently no heirs have come forward to make a claim.'

'Five years ago,' murmured Fabrizio. 'Five years ago is when that woman suddenly showed up here, and Reggiani told me she had been working as a housekeeper in Volterra ... Here, maybe?' He vaguely remembered Signora Pina mentioning something of the sort that first time he'd eaten at the trattoria.

'Seems strange to me. I've always seen it closed up. But I can try to find out. Someone must have lived here at one time. Here, see, take a look at this. This rectangle on the edge of the outside wall is certainly an air vent for the basement.'

'It'll be bricked up like the windows,' mused Fabrizio. 'Or closed by a grating.'

'We'll never know unless we go and look. Here, according to the map it's on the right wall when you're facing the facade, along Via Cantergiani.' She closed the file, turned off the computer and slipped it back into her bag. 'Shall we go?' she said, getting to her feet and walking towards the right side of the building.

Fabrizio followed her and together they began to search the solid, windowless ground floor. The long limestone wall was braced every five or six metres by vertical ribbing. Just behind one of these protrusions, they found the air shaft. Its heavy iron lid had been removed and it lay vertically on the wall, secured by a rusty ring. The shaft was closed by a grating of heavy iron bars that looked like it hadn't been moved in some time. Fabrizio tried to lift it but it wouldn't give a centimetre.

'I was afraid of this. It's sealed into the foundation.'

Francesca knelt to take a look. 'That seems strange to me. Usually these openings were also used for lowering barrels of wine into the cellars, or other foodstuffs that needed to be kept cool. Or anything they wanted to hide ... Thank God there's no one around,' she added, sticking her hand in the grating. 'If anyone saw us, Lord knows what they'd think.'

'Especially if that someone was Signora Pina!' said Fabrizio. 'Fortunately, it looks like she's closed tonight. I can't see any lights on in the restaurant.'

'Now that you mention it, you don't have a torch, do you?' asked Francesca.

Fabrizio rummaged through his backpack, found a torch and shone it at the grating and the edges of the hole, but the beam went straight down to the cellar floor.

'Hey, look at that!' he said.

Francesca peered at the muddy floor. 'Footprints ...'

'Little ones, I'd say. It's Angelo, I'm sure of it.'

'So how did he get in?'

'Through the bars.'

'That's impossible.'

'He's small and skinny, I'm telling you.'

Francesca shook her head incredulously and continued to feel around under the grating.

'Found it!' she exclaimed suddenly. 'There's a chain.'

She unhooked it and Fabrizio was able to raise the grating.

'I'm going first,' said Francesca, and let herself drop down to the floor. Fabrizio heard her swearing and shone the torch on her. She had slipped when her feet touched the ground and she was sitting in the mud. She got up and cleaned herself off as best she could, then looked up at Fabrizio. 'Pass me my bag with the computer. Drop it. Don't worry, I'll catch it.'

Fabrizio dangled the bag as low as possible, then called out to her and let it go.

'Got it,' rang out Francesca's voice underground.

Fabrizio lowered himself down as well and the two of them

looked at each other without speaking for long instants in the dim light raining down from the street.

'Let's hope no one falls in,' said Francesca. 'Leaving the grating open turns this into a real trap. If someone stumbles over it, they'll kill themselves.'

'Who do you think is roaming the streets at this hour of the night? You saw for yourself. There's not a living soul out there.'

'Well, I'd also like to know how we're going to get out.'

'We'll worry about that when the time comes. We could go through the front door – the place looks like it could use some airing out.'

Fabrizio was trying to make light of a fairly grim situation. The air was heavy in the intense darkness of the underground chamber and there was a strong musty odour. He pointed the torch at the walls and ceiling to get an idea of the dimensions and characteristics of the room and found another wall that crossed it from one end to the other, interrupted by a couple of round arched doorways made of big hewn tufa stones oozing dampness and covered with grey mould.

'Definitely ancient,' observed Francesca.

'Etruscan,' concluded Fabrizio, shining the ray of light from one end to another. He swept the beam across the floor to light up the line of small footprints leading away from them under the arch.

Francesca took out her laptop and turned it on. 'These cellar rooms may even be included on the map,' she said. 'The registry date is old enough. It goes back to the age of the Leopoldo dukes, if I'm not mistaken. OK, look at this . . . See . . . This is the wall with the arches, right? Good, we're here . . . Let's go on, this way.'

They proceeded about ten metres or so until they found themselves in front of an iron railing which flanked a ramp of stairs leading downward.

'Is this on your map?' asked Fabrizio, peering at the screen.

'No,' said Francesca, 'it's not. At least, I don't think it is.'

They descended seven grey stone steps until they found themselves in a completely empty room whose walls still displayed traces of colour and peeling plaster. At the corner opposite the bottom of the stairs was a sloping ramp. They continued down despite the fact that they could no longer make out any footprints on the stone slabs. There was no way of telling whether Angelo – if the prints they'd seen had truly been his – had continued in this direction.

'I can't believe the only way we can go is down. There must be a point where we can get up into the main building, right?' asked Francesca, as if thinking aloud.

'Yeah. I was just thinking the same thing,' admitted Fabrizio. 'But it doesn't look like we've got much choice.'

They stopped and took a look around. The entire room had been roughly carved out of a bank of tufa and Fabrizio made his way forward laying one hand after another on the damp surface.

'Do you realize where we are?' he asked all at once.

'We're at the ground level of the ancient city,' replied Francesca. 'The two archways we came across earlier must be from a section of the Etruscan city walls.'

'Well, we've reached the end of the line anyway,' said Fabrizio. 'There's no one and nothing here.'

They fell silent for a few moments, watching their breath as it condensed into little puffs of steam. They stared up and around at the walls and ceiling.

'Come on. Let's turn back,' said Fabrizio. 'I feel like I'm suffocating down here.'

Francesca nodded and followed him up the stairs until they reached the big underground chamber where they had lowered themselves down from the air vent. They examined the wall minutely with their hands until they discovered a narrow stairway enclosed and partially hidden between two brick walls. Fabrizio started up, followed by Francesca, but the feeling of oppression he'd experienced down below only increased as they made their way to the ground floor. They ended up at a little door clad with iron studs that let them into the palazzo's central hall, but as they raised their eyes towards the ceiling they were amazed by the vision of a spiral staircase reaching up several storeys all the way to the ceiling, free-standing in the middle of the space, without any central support.

'My God!' exclaimed Francesca. 'This is incredible! I'd heard this existed but I'd never seen it. It's absolutely perfect, a masterpiece! I believe it's attributed to Sansovino.'

Fabrizio pierced the elliptical cavity of the daring staircase with his torchlight, all the way up to the ceiling beams. 'Christ! It may be a masterpiece, but there's something really disturbing about it. It reminds me of the coils of a gigantic snake or the circles of hell! If you stare at it long enough, it looks like a monstrous screw. Isn't that strange?'

'Do you think Angelo might be here, hidden somewhere?' asked Francesca. 'Maybe he's watching us from the top of one of those ramps. Maybe he likes sliding down the banister! I'd always do that when I was little and I lived with my parents in the Annibaldi villa at Colle Val d'Elsa.'

Fabrizio stepped forward and tried calling, 'Angelo! Angelo, are you there?'

All he got back was an echo in the huge empty chamber.

'I'd like to go up. It's the only way to know whether he's here or not. Maybe he's fallen asleep somewhere.'

'If those footprints were his,' Francesca reminded him.

'Right,' agreed Fabrizio.

He tried pressing a light switch but nothing happened. The electricity had probably been disconnected years ago. They began to climb the staircase slowly, keeping to the outside, until they got to the second floor, where, to their left, they found another hall as long as the entire mansion. It was closed on one end by a huge set of French doors that must have led to a balcony over the main door at the front of the palace, where they'd seen the stone shield.

The odour of dust filled the place and as Fabrizio trained his torch beam down the length of the vast hall he jumped at the sight of two long rows of bizarre, grotesque figures that appeared to be glaring at him from either side of the room. An astonishing collection of stuffed exotic animals loomed to the left and right: lions, leopards, gazelles, antelopes, jackals and hyenas baring their yellowed fangs in dusty sneers.

Both Francesca and Fabrizio found themselves tiptoeing among the beasts of this unexpected taxidermy gallery.

'This guy must have been crazy!' gasped Fabrizio. 'Did you know this was here as well?'

'I thought the contents had been donated to a natural science museum . . . Perhaps they were, at one time, but no one ever came to claim them. Maybe it would have cost too much to transport all of them. Anything can happen in a country like Italy. Anyway, there are side rooms along both walls,' observed Francesca. 'And here's a candleholder. You go that way with the torch and I'll search this way by candlelight.'

They began their inspection of the side rooms, with Fabrizio constantly calling out, 'Angelo! Angelo! Are you in here?' But the rooms were filled only with more specimens of the grotesque collection of creatures. One featured night birds on their perches: long-eared owls and little owls, tawny owls, scops owls and screech owls. There were daylight birds of prey in another, ravens and crows in another, and yet another filled with fish, sharks and octopuses, all covered with a shiny wax and impaled on stands. They looked like suffering souls. He opened the last door and cried out, slamming it closed. The door banged so loudly that Francesca turned in alarm and ran over to join Fabrizio, who was pale and shaking.

'What's in there?' she asked.

Fabrizio shook his head. 'It's nothing. These things are just so weird.'

Francesca took him by the arm. 'We've seen dozens already.

What's so special about that room that has you trembling like a leaf? Let me see.'

She strode towards the door and opened it decisively, lifting her candle to see inside. She closed it instantly and leaned hard against it, drawing a sharp breath. 'Oh, Good Lord!' she exclaimed.

'I told you this felt like the circles of hell! But I never thought I'd meet up with him here.'

'Oh, God, you're right,' gasped Francesca. 'It's horrible!' She was still trying to catch her breath. 'Do you feel up to taking a second look?'

'Do I have a choice?' asked Fabrizio.

He slowly pulled the door open and shone the beam of light inside. At the centre of the room stood an animal which appeared to be identical to the beast he'd seen ripping out Pietro Montanari's throat two nights before. He turned to Francesca.

'It's pretty shocking, isn't it?' he offered, trying to keep his gut reaction under control.

'I don't know what to say,' agreed Francesca. 'It looks just like the animal we saw. My God, it's a monster. What kind of breed . . . Fabrizio, what does this mean?'

'I have no idea. Don't ask me. I only know I really want my life back – as soon as possible!'

'What's stopping you?'

'Nothing . . . No, a lot of things. I don't want to leave you on your own here . . . and . . .'

'And?'

'I want to know how this ends up.'

Francesca nodded and circled all the way around the stuffed animal. It was a kind of dog, with a dense, bristly coat. Its huge jaws were gaping in a show of enormous fangs. Its long, thick tail was also covered with shaggy hair. The stuffed creature was completely covered with dust, giving its black coat a greyish cast.

'Do you think this means the one we saw comes from here as well?' wondered Francesca.

'Who can say?'

'I'd always heard that Count Ghirardini had a real reputation for being eccentric. He was famous for his game hunts in Africa and other exotic places. I don't know much more than that, other than that he was quite private and reputed to be very strange.'

'I'd say there's little doubt about that. Anyway, this is Reggiani's dream: seeing that animal pumped full of lead and filled with straw in some museum.'

Francesca leaned closer to illuminate the creature with her candle, but all of a sudden, part of the fur caught on fire. She cried out and Fabrizio tore off his jacket and hit the animal's side hard to put out the flames.

'Careful with that thing! This whole place might have burned down!' he said.

Francesca held out her hand for the torch and shone it at the scorched coat to see how bad the damage was. She looked astonished at what she was seeing. 'Will you look at that . . .'

'Look at what?' asked Fabrizio.

'It's fake.'

'That's not possible.'

'Look for yourself.' She tapped her knuckles against the animal's side. 'It's wood. It's not an animal at all. It's an extremely realistic sculpture. As if Ghirardini, or whoever it was, had wanted to reproduce something that he'd seen but couldn't have in his collection. If we had the time to search through here, I'll bet we'd find sketches, drawings, notes. I'm sure of it.'

'So Ghirardini saw it too,' he said, raising his eyes to Francesca's. 'The animal has to be somehow connected to this place.'

'Do you want to scare me to death? Come on. Let's get out now. The little boy's not here, Fabrizio.'

She hadn't finished saying that when they heard a noise, in the distance, followed by a louder, sharper one.

'What was that?' asked Francesca.

'I don't know. It sounded strange.'

'Is it coming from outside?'

'No, it's coming from inside. From upstairs, maybe . . .'

'Fabrizio, it's definitely coming from outside. I can tell. Let's get out of here.'

'No, I was wrong. It's coming from downstairs. Hear that?'

'But there is no one downstairs – you saw that for yourself.'

'Maybe we didn't look closely enough.'

'Yes, we did. I want to leave, now.'

'To leave we have to go back downstairs, don't we? We can't just walk out of the front door.'

Francesca gave in. 'All right, then. Let's go downstairs to see. At least I won't have to look at these revolting animals any more.'

They descended the stairs to the first floor and then went down the narrow steps leading from the corner of the main hall to the floor below. The sound was becoming sharper and more distinct. Hammering, against something hard: the ground, perhaps, or a wall.

'See! I told you it was coming from down here,' said Fabrizio.

'I really am scared now.'

'Come on. Nothing's going to happen. Maybe someone else fell through the hole, ended up somewhere down below and is just trying to get out.'

'Fabrizio, there's nothing but an empty, doorless room down there, cut into the tufa,' said Francesca, grabbing on to his arm as he continued to descend slowly.

'So that's all we'll see,' replied Fabrizio, setting his foot on the last step.

A slight luminescence shone from the room below, like the

light of a candle. Fabrizio put his head around the corner as the noise stopped abruptly and directed the torch beam at the middle of the room. He stood gaping open-mouthed at what he saw.

It was Angelo, covered in mud from head to toe, and he was holding the missing bronze fragment in his hand. A candle stub at his feet let off a tiny glow.

The child smiled as if this were the most normal thing in the world.

'See?' he said. 'I know how to be an archaeologist. So, can I stay with you now?'

15

FABRIZIO DREW CLOSER carefully, slowly, as if he couldn't believe what he was seeing, as if that vision might vanish from one moment to the next. Angelo was standing hunched over in front of him, bowed under the weight of what for him was a very heavy bronze slab. He didn't seem frightened or upset, or even uncomfortable, in that dark underground chamber. He looked like he had been biding his time, waiting for this very encounter.

'Do you want to . . . give it to me?' asked Fabrizio, holding out his arms.

The boy nodded and handed over the slab.

Fabrizio took it as he nodded to Francesca. 'This is Angelo.'

'It's a pleasure, Angelo. I'm Francesca,' she said, extending her hand.

Fabrizio noticed a pickaxe at the corner of the room, along with a pile of freshly dug earth, and asked, 'How did you know where it was? Do you know who put it here?'

But the child seemed suddenly alarmed, as he strained to hear sounds that the others were unaware of. 'We have to get out of here before she finds us. Hurry. This way, fast . . . She's coming.'

He was frightened now. He had taken Francesca's hand and was tugging her towards the staircase. She gave Fabrizio a look and all three of them started up the steps. They reached the main hall and moved towards the front entrance. Angelo stood on tiptoe to push back the latch of the secondary door and

Francesca immediately went forward to give him a hand, but it was stuck and would not move. Fabrizio had no better luck: the door had been bolted from the outside.

Angelo seemed paralysed for an instant, then looked up at his companions and said, 'This way. Come on – follow me.'

He turned back and retraced his steps until he was halfway down the hall, then opened a side door and started to run down a long, dusty corridor filled with cobwebs.

Fabrizio was weighed down by the slab and was having trouble keeping up, but Angelo kept turning to say, 'Hurry! We have to get out.'

He moved easily through that sinister place, a labyrinth of corridors and rooms leading into each other like a strange set of dominoes. Rats and beetles, the denizens of those abandoned halls, would start at the sudden intrusion and the wildly aimed torch beam, racing for shelter under rickety, worm-eaten furniture and behind old picture frames leaning up against the walls. All at once, while running through a larger room, the boy stopped for a moment to glance at a big canvas that depicted a man who appeared to be the master of the house standing alongside a large desk bearing a marble bust of Dante Alighieri. Jacopo Ghirardini, perhaps?

'Do you know who that is?' asked Fabrizio, panting.

The boy didn't answer, hurriedly taking off down a very narrow final corridor, more of a passageway between two solid stone walls, at the end of which a milky light appeared to be filtering through from the outside. A thick iron grating covered an aperture of about fifty centimetres by one metre, secured by a bolt. Angelo slid the bolt open and pushed but nothing happened.

'You push,' he said to Fabrizio. 'You're stronger. Maybe there's something outside blocking it.'

Fabrizio set the bronze slab down and applied all his strength, but the grating did not budge. He stuck his hand through and his fingers curled around a chain closed with a heavy padlock.

'Damn. There's a chain. Didn't you know it was there?' he asked Angelo.

The little boy shook his head with a baffled expression. That curious air of confidence had completely vanished.

'The cellar,' said Fabrizio to Francesca. 'We'll go back down to where we got in and I'll push you up on my shoulders. Once you're out, you can help Angelo out too and I'll get out somehow as well. We have to hurry. I'm afraid the torch batteries are running down and we won't get anywhere if we can't see.'

Their haste and the child's bewilderment had made them frantic, as if the building itself were about to collapse around them from one moment to the next. They descended underground and stumbled back along the path they'd taken, but when they got to the air vent they saw that the grating had been returned to its original position.

'Damn! That's all we need,' swore Fabrizio. 'We're trapped.'

'Wait! Maybe not,' said Francesca. 'Maybe a policeman or night watchman came by and pushed the grating back in place so that no one would fall in. Help me get up there. I'll bet you it's still loose.'

Angelo was becoming more and more nervous. He kept checking behind him and begging, 'Hurry, please. We have to get out of here.'

When Fabrizio had put down the slab, Francesca took off her shoes and climbed on to his shoulders. She could easily reach the grate and gave it a big heave, but it didn't budge a centimetre.

Fabrizio heard her sigh, 'Oh, my God, no . . .'

'It's locked, isn't it?'

'It is,' she replied, dropping from his shoulders. 'From the outside. What do we do now?'

'We stay calm,' said Fabrizio. He switched off the torch to save on the batteries and continued: 'I really hate to look so stupid, but we have no choice. I'm calling Reggiani.'

He switched on his mobile phone but there was no signal.

'This is not looking good,' said Francesca in a tone that could not mask her rising panic.

'All right. If we can't get out from down here or from a side entrance, we'll get out from above. I'll go up that damned spiral staircase to the attic. There's got to be a skylight or dormer or something. We'll get out on to the roof, call Reggiani and have him come to get us.'

'That sounds good,' said Francesca without much enthusiasm.

'You and Angelo wait here. There's no sense going together. But I'll need the torch. You don't mind being in the dark for a while, do you?'

Francesca replied that she wasn't afraid, but he could see she was terrified. Fabrizio held her close and kissed her, then gave Angelo a pat and was off.

He made his way back to the main hall, looking carefully in every direction before starting up the spiral staircase. At each floor he was greeted by a spectacle similar to or worse than the one before: long rows of stuffed animals of every description – vultures and wide-winged condors, cats, skunks and weasels with sharp little teeth glinting in the pale beam of the torch, martens and wolves, dogs and foxes and even snakes, huge pythons, boas and anacondas, gape-jawed cobras immobilized in the act of pouncing on imaginary, unsuspecting victims.

He climbed the last ramp to the top-floor landing, opened the little door that led to the attic and shone the light inside. His heart jumped into his throat at the nightmare scene in front of his eyes: there were human beings in the attic, stuffed like the exotic animals downstairs. Tribal peoples from distant lands, nude males and females gripping spears, frozen in obscene expressions and wizened smirks. Fabrizio backed up and pulled the door shut, but then decided that he had to overcome his repugnance at that infernal vision and push on. He took a long, deep breath to restore a normal beat to the heart leaping about inside his chest, then opened the door and walked into that forest of mummies. Many had been gnawed at by rodents and their bones were showing. They all had glass eyes, like the foxes and vultures below.

He inspected the roof thoroughly without finding any exit – not a skylight, dormer or window of any sort. Between one beam and the next, the ceiling was completely lined with lead sheeting and he was unsurprised to realize that he couldn't get a phone signal up there either. The place was sealed shut. The whole huge building was as airtight as an intact tomb. When he returned to the cellar to give them the bad news he was wheezing and covered with cobwebs.

'You look terrible,' said Francesca. 'What else did you see up there?'

Fabrizio did not answer. He knelt next to the child and grasped him by the shoulders. 'Listen carefully, Angelo. Are you sure there is no other way out? I remember clearly that I saw you going into that little door at the front.'

'I watched where she put the key and when she didn't leave it, I got in and out that way, like today,' he said, pointing at the closed grating.

'What can we do?' asked Francesca. 'Unfortunately, no one even knows we're in here.'

'We'll wait until dawn and start yelling.'

'If there's anyone out there to hear us.'

'Right. Someone has to hear us.'

'Wait! Maybe I have a better idea.' Francesca switched on her computer again and started hitting the keys.

'What are you trying to do?' asked Fabrizio.

'I just remembered that there's an email I downloaded a couple of days ago but never got around to reading. It might be the updated map of underground Volterra incorporating the eighteenth-century Malavolti survey information. The topographical centre has been working on it for some time and they usually send me an update at the end of the month. So, let's take a look . . . See, here, if we're lucky . . .'

Fabrizio had turned off the torch and the only light in the underground chamber came from the glow of the computer screen, where Francesca had found what she wanted and was now exploring patiently, searching for an escape route.

Fabrizio turned to the child, who was trembling with cold and fear. He chatted quietly in an attempt to distract him: 'When I saw you slipping through that door the other day, I couldn't help but wonder why you were here, what you could be doing in a big old empty place like this all on your own. So, will you tell me now?'

'I come to see my father.'

'Where is your father?'

The child motioned upwards with his eyes.

'The painting?'

Angelo nodded.

'You're Jacopo Ghirardini's son?'

The little boy nodded again.

'Are you sure?'

Angelo began speaking in a strange little voice. 'My father is in here, I know he is. I come to visit him whenever I can. Without letting my stepmother know, or she beats me.'

'How do you get around in the dark?'

'With a torch.'

'A torch like this one?'

Another nod.

'You've got one in here?'

'Uh-huh.'

'So what were you waiting for to tell me? We need a torch badly.'

'If I give it to you I can't see my father any more. I'm out of candles and I don't have money for batteries. I stole the ones I'm using.'

Fabrizio touched his cheek. 'I'll buy you all the batteries you want. But please, let us use the one you have now . . .'

Francesca's voice interrupted him: 'Found it!'

'Found what?'

'The way out. Look. Here in the cellar, in the south-west corner.'

'We've already looked,' objected Fabrizio. 'There's nothing there.'

'Because the west wall shifts eastward in relation to the north wall and creates a kind of illusion so that it looks like a closed corner. In reality, there should be a passageway that leads to a tunnel that emerges above ground . . . in the Etruscan cistern on the Salvetti farm! Come on. Let's go and look.'

'If Angelo lets us use his torch,' said Fabrizio.

The boy took a few steps, rummaged in the dark under some stones and came back with a torch in his hand.

Francesca switched off the computer, got up and followed Fabrizio, who was carrying the bronze slab and heading towards the south-west corner of the cellar. She'd been right: there was a gap between the two walls hiding the entrance to a narrow passageway.

'So we walk out,' commented Fabrizio, drawing a long breath. 'If the tunnel is usable that is. If the walls haven't collapsed and—'

'We'll never know if we don't try,' said Francesca. 'Ready for an adventure, Angelo?'

The boy nodded and wordlessly handed Francesca the torch as she squeezed herself into the passage. They forged ahead without meeting any obstacles. The tunnel was cut into the tufa and after a narrow start opened up enough to allow all three of them to walk along comfortably. They would stop now and then so that Fabrizio could set down the slab a moment and rest his arms, before continuing again.

After a level stretch, the tunnel started to slope downwards, confirming what Francesca had seen on her computer map.

'Do you suppose Malavolti explored the entire length of this tunnel, then?' asked Fabrizio during one of their rest stops.

'That's what his notes say. He was a very serious researcher. I'd say we can trust him.'

Fabrizio shook his head. 'And to think how incredulous I was when Signora Pina told me there was a secret passage from this building to Lord knows which monastery.'

'There's always a kernel of truth in any old wives' tale. You should know that. I'm curious as to how the Etruscans could have created an underground connection between two places proceeding blindly and without instruments.'

'I imagine they did go on blindly, one stretch at a time at least, and then, when they emerged above ground, marked the spot with some sort of construction that wouldn't draw attention to the passageway below: a small sanctuary, perhaps, or a farmhouse.'

'You really think so? Look at the way this tunnel proceeds. Does it seem casual? Like it's proceeding blindly, any which way? I think the Etruscans had refined such a strong sense of orientation that they could perceive magnetic fields.'

'Like migrating birds?' asked Fabrizio.

'Well, yes, more or less.'

'And you accuse me of letting my imagination run away with me!'

The width of the tunnel – and the sensation that they were distancing themselves from the bowels of that creepy, labyrinthine building – helped to slowly alleviate the hysteria that had gripped them when they realized they were trapped inside. The tunnel widened enough for them to walk abreast of each other and Angelo took Fabrizio's hand. They continued until they found themselves at a fork. A couple of steps in the stone raised the floor by about thirty centimetres.

'Which way now?' asked Fabrizio. 'I don't remember seeing this in your map.'

'No, me neither,' replied Francesca, 'and I don't think there's enough power left to consult it again. So let's say we go straight. It should lead us out somewhere. If it doesn't we'll come back to this point and try the other direction. Anyway, I don't know whether you've noticed, but it seems to me there's a breeze, which must mean this leads out to the open air. I just hope the exit is big enough for us to get out of . . .'

'By this time Massaro will have noticed I'm not in the house and have informed Reggiani,' Fabrizio mused.

'And Reggiani will have unleashed his forces to discover where you are and what you're up to . . . He hates not being in control. He'll have tried me first, but my mobile's not picking up and my answering machine's on at home.'

'First he'll get angry as hell, then he'll start thinking it through. That's the part that worries me,' said Fabrizio. 'So let's put ourselves in his shoes and figure out what he'll do next.'

'We have no idea where we're going or what we're doing,' shot back Francesca. 'How could he?'

'OK, I guess what I'm trying to say is that I'm worried Reggiani will call an early start to the operation, hoping to catch us in his net before something else gets us—'

Francesca stopped suddenly. 'Shh! Did you hear that?' she said in alarm.

Fabrizio stopped as well and strained to hear. Angelo squeezed his hand more tightly: he'd heard as well.

It was a clear, distinct sound, distorted and amplified by the tunnel walls: the beast's snarl, its gnashing teeth, its hoarse, hissing breath. The entire length of the underground chamber was saturated with its presence and the stench was unbearable. The beam of the torch in Francesca's trembling hands pierced the darkness and shone straight into the monster's eyes.

'Oh, my God! My God! My God!' screamed Francesca in the throes of panic. 'Run! Get away!'

Fabrizio dropped the slab and all three took off in the opposite direction, racing back to the palace, well aware they had no chance. They could hear the panting of the animal, feel the hot huffing, knew he could spring from one moment to the next. As they reached the widening in the first part of the tunnel, Francesca tripped on the steps and sprawled to the ground. Fabrizio grabbed her arm and yanked her up. He flattened himself against the wall, instinctively covering the girl and the child.

The torch had fallen to the ground and lit the animal from below, making it look even more terrifying, if that was possible. It was approaching more slowly now, seeming to test the ground with its paws. Its enormous blood-drenched fangs were bared, its snout was wrinkled into deep furrows and the black hairs on its back were as bristly as the quills of a porcupine. It had evidently killed for the fifth time and was still on the prowl. Fabrizio gripped Francesca's hand, as if trying to communicate a last message before they died, but as the monster was about to lunge, the boy wriggled forward and placed himself squarely between his friends and the animal, shouting, 'No!'

Fabrizio and Francesca were incapable of moving a muscle. Paralysed by their terror, they could only watch as the little boy confronted the beast. Slender and defenceless, he was shaking, his hair was plastered to his forehead, his eyes were filled with tears, but he stood his ground. His courage seemed absolutely superhuman. And the miracle accordingly took place: the monster slowed its charge, cut short its leap and took a few steps towards the child, whimpering as if in pain. Then it backed off, raised its head again, stretched its jowls and let out a piercing howl, a cry of impotent ferocity and infinite suffering. It finally bounded into the side tunnel and disappeared from sight.

Fabrizio had reached the child and was hugging him. Francesca embraced the two of them at once as she burst into strangled weeping.

'It's over,' said Fabrizio. 'It's over now. Come on. Let's get going again. Someone else has lost their life and Reggiani will be doing everything he can to get his operation under way.'

A few minutes later, they stumbled on the bronze slab that Fabrizio had dropped and he picked it up again. They walked for nearly an hour until they could see the pale light of the moon filtering through a crack at the end of the tunnel. They'd reached the old cistern at the Salvetti farm.

Fabrizio squeezed out first, then helped Angelo and Francesca through. He held them close with tears in his eyes and led them around the ruined cistern, holding on to wild grape vines for support until they were above ground. The Tuscan hills loomed all around, veiled by an opaline mist pierced here and there by the sharp tips of the cypress trees. They breathed a long sigh of relief and set off in the direction of the regional road.

Fabrizio turned to Francesca and said, 'You know, when I found myself face to face with that thing, I was about to tell you something.'

'What?'

'That I love you, Dr Dionisi.'

'That's a strange way of telling me. But I'm glad.' She threw her arms around his neck and kissed him.

Fabrizio switched on his mobile phone and dialled Reggiani's number.

'Is that you?' answered the officer. 'Where the hell did you disappear to, damn you? As if I didn't already have enough trouble and as if I weren't pissed off enough on my own without you adding to it!'

'I know. It killed again.'

'Two this time. A young guy, a drug addict, and his father, who was trying to defend him. But how did you know that?'

Fabrizio ignored his question and went on, 'I have the missing fragment of the slab of Volterra. Come and get me, please. We're on the regional road near the Salvetti farm.'

'Who else is with you?'

'Francesca and a little . . . angel.'

'Don't move,' warned the officer. 'I'll be there in ten minutes with a couple of my men.'

ANGELO WAS curled up on the couch, under a flannel blanket, sunk in the deepest sleep. Every now and then he'd let out a little moan or a suffocated yelp, or he would shudder under his blanket as if in the grip of a nightmare. Francesca was making coffee for the four men sitting at the table.

'Who were the victims this time?' asked Fabrizio.

'Guy named Marozzi,' replied Reggiani. 'A farmhand, as big as they come and tough as nails. Hell itself wouldn't scare him. That's what got him. When he saw his son attacked by that monster, he ran after it with a pitchfork, of all things. Christ, what a massacre . . .'

A long, leaden silence followed, then Francesca spoke up.

'Have you checked whether these victims had anything in common with the others?'

Reggiani took a little notebook from his pocket. 'They didn't actually,' he said. 'The first ones were all tomb robbers or had actually broken into the Rovaio tomb, but these last ones—'

'I'll tell you what they have in common,' piped up one of the carabinieri, a youth of about twenty. 'I was born here and I can tell you that all of the guys who were killed are from families that have been in Volterra for generations and generations. They've always lived here, as far as I know.'

'As if it smelt the scent of their blood,' observed Fabrizio. 'Native blood . . . from Volterra . . . It hates this city with a fierce, implacable loathing.'

'And its den is under one of the oldest buildings in the city,' said Reggiani, shaking his head. 'Christ, what is all this?'

'We saw it with our own eyes,' said Francesca calmly, placing the tray with the coffee cups on the table. The look she gave them allowed no doubt.

'Well, then, we can set up a trap,' said Reggiani. 'This time it won't get away. I'll put enough firepower out there to exterminate a regiment.'

'You really think you can put it down, like a mangy stray dog?' asked Fabrizio.

'I've said it before: if it kills, it can be killed.'

Fabrizio looked straight into his eyes with a bleak expression. 'Death kills. But it can't be killed, right? You have no idea what this is. We had it right in front of us, just a metre or two away from us, for a few endless seconds. I have never seen anything like it my whole life. I am very certain that no animal of a like species exists. It's a monster, I tell you. A . . . chimera.'

Francesca's expression confirmed Fabrizio's words in full.

'I don't know about that,' replied Reggiani. 'Maybe it's the product of some experiment, you know? You hear about strange genetic experiments. Some mad scientist . . .'

Fabrizio thought of what he'd seen in the upstairs rooms of the Caretti-Riccardi palace and shivered. He drank his coffee in little sips, then looked up at the lieutenant. 'Marcello, don't make your move yet,' he said. 'You'd be making a terrible mistake. It's too soon and you'll have terrible losses. You won't be able to turn back. Wait.'

'I've waited long enough. As soon as I have word that we're ready to go, I'll unleash hell.'

'Wait, for the love of God,' insisted Fabrizio in a monotone.

'Wait for what? For this thing to exterminate every last person in Volterra?' He pulled a pile of newspapers from his black leather bag. 'Look at this! The news is all over the national papers. In an hour's time, people will be seeing this on the news-stands and they're going to panic. And that panic will spread. We have a catastrophe waiting to happen.'

'Wait,' Fabrizio insisted. He lifted the cloth covering the last fragment of the slab of Volterra. 'Until I've read this. Maybe . . . I think . . . it's the key to everything.'

'At this point,' said Reggiani, 'it's sixteen hours to green light. Not a minute more.'

'That'll have to be enough,' replied Fabrizio.

16

LIEUTENANT REGGIANI looked at the little boy, then at Fabrizio and Francesca. 'What do you know about him?' he asked.

'Not much. Nothing, really,' replied Fabrizio. 'He has more or less told us that his father is, or was, Jacopo Ghirardini, and that Ambra Reiter is his stepmother and that she beats him. He showed up at my house saying he didn't want to live at Le Macine any more and that he wants to be an archaeologist when he grows up. I've told you the rest.'

'Let me take a picture and see if we can find out anything more about him. You can never tell. Do you know how many kids disappear each year without leaving a trace?'

He went out to the car to get his digital camera and took a couple of close shots of the sleeping child. 'Keep him with you for now,' he said. 'No one has reported him missing yet. As soon as we're out of this mess, we'll worry about getting him settled.'

He swallowed his coffee down in a single gulp and left, racing off in his Alfa. Even before he was on the regional road he was on the radio to headquarters.

'Lieutenant Reggiani here. Who's that? Over.'

'It's Tornese. What do you need, sir?'

'Three vehicles and ten men set to move out right away. A search party. Have the warrant ready. Ambra Reiter at Le Macine. Look in the blue folder, top drawer of my desk. Is Bonetti from the archaeological protection team in yet?'

'He won't be here for a couple of hours.'

'Get him out of bed now and tell him to bring his gear.'

'You got it, sir,' replied the sergeant.

As soon as Reggiani arrived, he took the folder, picked up his men and vehicles and headed to Le Macine at top speed. They stopped about 300 metres from the building and he had the men scatter in a semicircle, hidden by the vegetation, so they would be able to converge on the objective and secure it.

He walked into the tavern alone and shouted, 'Reiter, Ambra Reiter, this is Lieutenant Reggiani. I have a search warrant!'

No answer. The place seemed deserted. He waved in the archaeological expert, who had just arrived. Bonetti set to work combing the floor of the room with a metal detector. He had no success until he moved behind the bar counter, when the needle surged past the maximum mark and the buzzer began to sound loudly.

'Under here,' said Bonetti.

Two of the men joined him and they knelt on the floor and started to scrape between the bricks with trowels until they found the edges of a well-disguised hatch. They used a crowbar to prise the lid up and an entire section of the floor opened up, revealing steps that led underground. Reggiani went down first, with a torch in one hand and his pistol in the other.

There was no one down there, but the place was a treasure trove. Bucchero pottery, a large red-figured Attic crater which was practically intact, an alabaster vase, a cinerary urn of alabaster as well, decorated with images of the deceased reclining on a triclinium, and even a fragment of a fresco with a dancing figure. It had been brutally hacked from its wall using a power saw. It was already partially packaged in Styrofoam and plywood, no doubt to be smuggled off in a truck headed for Switzerland. There were ancient weapons as well. Arrow- and spear-heads, a bronze shield and a couple of helmets, one of the Corinthian type, the other a rare Negau, dragon-shaped buckles with amber beads and others made of yellow granulated gold, a double-cone-shaped cinerary urn of the Villanovan era and metal fragments of a war chariot.

Bonetti, their archaeological expert, was an auxiliary officer who in civilian life was a researcher at Tuscia University. He dutifully jotted down a piece-by-piece description of the objects as Reggiani's torch illuminated them.

'Good Lord, Lieutenant, this stuff is worth millions.'

'I have no doubt about that. But I'm looking for something else here. Have them send me down a spotlight. I need to search this place centimetre by centimetre.'

One of his men connected the spotlight to an extension cord that he plugged in behind the bar, flooding the underground chamber with light. The chamber had been cut into a bank of tufa and had no flooring, although the ground was covered with a layer of yellowish earth; the same earth that Fabrizio had noticed on Ambra Reiter's shoes. The bright light revealed greenish traces on the ground over a rectangular area measuring about forty by eighty centimetres.

'Get me a sample of these oxides,' ordered Reggiani. 'I want to know what metal was lying there.'

'Bronze, most probably, sir,' answered Bonetti. 'A bronze object of rectangular shape was sitting here for at least a few weeks.'

'The slab of Volterra,' mused Reggiani.

Bonetti looked up in surprise. 'May I ask, sir, what you might be referring to?'

'To the hypothesis of a colleague of yours, Dr Castellani. Have you ever heard of him?'

'Fabrizio Castellani? Sure, I read a couple of his articles while I was at school,' replied Bonetti. 'He's a serious scholar and a smart guy.'

'Exactly my impression,' said Reggiani. 'You continue your work down here. I want a description of each and every piece. Write it all up in a detailed report. I want the original on my desk. Prepare a copy for the NAS director as well. But leave everything exactly where you find it for now. Massaro!'

Sergeant Massaro answered, 'Yes, sir, Lieutenant. I'm here.'

'You can send the others back as soon as they're finished here, but I want you to stay behind with three or four of your men. As soon as Ambra Reiter shows up here, arrest her for illegal possession of archaeological materials and inform me immediately. Don't let her get away. It's essential that I question her.'

'You can count on me, sir.'

'I will. I have other matters to see to. Remember, make no false moves here. Be careful not to give away your presence. Wipe out all traces of the vehicles and this search operation.'

He took a final look at a group of fabulous jewels glittering under the beam of the spotlight, then went back up the stairs and headed back to the city.

FABRIZIO SET the bronze slab on the table and started to clean it carefully with a bristle brush. Where the encrusted earth covering the text was too hardened to be brushed away, he set to work with a scalpel, using extreme caution.

'What you're doing is illegal, you know that, right?' asked Francesca.

'Of course. Partial restoration of the slab of Volterra with neither the permission nor technical assistance of the NAS. Furthermore, I'm holding an unpublished fragment of the same which has not been duly reported to the authorities. They could even put me in jail for this.'

'They could certainly put you in jail for this.'

'But my conduct is fully justified by the emergency conditions we're operating under and by the fact that the police are aware of the situation and have not made any objection.'

'Well, your friend Reggiani belongs in jail too.'

'That's why we get along.'

'So, then, why are you preventing him from carrying out his

operation? Military action might stop further deaths from happening.'

'It could provoke a far greater number of deaths. I have no idea what that animal is capable of, and nor do you or anyone else. What's more—'

His phone rang.

'Hello.'

'Hi there, handsome.'

'Sonia.'

'I see you still recognize my voice.'

'Not really. Your name just popped up on the display.'

'What a wanker you are.'

'I know you think I've been neglecting you . . .'

'Neglecting me! I could have dropped off the face of this earth and you wouldn't have noticed!'

'I deserve a good kick up the arse.'

'You certainly do! So when are you going to show up to collect it?'

'Why? Has anything new come up?'

'I'm done. With the animal, that is. The human bones are an entirely different story. The biggest piece is a few centimetres long.'

'Sonia, you're awesome. I can't believe you've finished. So what does it look like?'

'It's got me scared shitless. I can't wait to get out of this hole. If we put it on exhibition, the horror-flick crowd will all show up.'

'Listen, Sonia, I can't get over there just now because there's something big I'm working on here. It shouldn't take me more that a few hours . . . I hope. Then we'll do everything the way it should be done.'

'You've seen the papers, haven't you?'

'There's no need. I know what's in the papers.'

'What a bastard you are! You told me nothing!'

'I didn't want to frighten you. I wanted you to be able to

work in peace. And now that you've finished, my advice would be to go back home, where you'll be safe.'

'And miss out on what's happening here? I wouldn't dream of it!'

'Sonia, please listen. Nothing that's happening here is good. Exactly the opposite. I mean this as a friend: go home now, fast, while you can. We are all in danger, including you, I'm afraid. You've got to believe me, Sonia. I'll call you a few days from now, we'll meet up and I'll tell you everything, all right?'

No answer from Sonia.

'All right?' His tone was exasperated. 'Listen, if you go home like a good girl, I promise to introduce you to Reggiani.'

'You just want to get rid of me.'

'No, this time I'm serious. He wants to meet you.'

'I don't believe you.'

'Sonia, for God's sake, give me a break here. I'm trying to save your life!'

Sonia was silent for a moment as she began to believe he wasn't joking. 'I'll think about it,' she said. 'Maybe you're right. I do have a lot to do back in Bologna. Goodbye, then.' She hung up.

Fabrizio didn't know whether she was offended or angry or both, but it didn't really matter much for the time being. As long as she took his advice. He then put her out of his mind and got to work. Using the charts he'd drawn up while translating the other parts of the inscription, he began to transcribe the text, one word at a time. After a while, Francesca passed him a cup of coffee and he glanced over at Angelo.

'He still hasn't woken up!' he said.

'The shock was enormous,' replied Francesca, ruffling his hair gently. 'Rest is the best thing for him now.'

The boy turned in his sleep and tossed off his blanket, and Francesca leaned forward to tuck him in again.

'Wait,' said Fabrizio. 'What is that?'

'What?'

'Look. That bruise he has on his stomach, on his right side.'

Francesca paused with the blanket in hand as Fabrizio drew closer. 'I don't know. His skin looks red, as though he'd scraped it,' she said.

'How? It's right where his liver is. Don't you find that strange?'

Francesca covered the boy and looked into Fabrizio's eyes, lit up with a sudden realization.

Fabrizio sat at the computer and called up the image of the lad of Volterra.

'Do you see this?' he asked Francesca.

'This spot? It's right over his liver, exactly where Angelo has his.'

Francesca shook her head.

'What are you thinking?' Fabrizio said.

'What do you think I'm thinking? Angelo could have got that bruise in all kinds of ways. He's a kid and kids are always getting hurt. Why? What do you think?'

'What should I think?' replied Fabrizio. 'Here we have an apparently impossible sequence of events building up to a situation that we cannot ignore. The first time I heard the howl was the night the tomb containing the remains of the Phersu was opened, with its jumble of human and animal bones. Now that I've translated the inscription, I know that a horrible punishment was inflicted unjustly on a great, valiant Volterran warrior, Turm Kaiknas. At the same time I discover who the slender bronze statue of the boy in the museum portrays: little Velies Kaiknas, the son of Turm and his wife, Anait, the boy who was cruelly murdered together with his mother by their king, Lars Thyrrens.'

'Wait a minute,' protested Francesca, feeling as if she was grasping at straws. 'All that is in your inscription?'

Fabrizio remembered his dream and went on as if Francesca hadn't opened her mouth: 'The inscription that speaks of this atrocity was carved by Aule Tarchna, Anait's brother, diviner and priest of Sethlans, the god of lightning. He curses those

responsible for the crime, and those seven curses are inscribed
on to the bronze slab . . .'

Francesca's scepticism crumbled all at once and her eyes
filled with the same terror that had gripped her when they were
underground.

Fabrizio continued: 'When I've finished my work here, I'm
sure we'll know what fate awaits us.'

HE WORKED on for two more hours, fighting off the deadly
fatigue that threatened to overwhelm him. Francesca was dozing
in a chair and her regular breathing mixed with that of Angelo,
who was still deeply asleep on the couch.

The last barriers to understanding fell one after another, the
last knots unravelled and the ancient text unwound – with a
very few residual uncertainties and a couple of small gaps –
before his eyes:

> Aule Tarchna thus inscribes seven curses
> over the death of the Phersu
> May the beast [escape-leave?] [his] tomb
> May the hate and revenge of Turm and the [force] of
>   the beast
> sow death among the sons of Velathri
> May they die as he lives again
> to take [his] revenge
> May they scream in terror and [anguish?]
> and vomit blood
> May they die devoured by the beast
> May the beast devour the throat
> of [all those] who lied with their throats
> [those who falsely accused] an innocent man.

He wiped a handkerchief over his sweaty brow and his head
dropped in exhaustion. At that moment he heard a soft sound
and he turned. Francesca was standing there in front of him.

'Have you finished?' she asked.

'I still have a couple of lines to go. The nightmare is nearly complete. Have a look.'

Francesca leaned over and read the text that Fabrizio had transcribed on the computer screen.

'What about the seventh?' she asked.

'The part I've managed to translate is here,' said Fabrizio, showing her a notebook page full of arrows and corrections.

'Can you read it to me?'

Fabrizio read, his voice hoarse:

> 'The seventh death will [never] stop
> The beast will continue to kill
> [as long as] there is blood [to drink] in Velathri.

'Do you know how many people have been killed? Six. All Volterrans of many generations.'

'Good God. It feels like I'm living in a nightmare that I can't wake up from.'

'Here, take a look at this yourself.'

Francesca's eyes glazed over with tears.

'Then this little boy shows up. No one knows who he is or where he comes from. But he says that in that awful place, in the palazzo, is his father.'

'The man in the painting, Jacopo Ghirardini,' offered Francesca.

'If it is him in the picture and if he is Angelo's father. It seems that no one knows anything about Jacopo Ghirardini. Unless, perhaps, Ambra Reiter, but I can't see her telling us about it, unless Reggiani manages to convince her somehow—'

As he was speaking, the phone rang. Fabrizio lifted the receiver and mouthed to Francesca, 'Guess who?'

'What was that?' asked Reggiani's voice at the other end.

'I said, "Speak of the Devil and he will appear",' answered Fabrizio. 'We were just talking about you.'

'Saying bad things, I imagine.'

'Obviously. What's up?'

'That little boy you've got there—'

'Angelo.'

'If that's his name. He arrived in Volterra five years ago when he was four, or perhaps a little less, with Reiter, who claimed to be his mother. They say that she was quite a beautiful woman, and that there was something between her and the count . . .'

'No kidding! What else did you find out?'

'About the child? Very little. We're sending out a photo that one of our computer guys has touched up to make his face look five years younger. The program he's using was developed by headquarters and they say it's uncannily good. We'll be sending the image around to all the police and carabiniere stations and to Interpol abroad. Maybe he'll be recognized.'

'That seems like an excellent idea,' said Fabrizio, looking over at the sleeping child. The thought that they might find out who Angelo really was and that he'd have to be given back made him unhappy and uneasy, and he imagined that Francesca felt the same, from the way she was gazing at him.

'Listen, there's more, but not over the phone. I'll come by to get you. I'm already in the car . . . I'll be there in twenty minutes. Be ready. We don't have much time.'

He hung up.

'So what did he say?' asked Francesca.

'Angelo arrived in Volterra five years ago, when he was more or less four. So it's very unlikely that he's Jacopo Ghirardini's son. Although there may have been a relationship later between the count and Ambra Reiter. She certainly has the keys to the palace, the boy told us that himself. She's the one who locked us in, no doubt about it.'

'I'm sure you're right,' said Francesca. 'But then, who is the child's father?'

'He knows that his father lives in the palace, but the only

image he's ever seen·is the one in the painting. There may be another reality that he can't even imagine . . .'

'No, you can't be thinking what I think you are,' objected Francesca. 'That's pure folly, Fabrizio!'

'You think so? Then how can you explain that that blood-thirsty monster pulled up short like a puppy dog in front of the boy? You saw it yourself. Didn't we both think we were staring death in the face just a moment before? And how do you explain a nine-year-old child standing up to a murderous beast? It was as if a supernatural force were watching over him. Any other kid his age would have become hysterical or passed out.'

'He almost did.'

'No. In reality, he dominated the situation. He moved as if he knew exactly what to do. He actually ran towards the beast while you and I were paralysed with fear. And the mark that he has on his right side where his liver is, it's in exactly the same place as the spot that comes out when you X-ray the statue. Francesca, I think I understand. Do you remember the big underground chamber cut in the tufa underneath the Caretti-Riccardi palace?'

'Where we found Angelo?'

'Right. It was reworked in medieval times, but it's still recognizable. It's a large Etruscan chamber tomb from the fifth century BC. It must have been the Kaiknas necropolis.'

'You know that's impossible. The necropolises were always outside the city.'

'Exactly. What makes you think that the area of the Caretti-Riccardi palace was inside the walls of the Etruscan city? Didn't we see a section of the walls underground? Anyway, it's easily checked. I'm sure the survey records will prove me right.'

'That might be,' agreed Francesca, very confused now.

'I'm sure of it. The animal's den is down there because there's an Etruscan graveyard down there. The Kaiknas family tomb. Where Turm would have been buried had he died honourably, with his sword in his hand and his shield on his arm. As a warrior instead of as a scoundrel with his head tied in a sack, torn to pieces by a starving beast . . .'

Fabrizio stopped because Francesca's eyes were staring and flashing a message at him. A warning: be quiet.

Fabrizio turned instinctively and found the boy behind him. On his feet, his eyes wide open and filled with pain and surprise.

'Angelo, I-I . . .' he stammered.

Just then, the roar of an engine was heard and the screeching of tyres on gravel. Francesca went to open the door for Reggiani.

'No time to waste, friends,' the lieutenant called out, without even crossing the threshold. 'Are you ready, Fabrizio?'

Fabrizio had a moment of uncertainty. He looked at Angelo and then at Francesca, who gave him a quick nod of reassurance.

'Yes,' he replied, 'I'm ready.'

He took his leather jacket from a hook, gave Francesca a kiss and touched the boy's cheek, then got into Reggiani's car, slamming the door hard. It was only a few seconds before the roar of the powerful engine faded into the distance.

Francesca stood at the doorway with Angelo, who was squeezing her hand. She closed the door then and knelt to talk with him.

'You looked scared before. Fabrizio was telling a story of something that happened a long, long time ago. You needn't be frightened.'

Angelo did not answer.

'Are you hungry?'

The boy shook his head.

'Do you want to go back to bed? Are you still tired?'

Another shake.

'OK. Then just sit down here for a little while and wait. There's something I have to do.'

She went to the computer, opened the files with the inscription and the comparison chart and began working on the last two lines of the text. Fabrizio had already put the words in sequence and had hypothesized a grammatical structure. All that remained was to give meaning to the words. There had been no time to analyse the shadows of the opisthographic Latin text on the back of the slab. They could only work on the basis of the part that had already been translated, so Francesca hoped she wouldn't run into any words that had not already appeared.

Angelo sat in front of her with his hands on his knees, without moving, for the entire time she was working on the inscription. It was late afternoon when Francesca had managed to decipher enough terms to understand the general meaning of the last part of the text. She picked up where Fabrizio had ended:

> The beast will continue to kill
> [as long as] there is blood [to drink] in Velathri
> [Only] if the beast is separated from the man
> will vengeance be served [be placated]
> [Only] if the son is [returned] to the father.

Francesca turned to the child with her eyes full of tears, while somewhere in the distance, at that same moment, rose the howl of the chimera. Angelo jumped a little and turned in the direction of that long beastly lament, then looked back at Francesca.

'We have to go,' she said. 'There's not a minute to lose.'

She scribbled a message on a sheet of paper, left a bunch of keys on top, took the child by the hand and left the house, closing the door behind her.

17

'Do you remember the yellow mud?' asked Lieutenant Reggiani as soon as they turned on to the regional road.

'Of course. I noticed it right away.'

'You were right. I searched Ambra Reiter's place at Le Macine using a metal detector, with the guys from the archaeological protection agency, and we found a shitload of stuff down there: bucchero pottery, candelabra, shields and helmets, incredible jewellery, even a war chariot.'

'Yeah, I suspected as much.'

'We also have pretty solid proof that the slab of Volterra was stored in that underground room for a number of days, perhaps even several weeks. There are traces of oxide on the damp mud and I've had them analysed. They were left by a bronze slab of an approximately rectangular shape.'

'I'm not surprised. How did she get in and out?'

'From behind the bar counter. That's how she appeared that day from out of nowhere.'

'Where is she now?'

'She wasn't there when we searched the place, and I'm glad she wasn't. My plan was that if we found nothing, we would leave on tiptoe as we'd come in. But since all that treasure was found, I left Massaro there with three of the guys in hiding. When she waltzed in they arrested her; she'd been caught red-handed, all the objects were still in place and there was no way she could deny anything.'

'Have you already interrogated her?'

'No, I had her taken to headquarters. I'd like you to see the underground chamber and then, if you like, you can sit in on the interrogation. Undercover, that is. I know how tired you are, but I think it's essential that you be there . . . then I'll let you sleep.'

'Sleep,' groaned Fabrizio. 'I don't even know what the word means any more.'

They turned off on to the country lane that led to Le Macine and Reggiani parked in the courtyard. Sergeant Massaro was there waiting for them at the door. He put a hand to his visor and offered Fabrizio an embarrassed hello, mindful of the hours he'd spent guarding an empty house.

'News?' asked Reggiani.

'Bonetti has nearly completed his inventory, sir.'

'Good. Let's let Dr Castellani have a look.'

Fabrizio went underground and exchanged a few friendly words with Bonetti, who was busy scribbling in a notebook.

'Do you know where this stuff comes from?' asked Fabrizio.

'I'd say it's all local, except for a few objects imported from other cities, perhaps in ancient times. Like that candelabrum, which looks as if it comes from Tarquinia,' replied Bonetti, eager to share his technical competence with someone who knew what he was talking about.

'Yeah, I'd say so,' said Fabrizio without enthusiasm. Then he turned to Reggiani. 'Do you want me to call Balestra?'

The lieutenant hesitated a moment. 'Maybe not. Not yet. I'd like to finish interrogating Ambra Reiter first. Do you feel up to joining me?'

Fabrizio nodded and the two men returned upstairs and made their way to carabiniere headquarters, which was swarming with packs of journalists and television crews. As soon as he got out of the car, Reggiani was surrounded by a forest of microphones and TV cameras. The international press was already starting to show up as well.

The same questions were shouted at him from every direction.

Was it true that a monster was roaming the fields around Volterra? How many people had died? Ten? Twenty? Why hadn't they called in the army?

Reggiani raised his arms in a gesture of surrender and said, loudly enough to be heard by all, 'Please, ladies and gentlemen, there's nothing I can tell you now. In just a few hours, certainly before evening, I'll be calling a press conference and you'll have all the answers you want. Right now, could you please let us through? We have urgent business to attend to.'

He managed somehow to elbow his way through the crowd, followed by Fabrizio, and to enter the HQ building.

Ambra Reiter was sitting at a desk. She had her legs crossed and was smoking. She seemed perfectly calm and her only movement was an occasional shake of the cigarette over the ashtray. Reggiani had Fabrizio shown to an adjacent cubicle with an interphone, so he could hear what was going on in the interrogation room.

'Are you going to give her the third degree?' he asked Reggiani.

The officer shook his head with a half-smile, as he took off his cap and black leather gloves. 'That's only on TV. You've been watching too many old Clint Eastwood movies. All we're doing here is asking questions. That may go on for hours. Even days. Only we switch off, while the person being interrogated can't.'

'Doesn't she have the right to call a lawyer?'

'She certainly does. But she doesn't have a lawyer and the court-appointed counsel won't be here until tomorrow. He's just had a tooth extracted and he'll be in the clinic until tonight, if there are no complications. Let me repeat this: we're not doing her any harm. It's only a few questions. Sit down and you'll hear for yourself that no one is being tortured.'

Fabrizio approached the listening console; Reggiani entered his office and sat down on the opposite side of the desk and rested his cap and gloves on the table.

'I'm Lieutenant Reggiani,' he said. 'We've met before, at Le Macine, if I'm not mistaken.'

Ambra Reiter nodded.

'Your counsel will be here tomorrow. You have the right to remain silent. But I can tell you that if you collaborate with us you'll have considerable advantages in negotiating a plea agreement. As you can see, we're making no recording of this session and nothing you say will be held against you.'

'Why?' she asked. 'I've committed no crime.'

'Illegal possession of archaeological material worth millions is not a crime?'

'I just work at the bar. How do I know what's underground?'

'You certainly do know. When Dr Castellani and I came calling, you appeared behind us. You'd obviously emerged from the hatch behind the bar counter.'

'That's not true.'

'Of course it is. I immediately noticed your shoes were caked with yellow mud, the same soil we found in the underground chamber.'

Fabrizio couldn't help but smile at how Reggiani was taking credit for something he hadn't noticed at all, but he obviously wanted to make an impression on the woman as far as his investigative skills were concerned.

'In any case,' continued the lieutenant, 'if you are not responsible for the underground treasure trove, you'll have to tell me who is. I doubt that people can come through your tavern carrying vases and candelabra, shields and helmets, without you ever noticing. Tell me this. How did they dig up the chamber without you knowing?'

'Evidently it was already there, dug before I took over the tavern.'

'You know that's not true, Ms Reiter. We've already taken samples of the concrete on the walls and before evening I'll be able to show you an expert's technical report that demonstrates that the chamber was created no more than one year ago. What do you say to that?'

The woman gave him a hard stare. 'I have nothing to say, and won't say anything until I have a lawyer.'

'As you prefer, ma'am, but you must know you're running a great risk . . .'

The woman did not seem to acknowledge his threat and lit another cigarette.

Reggiani took a packet from his inside jacket pocket. 'Mind if I join you?' he asked.

But Ambra Reiter had withdrawn completely and gave no answer.

'As I was saying . . . you're putting yourself in grave danger,' Reggiani continued, lighting his own cigarette. 'You are aware, I'm sure, of how Pietro Montanari died.'

'Yeah. I heard about it,' said the woman after a few moments of silence.

'Yes, you must have been quite upset, seeing that you knew him so well. Unfortunately, you were the last person to have seen him before he was found murdered.'

Reggiani's suggestion seemed to startle her. 'You're making things up to frighten me and trick me into saying things that aren't true. Your tactics won't work with me.'

'They won't?' Reggiani pressed a button on the interphone and said, 'Massaro, can you bring me the La Casaccia file please?'

The sergeant came in and laid a file on the table. It contained several black-and-white photographs as well as some transparencies developed from digital images.

'Here you are,' said Reggiani, showing them to the woman. 'These are your tyre tracks. And we have a witness who saw you enter and then exit from Montanari's house at ten thirty p.m. The cadaver was found, in horrific condition I may add, shortly thereafter. Moreover, your fingerprints were present in multiple locations throughout the house, as were footprints that match shoes found in your home. Fortunately for us, and unfortunately for you, Montanari's courtyard was quite muddy . . . And that's not all. Tracks left by the tyres of your vehicle were also found at La Motola, not far from where Santocchi was murdered.'

Ambra Reiter seemed shaken.

'What's more,' Reggiani added, 'both Montanari and Santocchi were found with their throats ripped out, exactly like the other victims who died both before and after they did. Which would suggest a serial killer. No judge would believe the cock-and-bull story the papers are putting out about a werewolf prowling around the fields of Volterra. They will find the evidence I've produced much more convincing. It all adds up against you, doesn't it? If my past experience is any indication, you can be reasonably certain of spending the rest of your days in prison. I'd guess that you'll be serving hard time in one of those maximum-security prisons, obviously, since you seem to be in perfect mental health. I wouldn't wish that on my worst enemy actually . . .'

Fabrizio, who was following the conversation word by word, found it hard to believe that this bewildered, uncertain creature was the same woman who had haunted his nightmares, the voice that had sent his heart racing in the middle of the night, the mother who had bullied her child into running away from home. In this context, divested of her aura of mystery and power, she seemed quite harmless, fearful only of ending up in prison. How was that possible? Could she have some kind of personality disorder? He could perfectly call to mind the disturbing, imperious tone her voice took on when she warned him to 'leave the boy in peace'. And he remembered all too well the anxiety and trepidation in Montanari's gaze after she'd left his house that night of blood, chaos and gunfire.

He found himself wishing he could stare into her eyes.

Maybe something there would reveal how such a dreadful witch could transform herself into someone so totally different, someone who perhaps somehow had truly forgotten everything.

He heard her voice saying, 'What do you want from me?'

'First of all, I want to know where that stuff we found underground comes from. In particular, the bronze slab with the inscription.'

'I don't know what you're talking about.'

'OK, so we're starting off on the wrong foot. I'm talking about a bronze slab that was cut into seven parts and stored for at least several weeks on the ground in the left-hand corner of the room underneath your bar.'

The precise nature of his reference seemed once again to shock the woman into silence.

'Well?'

'You know I didn't kill Montanari.'

'That remains to be seen. All I can say is that all of the evidence points in your direction and that a lot will depend on how you answer my questions.'

'How do I know that, if I talk, you won't find new things to accuse me of?'

'Actually, you can't be sure. You'll have to take my word for it. My word as a carabiniere officer and honest man. If you answer my questions I will not charge you with homicide . . . I'll look for another cause. A werewolf, I guess.'

He stared fixedly at Ambra Reiter as his friend Fabrizio Castellani would have done if he'd been sitting there opposite her, searching in her eyes for the merest shadow of the monster that was terrorizing the city, but her gaze was absent, unemotional.

He sighed and said, 'Let's start from the beginning. When did you first arrive in Volterra?'

'Five years ago . . . in the autumn.'

'Where were you coming from?'

'Croatia.'

'Why did you choose Volterra?'

'I was looking for a tranquil place to start a new life. Things were terrible after the war back home . . .'

'And you found work with Count Ghirardini.'

'Yes.'

'Did you become his mistress?'

'What difference does that make?'

'I'll decide whether it makes a difference. Did you become his mistress?'

'Yes.'

'And you moved into his house – that is, the Caretti-Riccardi palace.'

The woman nodded.

'With . . . your son?'

'Yes.'

'For how long?'

'About a year.'

'After which Count Ghirardini suddenly disappeared. Strange, no?'

'He was a strange man. He had spent most of his life in exotic places. He could be anywhere in the world now. He may never come back or he may suddenly reappear like he did back then.'

'There are those who believe that the objects we found underground in your pub come from the count's private collection and that you smuggled them out, perhaps as recompense for services you rendered and were never paid for.'

'That's not true.'

'Then what is true? Careful of what you say, Ms Reiter.' He tapped a finger against his forehead. 'This is better than any recorder. I have the memory of an elephant.'

Ambra Reiter lowered her head and said nothing for a few moments, as if she were weighing her options, then spoke up again. 'Back then Montanari was working for the count as well, doing odd jobs. One night we heard noises underground and we went to see what was down there.'

Fabrizio, on the other side of the wall, started. Reggiani instantly became more attentive.

'What kind of noises?'

'I don't know . . . voices. It sounded like voices. Calling.'

'And you weren't worried about hearing voices in a place like that? What were these voices saying?'

'I don't know. You couldn't understand.'

'Could Montanari hear them as well?'

'Actually, no, he couldn't. But he couldn't hear very well anyway.'

'Continue.'

'We went down into the cellar and I kept saying, "That way. It's coming from over there," until we found a passageway. Steps cut into the stone that went deeper underground. I couldn't hear anything any more, but Montanari started saying there was an ancient cemetery there.'

'Etruscan.'

'That's what Montanari said. I didn't know anything about any Etruscans. But he said that the objects in the tombs were worth a lot of money.'

'So?'

'So he suggested we become partners since I had the keys to the palace and to the cellar. When the count was away, we could go underground and carry those things away, one at a time. That's what we did. If they were little, I'd put them in my pockets. If they were bigger, we'd do it at night. We'd load them up in the van and take them to La Casaccia. As soon as we started earning some money, I bought Le Macine and opened my tavern there. After that, Montanari dug out a room underground and we used it to store our stuff.'

'What about the inscription?' prodded Reggiani.

'Yeah, that too. It came from under there. Montanari found it under a layer of—'

'Of what?'

'Of bones. Bones of many different animals, big and small. Maybe even human bones . . . but I don't remember.'

'What did you do with them?' insisted Reggiani.

'Montanari threw them out. He said they weren't worth anything.'

'Why did you cut the slab into pieces?'

'He said the pieces were easier to sell and that we could get a lot of money for them.'

Reggiani grimaced. 'So then why did he contact the director of the National Antiquities Service?'

'Montanari was stupid. He ended up arousing the suspicion of the Finanza and he felt they were on to us, so at that point he thought he'd better contact the NAS. He told me that Balestra had promised him half a million as a finder's prize.' She stopped abruptly. 'I've told you everything I know. Can I leave now?'

Reggiani didn't answer.

'You promised me that if I answered all your questions you'd let me go.'

'I have one last question to ask you . . . for now.'

She eyed him in silence with her grey and apparently absent look, as if she wasn't even seeing him. Some time ago she must have been a woman of uncommon beauty, that aggressive, brazen beauty that can drive a man mad.

'You'll remember when I came looking for you that day at Le Macine with my friend Dr Castellani . . .'

The woman nodded.

'Why did you lie? Why did you say you had never telephoned him?'

Fabrizio started and leaned closer to the speaker so he wouldn't miss a syllable of that answer, if there was going to be one.

'I was telling the pure truth. I'd never seen him before and I would never dream of telephoning him.'

Accustomed as he was to listening to every kind of cock-and-bull story from every kind of insolent delinquent son of a bitch on earth, Lieutenant Reggiani felt sure that he would catch a glimpse of uncertainty in her eyes, but they remained hard and smooth as a slab of ice.

He said, 'You can go now, but I would advise you not to leave Le Macine. My men will be keeping an eye on you, so you'd best comply.'

'But I've already told you everything you wanted to know.'

'Not everything. There's one more question.'

'About what?'

'About that boy who lives with you.'

Ambra Reiter lowered her gaze and asked, 'Where is he?'

'In a safe place. To be frank, I would have expected you to put in a call to the carabinieri before now to report that your son had gone missing. Now you can go.'

'But—'

'You can go now, Ms Reiter.'

The woman got up to leave and, for the first time in eleven months, Reggiani lit up his second cigarette of the day.

Fabrizio emerged from his hiding place and walked into Reggiani's office.

'Can you believe the nerve of that bitch! I would have liked to look into her eyes while she was telling such an outrageous lie.'

'You've seen her do it before, haven't you?' replied Reggiani. 'Completely deadpan, as if she were reciting a phone number. I can assure you that if I didn't believe you I would have believed her.'

'If you doubt what I've told you, I can—'

'I didn't say that. I'm saying that she seemed to be telling the honest truth. You heard her yourself, right? My gut feeling was that she was telling the truth about everything. I think she realized that I will not hesitate to incriminate her if she doesn't cooperate.'

'What about the boy?'

'That's an entirely different matter. And if you want to know what I think, that's where the greatest mystery lies. I'm convinced I did well to make you come in here with me, even though you are so tired.'

'Absolutely . . . A lot of things are falling into place. Listen, just for a moment, let's examine the possibility that she's telling the truth.'

'About what?'

'About the fact that she's never seen me or called me.'

'You can't be serious.'

'I've never been more serious. Couldn't this be a case of split personality? It's rare, I know, but it can happen.'

'Just what are you saying?'

'Simply put, the Ambra Reiter who was talking to you a few minutes ago is not the Ambra Reiter who was calling me and whom I talked to at the tavern.'

'I don't think I'm following you.'

'Let's suppose that when she was calling me in the middle of the night, she was in a state of altered consciousness; her actions were controlled by a second personality.'

'Like when someone has taken some serious dope?'

'Something like that.'

'Can we analyse her?'

'I don't think you'd get anywhere.'

'So what are you thinking?'

'What if she were . . . a medium?'

Reggiani shrugged. 'Yeah, right, like the kind that makes tables dance around and spirits speak. Fabrizio, get serious. You'll remember that I brought up the idea of using a psychic to get to the bottom of this and you were the one who talked me out of it. I honestly think you're barking up the wrong tree here. This one may read cards, coffee grounds, that kind of thing . . . I'll bet she has Gypsy blood in her.'

'Well, before he died, Montanari told me that after they'd

found the slab something changed in her, turned her into a harpy. That she became unrecognizable at times. You have to admit there's something disturbing about her.'

'There's no doubt about that,' he said, as his attention was attracted by the noise outside. 'Listen to the racket those journalists are making out there. I'm here with six cadavers on my back and I still don't have a clue. What do I tell the Secretary? The werewolf story?'

'The Secretary?'

Reggiani rolled his head and sighed. 'Ah, yes. The Home Secretary will be paying me a visit tonight, along with our Commander General. Both sure to be in a foul mood. You know what that means, right?'

Fabrizio looked at his watch. 'That in four hours you'll be sending out your shooting party.'

'Let's say two, as soon as it gets dark. Unfortunately, the situation has changed radically. And you can be sure we'll be hearing the beast's howl tonight as well. But this will be the last night, I'll promise you that.'

Fabrizio paled. 'But wait, you promised—'

'I'm sorry, my friend, but this can't wait. The lives of too many people are at risk.'

'Listen, just give me another hour, two at the most. I have to figure out what the last part of the inscription says ... There's a ... How can I get this across? ... You'll be putting the whole city in dire danger. It could be a disaster ...'

'Mediums ... dire danger ... Sounds like your brains are fried, my friend.' He took his pistol out of the drawer and drew back the bolt to load it. 'You want to know what I believe in? This.'

'What's going to happen?'

'My men are stationed at the exit to the old cistern. We've cleared the area for half a kilometre all around. As soon as the creature shows up, we'll unleash hell. Whatever it is, there won't be a hair left of it. I'm sorry, Fabrizio. I have to go now.

I had you come in here because I wanted you to know how we were proceeding, and I wanted you to hear Ambra Reiter's story with your own ears. I felt I owed it to you.'

'You're crazy,' said Fabrizio. 'It's going to be a massacre.'

Reggiani didn't answer. Fabrizio watched as he pushed his way through the crowd of journalists waiting in the front hall.

The lieutenant then went into the locker room, took off his uniform and put on his combat gear.

18

FABRIZIO MET the press himself shortly afterwards. Special correspondents and TV reporters thrust their microphones at him, figuring he must be involved somehow with the story.

Those crowding in behind the first row asked, 'Who's this guy? Was he with Reggiani? Does he know something?'

Others provided partial answers: 'He's an archaeologist . . . Someone said he's an archaeologist. There's got to be some connection . . .'

Then one said, 'His name's Castellani. Dr Castellani, a question, just one question, what were you doing with the lieutenant? What did he tell you? Is it true a woman has been arrested? Please, give us a hand here!'

Fabrizio shoved his way through, ignoring the insults and abuse hurled his way, especially from the notoriously rude Italian TV operators from Rome, and began to run down the city streets, trying to lose them in the maze of the city centre. He reached the museum and saw Mario at the security guard's booth.

'Dr Castellani! The director has been looking for you all week! Where have you been?'

'I can't just now, Mario. Please tell the director I'll report to him as soon as possible. Is Dr Vitali here?'

'No. She left half an hour ago but didn't say where she was going.'

Fabrizio nodded. He swiftly made his way to the taxi stand in the nearby square and hailed the first cab he could find.

'Take me to the Semprini farm, as quickly as you can.'

'The place in Val d'Era?'

'Yes. I'll tell you the best way to get there.'

The taxi set off and Fabrizio phoned home. No answer. He tried Francesca's mobile but it was off. Anxiety welled up inside him like a black tide, crushing him back into his seat. The regional road, then left, Val d'Era and then the track.

When the cab stopped outside the front door, Fabrizio had the fare ready. 'Keep the change,' he said, and jumped out. The taxi backed up and drove off.

The house was deserted, but the computer was still on, with the translation of the last part of the inscription. He noticed the handwritten note that Francesca had left for him and his heart plummeted. He feverishly dialled Reggiani's mobile number and listened as it rang one, two, three times, his teeth clenched as he spoke aloud: 'Answer, goddamn it, pick it up—'

'Where are you?' asked the lieutenant curtly at the fourth ring.

'At home. Marcello, for the love of God, listen to me. Francesca's down there.'

'Down where?'

'In the palace, underground.'

'What the hell . . . Is she crazy?'

'She translated the last part of the inscription and I think . . . I think that . . .'

'What! Talk! You know my minutes are counted!'

'I think that she believes . . . that she believes in the words of the inscription. She thinks she can stop disaster from happening. It's too long a story to explain it all now, but do you have a flame-thrower?'

'A flame-thrower? You've lost it, Fabrizio. What do you want with a flame-thrower? That's an assault weapon, used by the special forces. I'd have to ask the ROS guys.'

'Shit, Marcello, you are an ROS guy! You must have a flame-thrower.'

'I'm no longer operative, and even if I wanted to get one, there just isn't time enough. Listen, don't screw things up here. I'm about to launch the operation. Do not interfere, Fabrizio. Do you hear what I'm saying? You'd risk fucking up the whole thing, putting your own life at risk and Francesca's as well. Wherever you are, go back to headquarters and do not move from there until it's all over. We will find Francesca, understand? We will find her. You—'

The line went dead and whatever he had meant to say was cut short. Fabrizio immediately dialled Sonia's number.

'Hi there, handsome,' said her voice. The connection was scratchy.

Fabrizio tried to keep calm and speak in a normal tone of voice. 'Sonia, where are you?'

'You said you wanted me out of your hair and I took the hint.'

'Where are you?' he repeated in an even, if not calm, tone.

'I've just turned on to the regional road for Colle Val d'Elsa. Hey, what's up? You sound funny.'

'Sonia, stop as soon as you can when you see the signal is good. I have to be able to hear you clearly. First of all, I need to know if you've finished your work.'

The line was stronger now; Sonia must have found a place to stop.

'Yeah, right, I told you I had. Why?'

'What I need to know is if all the animal's bones have been separated from the human bones. All of them, to the very last fragment. Do you understand what I'm asking?'

'What kind of a question is that? No, obviously not. How can I tell whether all those remaining fragments are human or not? Probably some of the dog's bones were chipped as well. You'd need a very close analysis. I'd have to take it to a lab . . . Why do you care? The skeleton looks great, so who cares about a few fragments? But now that you're asking, maybe there are a few pieces missing. How can I be sure? First of all you scare me to death and tell me to get out of here as soon as I can, and then you tell me I should have used a microscope to finish the job. I can't figure you out, Fabrizio. I just don't get why you're putting me on the spot like this.'

'Sonia, there's no time to explain, but if you are willing to complete the job – that is, to separate all the animal bones from the human bones – please, turn back and do it. Go back down there and sort out all the bones and then don't move from there. Lock yourself in and open the door only if you hear my voice. Sonia, please, please, please do this for me!'

His voice sounded so desperate that Sonia's mood changed completely. 'Are you sure you're all right?'

'Sonia, when it's time I'll tell you everything and you'll be glad you helped me. Just tell me that you'll do it, right away.'

'Maybe there is a way to figure it out. The colour is slightly different, but that means I'll need a solar colour-temperature light . . . Right, OK, I think I can handle it. You call Mario and tell him to let me in. I'll take care of the rest.'

'Thank you, Sonia. I knew I could count on you. I'll call Mario right away.'

'Listen, so when are you coming?'

'As soon as I can, but I have to find something first. You don't move from there and don't open the door for anyone but me, understand?'

'I understand,' said Sonia, and hung up. 'I understand that you're completely bonkers,' she continued, mumbling to herself, 'but I'm too curious to see where this wild ride will end.'

FRANCESCA made her way through the rooms under the Caretti-Riccardi palace, lighting her path with a torch and holding Angelo by the hand. The child was strangely calm and placid.

She whispered, 'Only you can stop him, little guy. No one else, understand?'

'Will they kill him?' asked the boy.

'Maybe not,' replied Francesca. 'Maybe not, if you can stop him.'

She looked at her watch: it was nearly seven o'clock. At that moment the underground chambers filled with the beast's long howl. A deep, gurgling sound, far and near at the same time, refracted and disrupted by the subterranean labyrinth.

'I think . . . he's still down here. Maybe in that side tunnel we saw yesterday, remember?'

Angelo nodded and tightened his grip on her hand.

'Maybe we're still in time to stop him . . .'

The boy was trembling all over now and squeezing Francesca's hand hard. She could feel the sweat on his small fingers.

'Don't be afraid,' she told him. 'We're trying to save a lot of people. We're trying to put an end to hatred that has been festering for a very long time, to heal an old, old wound . . .'

She was talking to herself more than to the child. She didn't even know if he was listening, but as they walked down the tunnel that led to the old cistern, she had a distinct sensation of heat coming off the boy's hand, a spark of violent energy that ran up her arm and through her body. Her face felt hot. They were getting closer and closer to the fork where the monster had run off down the secondary tunnel the day before. The snarling was louder now, and clearer, and another noise could be heard as well, still far away for the moment: the sound of claws scratching the tufa as the animal ran towards them.

SONIA SPED through the maze of streets in the old city until she reached the museum. Fabrizio must have phoned, because there was Mario with keys in hand, waiting for her.

'Back so soon, Dr Vitali? Did you forget something?'

'Well, yes,' replied Sonia. 'I left a book of notes downstairs, and since I had to come back for them, I thought there were still a few things I could usefully do.'

She moved swiftly downstairs to the storeroom with Mario,

who inserted a key in the door for her. As Sonia slipped in, she said, 'Please go on home, Mario. When I've finished I'll set the alarm and pull the main door shut behind me.'

She closed the door before Mario could answer. He slowly climbed the stairs up to the ground floor. He was used to the strange habits of academics and researchers: people who lived in another world, just like Balestra, the director, who closed himself up in his office for weeks on end, studying Lord knows what. He hung the keys on a hook in the security guard's booth, put on his coat and walked outside. There were just a few steps between the museum entrance and the front door to his house, but he felt as weighed down as if he were wearing shoes of lead. A strange feeling he'd never experienced before.

Meanwhile, in the basement, Sonia switched on the overhead light as well as the spotlight that was trained on the big skeleton standing on a wooden platform at the end of the room. She had wired the bones together using a system of steel bindings she had devised herself. For the first time, she saw it with new eyes: no longer as a palaeozoological specimen but as a fleshless monster, a Cerberus straight out of hell.

She drew in a long breath and approached the pedestal. She had collected all the leftover bone fragments on a piece of white felt. She knelt down and began to pick out the pieces that surely belonged to the human skeleton: fragments of the skull – several of which still bore the marks of the fangs that had crushed it – and of the long bones, the humeri and femurs cruelly snapped by the bite of powerful jaws. She then began to examine the remaining fragments: ribs, vertebrae, phalanxes, astragali . . .

She sighed. What criteria could she use in separating them? There were certainly a number of options, all of them reliable, but given the conditions and the urgency – what emergency could Fabrizio possibly be on about? – there was just one fast, sure way: colour. The animal bones were a bit darker.

'I guess I'll just have to make do with what I have,' she mused aloud.

She took some of the plastic boxes they used for collecting archaeological finds and stacked them up next to the bone fragments on the white felt. She took a Polaroid camera from her bag, climbed up her improvised staircase and snapped one, two, three shots at slightly different angles. She examined the prints one by one, chose the best and then ran up to the first floor. There was no one in any of the offices. She reached the laboratory and switched on the highest-resolution scanner. She framed a single fragment and took that colour tone setting, then programmed the machine to recognize all objects having the same tone and to highlight them. In just a few minutes the printer provided an image with all the selected fragments. Sonia shut off the machine and the lights and ran back underground, carefully bolting the main door as Fabrizio had ordered. Then she placed the printout on the ground and began to sort out each one of the highlighted fragments, laying them carefully on the wooden pedestal beneath the skeleton.

FRANCESCA grasped Angelo's hand without taking her eyes off the opening to the tunnel, which was framed by the beam of torchlight.

'We're here. Come on, little guy. Let's give it a go.'

They started to advance, very slowly, clinging to each other, preparing to meet the beast's charge. And all at once the sound of powerful legs, the scraping of sharp claws on stone, got closer and closer until they were face to face. Huge, dreadful, mouth foaming, eyes shot through with blood, monstrous fangs bared to the root. The child screamed and Francesca shouted out loud to release a burst of unbearable tension. The animal responded with a furious roar. Angelo and Francesca cowered against the wall, overwhelmed by horror. The snarling beast drew closer, a deep rattle coming from its throat, and Francesca understood that what she'd done was insane. She shielded the boy with her own body, hoping that the monster would be sated by her blood alone.

SONIA heard the doorbell ringing insistently and then a furious banging of fists on the door. The main entrance! She'd forgotten the bolt on the door upstairs! She left the room, ran up the steps and towards the door, yelling as she went, 'Who's there?'

'It's me, Fabrizio! Open the door, fast. Now, Sonia! We only have a matter of seconds. Open up!'

Sonia slid the bolt and found Fabrizio soaked with sweat and brandishing a heavy gas canister connected to a blowtorch. His car was blocking the deserted street, its headlights on and door wide open.

'What in heaven's name . . .' she blurted out.

But Fabrizio was already dashing along the corridor and down the stairs, shouting, 'Get over here! Did you finish what I asked you to do? Have you separated all the fragments?'

Sonia ran after him breathlessly without even closing the door, shouting back, 'Yeah. I think so, at least, but what is that thing you've got in your hand? What the hell are you going to do with it? Burn down the place? Talk to me, goddamn you, Fabrizio! I swear I'll sound the alarm unless you stop right now. I swear I'll do it! Stop and listen to me!'

But Fabrizio seemed possessed. He ran carrying the heavy iron canister as if it were made of paper. He reached the skeleton, recognized the human bone fragments lying on the felt, then turned back to the skeleton and the animal bones that Sonia had piled up on the wooden pedestal. He opened the gas valve, pulled a lighter out of his pocket and applied it to the burner. A blue flame burst from the torch and Fabrizio moved towards the skeleton.

'No!' shouted Sonia. 'No! What are you doing? Damn you! You can't do that! Don't destroy it! Stop!'

She jumped at him to make him stop, sure that he'd gone mad, that he'd lost his mind. But he spun around and hit her hard in the face, knocking her to the ground. He directed the blowtorch at the skeleton, which started to burn. The metal bindings became incandescent and twisted in the flames, the structure collapsed and the skeleton of the beast, so patiently and laboriously reassambled, disintegrated one bone at a time, crumbling on to the wooden base, which burst into flame all at once. The fire grew in intensity as the great skeleton turned to ash.

AT THAT same instant, in the underground tunnel, just as the beast was about to spring, it was enveloped in a whirlwind of flames. Francesca watched incredulously as it reared up on its hind legs, writhing in the grip of powerful convulsions. It let out a terrifying roar, a cruel and desperate howl of pain that almost seemed human. The girl turned and hugged the child tight, flattening herself against the wall, frantically covering his eyes and his ears to spare him the sight of such horror and the sound of such unending suffering. The entire tunnel trembled, as if shaken by a violent earthquake, as the walls echoed the cries of the dying beast. The howl disintegrated into a shriek of pain and Francesca's ears filled with moaning and sobbing, suffocated words in a forgotten language, prayers and imprecations welling up from the abyss of millennia. Then everything was plunged into a silence deeper than death.

FABRIZIO extinguished the flame and mopped the sweat from his forehead. He was completely drenched from head to toe, as if he had accomplished the most strenuous task of all times.

He turned immediately to Sonia and blurted out, 'I'm so sorry. I didn't mean . . .' But she was gone.

He turned off the gas valve, ran back upstairs through a thick curtain of smoke and rushed out into the street, where he was nearly run over by Reggiani's police van.

'Your colleague Sonia Vitali just called me. What the hell do you think you're doing? Get into the car now. I'm going to keep you under lock and key until all this is over.'

Two soldiers flanked him while Reggiani turned to his radio and instructed, 'Open fire as soon as it comes out.' He turned back to Fabrizio then and said, 'There's no chance of it getting away. The moment it surfaces, it'll be blinded by half a dozen two-thousand-watt photoelectric cells and riddled with shots.'

'No!' shouted Fabrizio. 'You don't understand! Francesca and Angelo are down there and they might be trying to get out. You risk killing them instead of the animal. They're still underground, I'm telling you! Listen to what I'm saying – I heard it howling, just moments ago, but it was different this time. It was horrible. I'd never heard anything like it before. Come on, Marcello, for the love of God! Order your men to hold their fire, please! I'm begging you!' He was weeping openly.

'All right!' growled Reggiani. 'But let's get moving, damn it!'

Fabrizio took off at a run towards the Caretti-Riccardi palace with Reggiani close behind and the police van following. Sonia, her eyes full of tears and her face swollen, emerged from a dark corner and went back to the museum entrance, but she didn't even have the strength to go up the stairs. She collapsed on to the step at the threshold and, with a long sigh, leaned her head back against the door.

Fabrizio burst into the square and ran towards the main entrance to the palace. He pushed at the side door at the centre of the facade and it yawned open without any resistance. He dashed in while Reggiani quickly grabbed the van's radio.

'Do not open fire unless you are absolutely certain you have the animal in your sights. There are people underground who may be trying to escape through the cistern. I repeat, people are present.'

'Roger that, sir,' replied Tornese's voice. 'We'll be careful.'

Reggiani replaced the transmitter and took off after Fabrizio, followed by a couple of his men. They ran breathlessly to the end of the great hall, which rang out with the pounding of their combat boots. They tramped down the stairs and through the cellar, trying to keep up with Fabrizio, who was racing along as if he could see in the dark. He finally entered the tunnel without ever pausing for breath and ran until he found Francesca, who was sobbing disconsolately. She had collapsed to the ground and was holding the child tenderly in her arms. The animal was nothing more than a dark, shapeless, burnt mass on the tufa floor.

'It's all over,' said the girl between her sobs.

Fabrizio had pulled up short, paralysed by what he was seeing. He whispered, 'Only if the beast is separated from the man . . .'

'Only if the child is returned to the father . . .' continued Francesca, and she opened her arms. 'He's dead. Angelo is dead. His father took him away with him.'

Reggiani shouted to his men, 'Call an ambulance! A doctor, fast!'

Fabrizio lifted the child and laid him gently on the ground. He began a cardiac massage and tried blowing air into his lungs. He could feel heat and got a whiff of his little boy's smell: life couldn't have completely abandoned him yet. Francesca was leaning against the wall and crying hot tears in silence. Reggiani was frozen in place, his loaded pistol still in hand, a wordless witness to the scene.

All at once Fabrizio distinctly felt a draught of cold air coming from the side tunnel and he seemed to be struck by a sudden awareness. He got to his feet, still holding the little boy to his chest, and began to advance down the dark passageway.

Reggiani started. 'Where are you going?' he said. 'Wait!'

He moved off after them, still holding his pistol in his right hand and a torch in his left. They continued for ten or twelve metres, until the tunnel walls squared off suddenly and came to an end at a carved doorway.

'My God!' murmured the officer, astonished at the sight. 'What is that?'

Fabrizio had already entered and Reggiani could see a beautiful fresco beyond him, on the opposite wall, depicting a banquet scene with dancers and flute players draped in light, transparent gowns.

'It's their tomb,' replied Fabrizio with a tremble in his voice. 'It's the Kaiknas family tomb.'

Fabrizio turned and saw a large sarcophagus bearing the image of a husband and wife, reclining on their sides: the lady was beautiful and her spouse had the powerful build of a warrior. His arm was wrapped around her shoulder in a gesture of love and protection. Reggiani directed the torch beam on them and remained speechless in contemplation of their timeless faces and enigmatic smiles.

Fabrizio fell to his knees in front of the sarcophagus, stretching the still body of the little boy forward towards them. 'Let me keep him!' he pleaded. 'Let him live! He can't die twice! I beg of you, leave him to me!' He burst into tears and clasped the little boy's body close to his chest.

The dark underground chamber was once again invaded by that cold, mysterious, sudden breath of air, and Fabrizio heard a sound that roused him from his weeping: a whisper more than a sound; a long, sorrowful sigh.

'Did you hear that?' he asked Reggiani.

The officer shook his head, regarding Fabrizio with a pitying expression.

'Francesca . . .'

'Who said that?' asked Fabrizio in surprise, but as he spoke he felt a shudder run through the little body he was clutching and then he felt the rhythm – hiccuping at first and then slow and even – of the child's breathing.

'Shine that over here!' he shouted frantically, and Reggiani illuminated the face of the little boy, who blinked in the sudden harsh light. The two men stared at each other without managing to get a word out.

'Where's Francesca?' repeated Angelo. 'What is this place?'

'Francesca? We'll find her. She's right here, close by,' replied Fabrizio, trying to control his emotions and speak as normally as possible.

They walked back towards the main tunnel, while the

mausoleum of the Kaiknas family sank into darkness and silence again.

They joined Francesca and tried to retrace their steps, but the tunnel was obstructed by a landslide, as if there had been an earthquake.

'All we can do is go on towards the cistern,' said Francesca. 'We have no choice. I hope your men aren't feeling trigger-happy,' she added to Reggiani.

They walked for about twenty minutes in the dim glow cast by the torch. When they were approaching the cistern, Reggiani called out, 'It's us! We're coming out!'

'We're waiting for you, Lieutenant! It's safe to come out,' came back the sergeant's voice, followed by a thump and a loud buzz as the photocells flooded the cistern well. The four people who had been feared buried alive came out one after another, last of all Fabrizio with the child on his shoulders.

An ambulance soon pulled up and a couple of nurses came out with a stretcher, accompanied by a doctor.

'He's fine now,' said Fabrizio. 'He fainted, but he's better now.'

'I'd still like to have a look,' said the doctor, who had been given a much more alarming prognosis by Reggiani's men. 'I think it's best we keep him under observation for the rest of the night.'

Francesca took Angelo's hand. 'I'll go with him. Don't worry. We'll see you in the morning.'

Fabrizio kissed her and held her tight. 'You were very brave. I never would have forgiven myself if anything had happened to you . . . I love you.'

'I love you too,' replied the girl, leaving him with a gentle caress.

Lieutenant Reggiani mustered his men. 'The operation is suspended,' he announced. 'The animal has been destroyed.'

'Destroyed?' repeated Sergeant Massaro. 'How?'

'With . . . a flame-thrower,' replied Reggiani curtly.

'A flame-thrower, sir?' asked the sergeant incredulously.

'That's correct. Why? Is there something strange about that?'

'No, nothing. I was just thinking . . .'

'No need to rack your brains, Massaro. Everything's fine, I can assure you of that. You can demobilize now and return to headquarters. It's all over. There will be no more deaths. All I have to do now is face the Home Secretary and the press, but at least they don't bite . . . At least, I hope not.' He turned towards Fabrizio. 'Where can I drop you off?'

'At the museum. My car is still in the middle of the road and . . . there's something I still have to do.' He switched on his mobile phone and called Sonia, but her phone was off and when they reached the museum there was no trace of her.

'I'll call her tomorrow,' he said. 'I have to ask her to forgive me. Or . . . would you like to call instead?' he asked Reggiani, guessing at his thoughts. 'Yeah, I think that's a better solution. Here, this is her number. Tell her that I'll call her as soon as I can and that I'm very, very sorry, but that I had no choice. You know why.'

'I'll take care of it,' promised Reggiani. 'What's next?'

'Come in. There's something I want to show you.' He took the key from his pocket, opened the door, crossed the hall and walked down the stairs to the basement. The room was still full of smoke and invaded by an intense, acrid, scorched smell.

Reggiani noticed the gas canister and burner. 'You could have blown up the whole place. You're completely irresponsible.'

'I told you I needed a flame-thrower and this was all I could find. Thank God I did! I remembered seeing a roadworker using something like this once to melt tar.'

'I think you owe me an explanation,' said Reggiani. 'Even if this is all over, I want to know what set the whole thing off and how.'

Fabrizio took a folded sheet of paper out of the inside pocket of his jacket and handed it to Reggiani. It was the translation of the inscription. 'Read this. You'll understand everything. It's the text of the slab of Volterra. Complete.'

As the lieutenant scanned the crumpled sheet in disbelief, Fabrizio bent down and carefully gathered the bones of the Phersu that Sonia had painstakingly separated from the animal's bones. He walked towards the sta...

Reggiani turned towards him, still shaking his head. 'Where are you going now? Haven't you got into enough trouble for one night?'

'I'm going back down there,' he said without turning. 'I'm going to take Turm Kaiknas's bones to the family tomb, so he can rest alongside his wife and his child. I'm certain about one thing at least. The statue of the young lad in room twenty above our heads, the one I came to study, comes from that tomb. Have all the entrances to the tunnel closed tomorrow in secret if you can. No one must ever disturb the sleep of Turm and Anait again, for any reason.'

Back up in the front hall, Fabrizio turned out the lights and set the alarm before leaving. 'In a few days we'll be asking ourselves if we dreamed it all. You know we're going to forget this, don't you? That's what happens to the human mind when events are too difficult to accept. Anyway, I think we've done the right thing. And what counts is that your case is solved, isn't it, Lieutenant?'

'No, not completely,' objected Reggiani as they walked towards the car. 'We still don't know where Angelo comes from.'

'Maybe Ambra Reiter will tell you the next time you question her.'

'You think so? I'm sure she'll come up with the most obvious story possible. That when her first husband died he made her promise to bring the child to safety in Italy. She may even have an ID card, documents.'

'Maybe . . .' said Fabrizio as if talking to himself. 'But the wounds of the past can come back to bleed again in the present.

Sometimes they can even hurt. Debts have to be settled, sooner or later. The truth – if it exists – is buried deep in the mind of that little boy, lurking in his dreams, waiting for the shades of twilight to come calling.'

Two DAYS LATER, Lieutenant Reggiani was back in his office at seven a.m. His expression gave no hint of the hellish events of the past fortnight. Instead, his face wore the perplexed expression that he got when he was trying to work his way through a complicated problem. He sat at his desk and began to sketch out a diagram with all the individuals who had played a role in the case and the relationships between them. After a couple of good nights' sleep, his mind was functioning again as usual and was refusing to accept an explanation that had nothing rational about it. As time passed and he got over the shock of what he'd seen down in that tunnel, he wondered whether the case was solved after all. Might there not be another murder that very night, or in two or ten days' time? In the end, all he had seen in the tunnel was a black mass on the ground that could have been anything. And a woman and child crying. He was startled from his thoughts by a knock at the door.

'Come in!' he called out, without looking up from his chart.

Sergeant Massaro stepped in and saluted him respectfully. 'Good morning, sir.'

'Good morning to you, Massaro. News?'

'Big news, sir.'

'What's that?'

'We've been following Reiter, as you instructed, and we've received the information we requested from the database at headquarters and from Trieste as well, where she was first picked up for questioning. I think we've got this solved, sir.'

'If that's the case, Massaro,' replied Reggiani, 'I'm recommending you for a promotion. Let's hear.'

'The child, Angelo that is, may have a first and last name: Eugenio Carani. That's the name of the child who disappeared from a household where Ambra Reiter had been employed as a housekeeper. When the child's parents reported him missing, she was tracked down near Colloredo and arrested, but there was no trace of the child. She was interrogated at length but nothing came of it. She denied knowing anything about the boy's whereabouts. What did become evident was that she was suffering from mental illness. She was diagnosed as borderline, with a dissociative disorder. Suspected schizophrenia, even. Her medical record is very complex.'

'And the family she was working for never noticed anything?'

'Apparently not. They said she was moody, but nothing out of the ordinary.'

'So?'

'So, after a three-month stint at a psychiatric clinic in Pordenone, she was released, and that's where we lose track of her,' continued Massaro. 'I'm thinking that's when she showed up here in Volterra. Even if she had the child with her at this point, no one recognized her, no one reported her. After all, there was no warrant out for her arrest, and the boy's disappearance wasn't front-page news any more. She must have kept him hidden somewhere while she was in the clinic. Maybe she had an accomplice.'

'Or maybe the child was already here with Ghirardini. He had no children of his own and they say he was obsessed with having an heir. That would explain why Angelo told Castellani that his father was in the palace,' mused Reggiani. 'Continue.'

'Well, I don't know how to say this, but I think we were this far away from finding . . . the animal.'

'What are you saying? The animal's dead.'

'Exactly. The other night, while you were out on operations, we stopped Ms Reiter as she was pulling up at Le Macine in her van. In the back she had a big cage, with iron bars as thick as my fingers, as if inside it she were keeping—'

'That's not possible!' said Reggiani softly, taken aback.

'We asked her what she kept in the cage and she said, "My

dog." I asked her where it was and she said it was dead, and that she'd buried it. She refused to tell me where.'

'The van and the cage,' Reggiani said to himself, 'that would explain the tyre tracks near the murder sites. Castellani himself mentioned the sound of an engine making him suspicious. Didn't you insist with Reiter?'

'Of course, but it was like talking to the wall. I sent a couple of guys out looking, but they haven't turned up anything yet. Anyway, that lady is a real nutcase, sir. She goes on and on about spirits, reincarnation, paranormal powers. When she looks at you with those wild eyes, it's like she's possessed or something. Then she clams up completely, turns totally blank. Sometimes she seems perfectly normal. But her normality is even scarier than her craziness, if I may say so.'

Reggiani nodded in silence.

'What shall we do?' asked Massaro. 'She's still under close surveillance.'

'We can't risk her disappearing on us. She's dangerous. We need to get her committed. Start working on the papers.'

'Yes, sir. I'm sure that's the best course of action. Permission to leave, sir.'

Massaro saluted and went to the door. Reggiani called out a moment before he'd closed it.

'Massaro.'

'Yes, sir.'

'By any chance, did you ask Ms Reiter when her . . . dog . . . died? I know it's a silly question.'

'No, it's not silly at all, sir. Of course I asked her.'

'And?'

'She said it happened the day before yesterday, in the evening. About eight p.m. All she said was that he died very suddenly. And she had tears in her eyes.'

'Thank you, Massaro. You can go now.'

Reggiani remained alone, mulling over those words. The day before yesterday. In the evening. Eight p.m. That would have been just about when Francesca and Angelo were down in the tunnel and Fabrizio was down under the museum with his skeleton. Crazy coincidence. But at least now he had the option of choosing not to believe in spirits. He sighed, then opened his appointment book to see what the new day would bring.

Epilogue

Some time later in Siena, Fabrizio and Francesca received an invitation from NAS director Balestra to attend the press conference formally announcing the discovery of the slab of Volterra, the most complex example of Etruscan epigraphy ever found.

At nearly the same time, they received an email from Lieutenant Reggiani which said, among other things:

> Our investigation into the origins of little Angelo has produced positive results. Ambra Reiter kidnapped the child from a couple in Trieste who she was working for at the time. The abduction had been commissioned by Count Ghirardini, who wanted an heir at any cost and contacted a criminal organization who arranged illegal adoptions. The child, I'm told, has been reunited with his parents. He has adapted well to his new/old family and is happy, according to the reports I've received. I'm enclosing a photo.

Fabrizio observed the image that pictured a fit, handsome man of about forty-five and a striking, elegantly dressed woman about ten years younger. Angelo was standing between them and smiling broadly.

The email continued:

> His real name is Eugenio and he's promised to come to visit as soon as he can, with his parents. As you may have learned, I delivered the final fragment personally to the NAS director, along with a complete report on all of the objects found in the underground hide at Le Macine. I think I can say that

245

everything's gone as smooth as silk. The animal that held us, and all of Volterra, in its thrall is dead. In one way or another, or in both ways, it's dead. We've spoken about this on the phone and I'm sure you'll soon come around to my way of thinking. Give me a call when you can, Marcello.

A PS followed:

Sonia has requested a transfer to the NAS offices of Florence and she hopes to be assigned to the Volterra museum. If that should fall through, I'll ask to be transferred to regional headquarters in Bologna.

Fabrizio looked at the photo again. 'I would have kept Angelo, if they'd let us,' he said.

'That would have made me happy too,' replied Francesca. 'He's a very special child. So sweet, sensitive, bright.'

'Do you have any idea of what Balestra's translation is like?' asked Fabrizio, turning the director's invitation over in his hands.

'More or less . . .'

'And?'

'From what I know, it will be a partial, hypothetical version . . . and no announcement of the opisthographic text will be given, at least not yet. The inscription will be hung on the wall in the museum and show only the Etruscan side. The complete translation is in the hands of a notary, who will keep it locked up in a safety deposit box for some time.'

'For how long?'

Francesca smiled. 'Long enough for all of us to accept a natural explanation for the events we lived through. Don't worry. Your friend Aldo Prada won't say anything. He won't want people thinking he's a crackpot.'

'Do you think it will be possible to keep it quiet?'

'Why not? If those who could speak up decide not to, everything will return to normal. As if nothing ever happened.

You're the only person who stands to suffer. I don't believe you'll ever publish your findings about the statue of the lad of Volterra.'

'Well, Sonia won't ever publish her skeleton either . . . The official explanation is that it was destroyed in a fire caused by a short circuit. But at least I found you.'

'You really were fond of that little boy, weren't you?'

'Yes.'

Francesca smiled again, this time with a teasing expression. 'Then we'll have to call ours Angelo,' she said. 'He'll be the only real thing to come out of this whole story.'

www.panmacmillan.com